the
SERVICE
of the
DEAD

the

SERVICE

of the

DEAD

A Kate Clifford Mystery

CANDACE ROBB

PEGASUS BOOKS

NEW YORK LONDON

THE SERVICE OF THE DEAD

Pegasus Books Ltd.
80 Broad Street, 5th Floor
New York, NY 10004

Copyright © 2016 by Candace Robb

First Pegasus Books cloth edition May 2016

Interior design by Maria Fernandez

Library of Congress Cataloging-in-Publication Data is available.

ISBN: 978-1-68177-127-4

10 9 8 7 6 5 4 3 2 1

Printed in the United States of America
Distributed by W. W. Norton & Company

For my dear friend Richard Shephard
for rekindling my fascination with York Minster.

GLOSSARY

—◦◦◦◦—

AFFINITY: the collective term for a lord's retainers, who offer military, political, legal, or domestic service in return for money, office, or influence

ASHLAR: paint on stone or plaster to create the appearance of square-cut stone

THE BARS OF YORK: the four main gatehouses in the walls of York (Bootham, Monk, Walmgate, and Micklegate)

THE BEDERN: the area of York, part of the minster liberty, housing the vicars choral

BUTT: a target for archery practice

CORONER: the official in charge of recording deaths and inquiring into the cause of deaths, among other duties regarding the crown's property

MINSTER LIBERTY: the area of the city under the jurisdiction of the dean and chapter of York

MAISON DIEU: "house of God"; an almshouse, a refuge for the poor

MESSUAGE: the area of land taken up by a house and its outbuildings

STAITHE: a landing stage, or wharf

VICAR CHORAL: as a modern vicar is the deputy of the rector, so a vicar choral was a cleric in holy orders acting as the deputy of a canon attached to the cathedral; for a modest annual salary the vicar choral performed his canon's duties, attending the various services of the church and singing the liturgy

Kate Clifford's
14th Century York

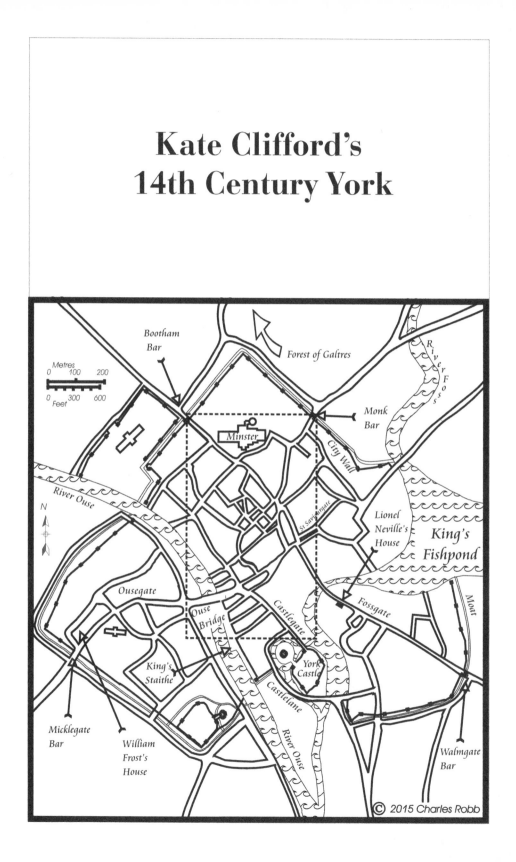

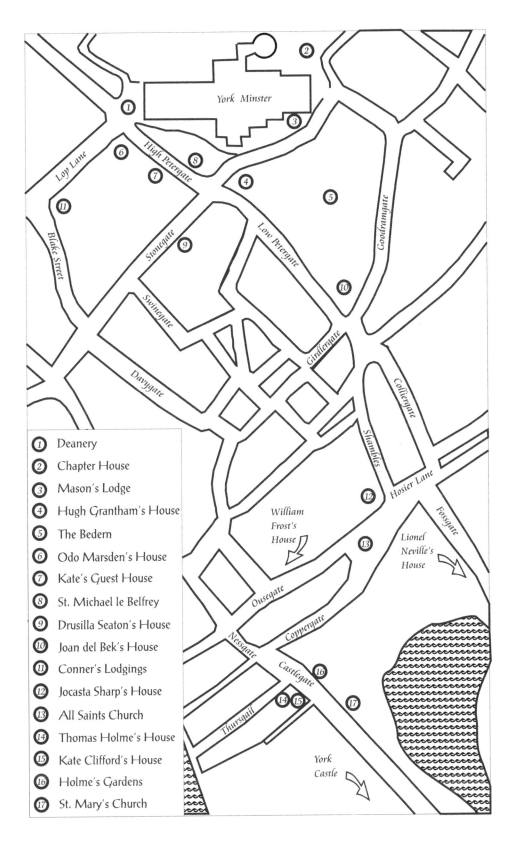

York Minster

Lop Lane

High Petergate

Blake Street

Stonegate

Swinegate

Davygate

Low Petergate

Goodramgate

Girdlergate

Colliergate

Shambles

Hosier Lane

Fossgate

William
Frost's
House

Lionel
Neville's
House

Ousegate

Coppergate

Nessgate

Castlegate

Thursgail

York
Castle

① Deanery

② Chapter House

③ Mason's Lodge

④ Hugh Grantham's House

⑤ The Bedern

⑥ Odo Marsden's House

⑦ Kate's Guest House

⑧ St. Michael le Belfrey

⑨ Drusilla Seaton's House

⑩ Joan del Bek's House

⑪ Conner's Lodgings

⑫ Jocasta Sharp's House

⑬ All Saints Church

⑭ Thomas Holme's House

⑮ Kate Clifford's House

⑯ Holme's Gardens

⑰ St. Mary's Church

AUTHOR'S NOTE

York, 1399. England is rife with rumor, tense with suspicion, and months away from invasion by the exiled Henry Bolingbroke and his supporters. The historical figures seeded among the fictional characters in the Kate Clifford mysteries are caught up in the crisis as it affects York. The stage is set for betrayals and murder.

Much ink has been spilled over the causes of the crisis between King Richard II and his cousin, Henry Bolingbroke—Earl of Derby (in 1398, Duke of Hereford) and eldest son of John of Gaunt, Duke of Lancaster. Muddying the waters is the contrast between how much was documented about Richard's life prior to 1399 as opposed to what was recorded about his cousin, Henry; Richard became king while in his early teens and was thenceforward always in the public eye, whereas Henry spent his youth and early adulthood in relative obscurity, overshadowed by his formidable father. What we do know about Henry is that he excelled at tournaments, though he had little to no experience in battle. That does not tell us much about his character at thirty-two, his and Richard's mutual age in 1399.

Years earlier, a group of powerful barons, calling themselves the Appellants, had risen up in protest against Richard's policies and his favorites at court. Henry had joined them. This was both a personal and a political betrayal—Henry had grown up in Richard's household, and many believed that the king, as yet childless, meant to honor the wishes of his uncle, John of Gaunt, in declaring Henry the heir to the throne if he did not, in time, sire a son. The Appellants could use Henry's presence in their ranks to threaten Richard—*we have in hand your heir, ready to take your place if we deem it necessary.* Henry eventually returned to court, and regained his royal cousin's affections. But one wonders just how much trust existed between them. In the novel I have Kate professing what appears to have been a popular notion, that Henry had gone back to court to reason with his cousin.

A decade later, Henry (now Duke of Hereford) repeated to his father, John of Gaunt, a tale of a plot against him that implicated the king. I will not go into the detail here—it is carefully laid out in Nigel Saul's *Richard II.** Suffice it to say, Thomas Mowbray, Duke of Norfolk, warned Henry of a rumor that King Richard meant to overturn the pardons he had given after the earlier rebellion. Even further, he might reverse an order dating to the reign of Richard's great-grandfather, Edward II, that had reinstated the Lancastrian inheritance after Thomas of Lancaster's rebellion in 1314. This reversal would wipe out the wealth and lands of a number of barons, but especially Gaunt, and, after him, Henry as the heir to the duchy. Belatedly realizing that Henry would warn his father, who would then approach the king, Norfolk attempted to ambush John of Gaunt. Upon his failure, the two, Henry and Thomas, were brought before the Parliament, where Thomas denied it all. Parliament ruled that the issue between the two men should be decided in "the court of chivalry." On September 16, 1398, Henry and Thomas presented themselves at the lists in Coventry. And just as Henry made the first advances toward his opponent, King Richard rose up and cried, "Hold!" The upshot: he exiled both of them, though Henry would be permitted to return, in time, and claim his inheritance.

---

* Nigel Saul, *Richard II* (New Haven, CT: Yale UP, 1999), chapter 15.

Shortly after Henry went into exile, his father died, and it was rumored that Richard had changed his mind. Henry's inheritance from Gaunt would be forfeit. In mid-March 1399, the court verified the rumor. King Richard intended to distribute the Lancastrian lands among the barons currently in favor. No one expected Henry, now considered by most to be Duke of Lancaster, to accept that without a fight.

Hence the tension building in England.

--◦⟨⊙⟩◦--

In May 1396, King Richard II granted to the city of York a charter giving it the status of a county. Essentially, it afforded the citizens full internal self-government. Such privilege came at a price, but the affluent merchants and guild members considered it a satisfactory trade, and a familiar process. The crown regularly contracted loans with the wealthy citizens; indeed, by the second half of the 14th century, this was such standard practice that groups of merchants in Bristol and York devised a way to share the risk among themselves by making these loans as corporations rather than as individuals. It was a risky business, lending money to the crown, which was perennially in debt. King Richard's grandfather, Edward III, borrowed with such abandon that he brought down several Italian banking families, which is why the king now looked to his own subjects, the prosperous merchants who relied on smoothly running mechanisms of state for their trade, for loans. So in 1399, as the tension between the king and his powerful cousin grew, the merchants were understandably edgy.

In this series I've cast Kate Clifford as a cousin of the historical William Frost, who, as mayor of York during both of King Richard II's visits to the city in the 1390s, played a major part in the negotiations leading to the grant of the royal charter described above. Frost was married to Isabella Gisburne, daughter of the late John Gisburne, a powerful but controversial York merchant. The couple acquired Gisburne's great house on Micklegate, complete with four adjoining shops. Frost seemed to stand in high favor with King Richard, so one might expect him to be fiercely loyal to him; but he proved to be a complex character.

Kate's late husband, Simon, and brother-in-law, Lionel, are fictional members of the very real, powerful Neville family. The patriarch of the Neville clan, Ralph, Earl of Westmoreland, was a historical figure of great significance in the coming conflict. Archbishop Scrope; Thomas Holme and his wife, Catherine Frost; Hugh Grantham; and Joan del Bek are all actual historical figures from the York records.

Richard Clifford, dean of York, is also borrowed from the archives. As dean of York and Lord Privy Seal, as well as recent Keeper of the Great Wardrobe, Richard Clifford was close to the king. I placed Kate in the Clifford family because of that royal connection and the Cliffords' influence in the North, particularly in Northumberland, as well as their occasional service as Wardens of the Northern March (the English/Scottish border). The border country was volatile, dangerous, and difficult to govern. I wanted Kate to have grown up in that atmosphere; it forged her character. And although her family was not as powerful as the Percy and Neville clans, they had significant roles to play in the coming conflict.

Suggestions for further reading are on my blog, which you can reach through my website: www.candacerobb.com.

We should profane the service of the dead
To sing a requiem and such rest to her
As to peace-parted souls.
                —*Hamlet*, act V, scene 1, lines 236–238

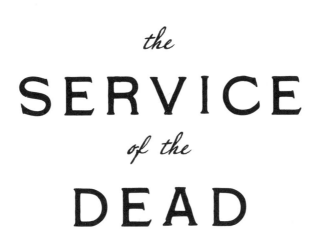

the

SERVICE

of the

DEAD

1

A RUNAWAY WAGON,
A BOX OF CINNAMON

York, early February 1399

One moment Kate was laughing as Griselde called Matt back for yet
another "final" instruction, and the next she was watching in horror as
the young man stepped into the street, cried out, and fell beneath a runaway wagon. She rushed into High Petergate calling out for someone to
help her lift the wagon and was quickly surrounded by a cluster of men,
one of whom barked orders.

The housekeeper tried to draw Kate aside. "Come, come, Mistress Clifford. Best not to look," Griselde murmured.

Kate shrugged her off. Bloody, mangled bodies were nothing new to
her. Carts and wagons and the animals pulling them were dangerous in
York's crowded, narrow streets. Kate had seen a man decapitated when a

cart pinned him against a stone wall, a boy's arm severed by a wheel, an infant crushed by a frightened horse. "I will see to him," she said to the housekeeper. Griselde withdrew.

The men had moved the wagon to one side. Matt lay on the cobbles—limp, unconscious, but whole.

"Bleeding from the back of his head," one of the men said. "Should we lift him?"

Griselde had disappeared back into Kate's guesthouse and now returned, holding out a blanket. "Roll him onto this, bring him inside." She crossed herself as they carried him past. "God walks with that young man."

Kate said nothing. She did not believe in miracles. Matt's reflexes had saved him. He had managed to roll between the wheels. She collared a passing boy and offered him a penny to fetch Matt's father from the Shambles. When she turned back to the house she was shaking so badly she paused for a few breaths to steady herself and find her legs. A crowd had formed round the wagon, discussing it, arguing about who owned it, who was responsible, who was to blame.

⁖⊙⊙⊙⁖

By midmorning, Matt had been removed to his father's house under the watchful eyes of his cousin, a healer. She'd listed his injuries as a bruised head, a deep cut on his ear, scraped hands, and a badly sprained leg—nothing life-threatening. Kate was not so certain. She had seen how hard he'd fallen. His head had hit the cobbles. Time would tell.

She sat in the guesthouse kitchen cupping a bowl of ale in her hands, trying to think what to do. The fact was, Kate needed Matt, and she needed him now. With his strength and agility, his smiling, easy nature, and his remarkable patience, he was the perfect manservant for the couple who ran her guesthouse. Heaven knew the elderly couple needed all the assistance Kate could provide them in the coming weeks. Lady Kirkby, a prominent noblewoman, was coming to stay, and she would be accompanied by a household of servants and retainers. She would arrive the day after tomorrow, and she planned to entertain prominent citizens at dinners in the guesthouse hall. Kate must find someone to replace Matt for the time being. A selfish consideration, but business was business.

"I could spare old Sam today," Kate offered Griselde, who had just settled down with her own cup of ale. "Could you use him?"

"Do not trouble yourself. I am ready for this evening's guests. But I would welcome help tomorrow. Perhaps someone with a bit more strength than Sam?" The housekeeper shook her head. "Whose wagon, that is what I would like to know." No one had claimed it yet. The men had moved it beneath the eaves, tucking it up against the front of the guesthouse. "Filled with stones, did you notice?" Griselde stared down into her cup. "I'd wager it was a servant, and he's run off to avoid punishment."

"The owner will turn up then. When Master Frost comes this evening, you might have a word with him. He has the mayor's ear. Someone must take responsibility for this."

Griselde promised to mention it if she had a chance.

Kate glanced round the room. "Is Clement abed?" The housekeeper's husband was infirm with age.

"He is. Gathering his strength for tomorrow." Griselde leaned forward. "But he can barely wait to learn how Master Lionel explained the discrepancy on the accounts."

"I will tell him myself on the morrow, after I've spoken to my brother-in-law. We meet this evening." Kate rose. "Young Seth Fletcher might do to help you. His father's asked whether I had work for him. In any case, I will arrange for someone to come to you tomorrow."

Out on the street the wind had picked up, twisting Kate's skirts about her. She moved back under the eaves and regarded the wagon with its load of stones. She noticed that some were caked with mud as if recently dug up. Someone building a wall? Kate drew a shaky breath, then pressed her hand to her stomach at the vivid image that rose in her mind of Matt crushed beneath the weight of the load. It might have been so much worse.

Passersby paused to ask after Matt. Kate kept her answer simple and consistent, that he should recover in time. Until she had more information to share, she would say as little as possible. What if Matt lost the leg? Or his head did not clear? The accident bothered her. Was it possible someone wished Matt harm? Why? He was young, inexperienced, of no standing in

3

the city. Had he not been the intended victim? The street had been fairly crowded. Had his appearance at just that moment foiled someone's plan? Suspicion was a habit she had developed in her youth on the northern border with Scotland, and she had been in York long enough to know that the absence of Scots did not guarantee peace. Merchants squabbled among themselves, and the nobles likewise. Faith, even the king was quarreling with his cousin and heir, an enmity that many feared could lead to civil war. Neither had the temperament simply to agree to disagree; one of them must die.

It put her own problems in a less threatening light. Small comfort.

She suggested to a few of the curious that they send for one of the sheriffs to take charge of the wagon and remove it, clearing the street. At last she found someone eager to do just that. He hurried off with an air of gleeful conspiracy.

She put up the hood of her cloak and set off down Petergate into Stonegate, avoiding the frozen mounds of refuse uncovered by the partial thaw. Snow was glorious in the countryside, a nightmare in the city. As she crossed St. Helen's Square and turned down Coney Street, she jumped aside to avoid a tinker and his cart. She'd overreacted, skittish because of Matt. The tinker had seen her and veered to one side. This time. In truth it was a wonder there were not more disasters in the city. It was not natural to live so close, so packed together. She told herself that the earlier incident might well have been nothing more than an all-too-common accident.

She eased her vigilance as she turned onto Castlegate and the prospect opened up, gardens bordering the street, a wide swathe on both sides bare of buildings—Thomas Holme's manor within the city walls. The wealthy merchant, her late husband's partner in trade, owned most of the land on either side of Castlegate between Coppergate and the grounds of York Castle, and he had clustered the buildings in a way that allowed for beautiful gardens to surround his house. They spilled across Castlegate, round the back of St. Mary's Church with its small *maison dieu*, and down to the River Foss. Kate's own house was on a small messuage just beyond Holme's house. Here she could breathe more easily than in the cramped streets closer to the minster. A low building fronting the street afforded small but private chambers for two of her servants and room for a tenant with a shop. That was currently empty. Another item on Kate's ever-lengthening list of chores. She crossed beneath the archway into the yard of her house and felt her tension ease a bit more as her wolfhounds came bounding out to greet her. And as she knelt to pet them, she realized her eyes were brimming with tears.

-◦◦⊙◦◦-

As the bells rang for vespers, Lionel Neville knocked on the hall door. Promptness was his one virtue, though the man's vile temper if kept waiting for the space of but a breath transformed it into an act of aggression. Kate let him enjoy a few moments out in the falling snow before opening the door to his curses.

Smiling, she welcomed him in. He swept past her without missing a beat in his complaint about the never-ending winter and lazy servants, pausing only to hand her his wet cloak. She indicated a hook by the door.

"You might offer me the courtesy of drying it by the fire."

"Of course. You are welcome to drape it on the back of your chair. I've set the table by the fire so we might be comfortable, and I've set the children and my servants to other tasks so we would not be disturbed."

Lionel grunted, but he crossed the room and did as she suggested, making a show of shaking out his wet cloak before draping it on the chair. "I heard about your manservant's accident," he said as he took his seat, then glanced round the hall. "I half-expected to find you attending him here."

It did not surprise Kate that in her brother-in-law's opinion no self-respecting mistress of a household would care for an injured servant. Her late husband often entertained her with a litany of his brother's prejudices. "How good of you to express concern about Matt's injuries. He is in capable hands, I assure you."

"I am much relieved," Lionel sneered. "I pray you, come to the point of this summons, Katherine."

What a relief it would be to shut the door behind him. Taking her seat beside Lionel, Kate opened the ledger that Griselde's husband Clement kept for her. "I found a discrepancy in the records of our recent shipment."

A small but valuable box of cinnamon had gone missing on their ship that had just returned from Calais. Lionel had been in charge, serving as factor. She'd long suspected him of pinching a little here, a little there, just enough to pad his purse and add to her debt.

Lionel snorted. "Thieving curs. I knew they'd removed something."

"Who?"

"The king's men. They boarded and searched the ship in Hull." Always had an answer, this one. "You can be certain they are using the king's order to their advantage, stealing whatever they can get away with, small things we won't detect beneath their cloaks. The spice was the perfect spoil."

It was, she agreed. "But it was your responsibility. You or someone you trust should have accompanied the king's men round the ship."

"They told us not to follow."

"On your ship you insist. Are they searching all vessels, or just ours?"

"Most of the ships coming from Calais, Ghent, Antwerp. Wherever there have been rumors of the exiled Duke of Lancaster. These are treacherous times, Katherine. You have heard that the king means to split up the Lancastrian lands, deprive Duke Henry of his inheritance."

"Yes, I have heard the rumor." And she accepted Lionel's excuse, but warned him again that it was his responsibility to escort the searchers and keep them honest.

"What you ask is dangerous."

Oh yes, it was. And with any luck . . . Best not follow that thought.

The people depended on the king for the health of the realm. But, much to their misfortune, King Richard believed he did not need his nobles, that he was an island unto himself. He did not understand that his strength was in appreciating and making use of the talents of his nobles and other powerful men who would in turn use them for the good of all his subjects. A dozen years ago they rose up—a warning. His cousin Henry Bolingbroke, son of the Duke of Lancaster, had joined the rebellion, but then returned to Richard's side for the sake of the realm, hoping to reason with him, cousin to cousin.

The nobles remembered Henry's doings, and wondered at Richard's subsequent treatment of his cousin. Henry had come to the king with proof that Thomas Mowbray, Duke of Norfolk, was speaking treason. Richard agreed to let Henry challenge Thomas before the court of chivalry. But at the last minute he changed his mind and exiled both of them. Where was the justice in that? And then to suggest on the death of Henry's father, the king's loyal uncle Lancaster, that Henry had forfeited his inheritance? How so? The nobles saw King Richard's recent acts as proof that no one was safe from his arbitrary punishments. Who could trust such a king? They would all suffer from his blindness.

The truth was, if the king decided the Nevilles were a threat to his reign, Kate might be ruined with them. Though she had never taken the name, she had married a Neville, and one branch of that family, led by Sir Ralph Neville, now Earl of Westmoreland, had risen quickly by dancing attendance on both King Richard and his uncle Lancaster. Not that the Clifford name was any safer. Her own uncle, Richard Clifford, had coerced her into hosting Lady Margery Kirkby, the wife of a man who had withdrawn from the public eye shortly after Duke Henry's exile. But her uncle was the dean and chapter of York Minster, and Lady Kirkby's fortnight's visit with a full entourage would bring in much-needed cash to High Petergate. Life was complicated.

Which was why she still wondered about Matt's "accident."

"Is your man Sam about?" Lionel asked as he rose.

"Not at the moment. I sent him to the Fletchers to see about young Seth taking Matt's duties for a while. Why do you ask?" Her brother-in-law's long face was in shadow, but she realized that he'd been gazing around ever since he arrived, as if expecting something—what? who?—to suddenly appear. "Have you business with Sam?"

"It is nothing. I had a question, that is all. About my late brother. It can wait."

Sam had been Simon's manservant, the only one she had kept on after her husband's death.

Lionel rose, once again shaking out his cloak. An edge caught in a hook on the side of Kate's vertical loom. "Peasant furnishings," he sniped.

"Your brother had this built for me," she reminded him. "Godspeed, Lionel. Hasten home before your good wife worries about you out in the snow." She let herself imagine it—frozen to death, his corpse discovered in the spring thaw. Kate doubted anyone would miss the unpleasant man.

2

BRAIDED SILK

———❧❧❧———

Griselde tied back the heavy bed curtains with a length of braided silk, a thick rope in the colors of the brocade curtains and counterpane—azure, deep crimson, green, gold. Such vibrant hues. She ran her gnarled hand along the counterpane, skimming the surface so as not to snag the silk with her rough hands, taking pleasure in the smoothness of the costly fabric. Her husband muttered in his sleep as he turned from the light, and Griselde winced to hear the bristles on Clement's unshaved cheek rasp against the fabric. The curtains and counterpane were of the same quality as those in the guest chambers in the solar above, and a gift from Mistress Clifford for loyal service.

In truth, Griselde's position as housekeeper in this guesthouse was a gift to Clement for his years of service as factor to Mistress Clifford's late husband. A substantial two-story tenement on the fashionable High Petergate, near York Minster, it had been fitted for them on the ground floor with a bedchamber in the back of the hall. The kitchen was a few steps from the rear door. It was the perfect arrangement for her ailing husband, who could no longer climb steps, but could help out in the kitchen, the hall, and the garden on his good days.

The two airy guest chambers up in the solar were reached by a partially covered outer stairway that wrapped round the back, with a landing that provided privacy to Mistress Clifford's customers, guests of the dean and chapter of York Minster. And, when no long-term guests were in residence, it afforded privacy to the worthies of York and their mistresses.

Seeing Clement's eyelids flutter, Griselde plumped the pillows behind him, turned down the bedclothes, and reached out to assist him in sitting up.

He waved her away. "I pray you've no cause to regret your softness, wife." Clement grunted as he worked his way upright and leaned back against the pillows to catch his breath. "This very morning you must hie to Mistress Clifford's home and confess to her that this night past we hosted not her cousin William Frost and the widow Seaton, as she'd expected, but a stranger accompanying Alice Hatten, a common whore. She will not be pleased."

"Chiding is your morning greeting? No smile? No kiss?" What a choleric old man he had become. "I know what I must do. You need not nag. Chiding." She muttered the last word as she poured him a cup of ale. But, glad that he sounded more himself this morning, she kissed his stubbly cheek before she placed the cup in his hands.

"Bless you, wife. I just pray you have not lost us our comfortable living."

"Husband, Master Frost vouched for the man and assured me the guests knew they must depart before dawn. I'll just step up and knock on the chamber door to make certain they're awake. But first I must stoke the fire out in the hall. It's a cold morning." Griselde made a show of confidence striding out of the room, but once out of sight of her husband she crossed herself and whispered a prayer, continuing with Hail Marys while she knelt to stir the glowing embers in the fire circle. She had not told him all the story, how when she had noticed in the early evening that it had begun to snow, she had gone to see whether it blew enough to collect on the outer stairway. The steps were tucked beneath wide eaves so that the wooden treads were passable in all but the worst storms. So far they looked clear at the bottom, but the lantern halfway up had gone out. Muttering about the poor quality of the wicks in the market she'd climbed up to fetch the lantern and change the wick, but found she had no need. It had not gone out; someone had closed the shutters. Wondering whether it meant the couple had already departed, she continued the climb up to the landing that wrapped round to the rear of the house, and the doors to the guest chambers. Hearing voices, she began to turn away, but paused, puzzled, for she could swear she heard not a man and woman conversing, but two men. She blushed with the thought that the stranger had invited another to join him in partaking of Alice's favors. This was not at all Mistress Clifford's intended clientele, two strangers and a common whore. But Griselde could hardly barge in and demand that they leave. It was not her place. All she could do was check again that the lamp was lit and wait until morning to report to Mistress Clifford.

Then, after seeing to her husband's needs—it had been one of the nights he could not move his legs, so she must do everything for him—Griselde had settled down with a second cup of wine and fallen into a deep sleep. Too deep, too early. She had no idea whether or not both men had stayed. Bad luck that this had happened when her manservant Matt had suffered a bad fall and his replacement could not come until the morrow. It was too much for a woman of her age to care for both her crippled husband and the guests by herself. She should have accepted Mistress Clifford's offer of more help, she thought. Sam had stopped in during the afternoon to deliver the cask of wine, but left quickly on another errand. Such strong wine. Both she and Clement had slept like the dead after sampling it. She prayed the guests had not drunk so much they were still abed.

Now she lingered over the fire, warming her hands, dreading the climb up to the guest chambers, and assuring herself that she had done nothing wrong in trusting Master Frost. After all, he had been the mayor of York, was a respected man in the city, and was not only Mistress Clifford's cousin but also one of her late husband's partners in trade. Surely it had been right to trust him. But had Clement not been so impaired, or had she a servant to send across the city to Mistress Clifford's home on Castlegate, Griselde would have reported the change in plans immediately. How unfortunate that Master Frost had informed her of the substitution after she had sent Mistress Clifford and the Fletchers on their separate ways.

Now easing herself up, her old knees popping, the housekeeper wrapped her cloak round herself and walked out into the pale dawn, the yard made beautiful by a blanket of snow. Looking up the stairway she saw that white triangles had collected in the inner corners of the steps, leaving the treads dry. But down at the foot of the steps the snow was well trampled. She hoped it meant the guests had departed, and rather than have the unpleasant task of waking them and insisting they leave within the hour, she might strip the bed for the laundress and air the chamber. It would be good to have an early start; she and the new servant would have much to do in order to prepare for tonight's guests in the smaller of the two guest chambers, as well as for the houseful that would arrive on the morrow. Lifting her heavy skirts, she began the climb up to the solar.

Halfway she paused to check the lantern. Someone had shuttered it again. If the guests had already departed, they had done so in darkness. Honest folk would prefer a lantern to light the way down the steps, particularly on such an icy morning. And if they had not departed, who, then, had shuttered the lantern? The light hung round the corner from the one window in the chamber, and down eleven steps. Surely the light could not have bothered their rest.

If only Matt had not been injured. He had the ease of a man comfortable with his strength and quick to move to protect himself—as her Clement had before the illness that was wasting him. Crossing herself and praying for strength, she continued up to the landing, forcing herself to keep up the momentum all the way to the door of the larger chamber. She knocked. Firmly. But not so firmly that the door should swing open as it did.

Inconsiderate guests! Had a good gust come round the corner the room might have been exposed to the weather. Men never considered such matters, but Alice Hatten, that slattern, she should have known better than to leave the door ajar. Grumbling, Griselde stepped into the room calling out, "Is anyone there?" Silence. So they had left. But Mother in heaven, what was that horrible smell? Had they left a full chamber pot to ripen? She was crossing the room to open the shutters for more light when she noticed something large lying beside an upturned chair. Had one of them been so drunk they had spent the night on the floor, and fouled themselves? Furious now, she fumbled with the latches of the shutters in the dim light, flinging them open to let in the fresh air. Still grumbling, she turned round.

Merciful Mother. She crept closer, holding her breath. The man lay with one arm flung wide, one holding something on his chest. Another step, and she leaned close. Oh, heaven help her, it was the devil himself, eyes bulging out of his blackened face, tongue poking through purple lips. . . . He was holding the end of one of the braided silk ropes. Oh no, no, someone had wound it tightly round his neck. Her hands fluttered toward it, wanting to relieve him, and she fumbled with it a moment, wrinkling her nose at the stench. He *had* fouled himself, and now he lay in it. A sob escaped Griselde as her cold fingers slipped on the silk. She could not gain a purchase, his flesh had swollen so around it. Thinking to move him closer to the light, she tugged on his feet. Too heavy. She managed to move him only a few inches, and the motion stirred up the foul odor. Blinking back tears of frustration, she fell back, clutching the side of the table to steady herself. A breath. Her mind cleared.

Oh, foolish woman, he is dead. You waste precious time. You cannot bring him back. He is dead. You must fetch Mistress Clifford. You must tell her what has happened. She will know what to do. God help her. God help us all. God help that poor man. Griselde used the table to pull herself up, then backed from the room, whispering to herself to keep herself focused. *He is dead. The stranger is dead. I must not scream, I must not wake all of Petergate. Mistress Clifford would not want the neighbors involved. Mistress Clifford will know what to do.*

She shut the door firmly, vaguely noting that church bells were ringing. Surely not for the dead man. Surely no one knew. Her head spun and she clung to the railing as she worked her way across the landing and down the steps, her legs shaking with the enormity of the trouble she had brought on her kind, generous employer by receiving the stranger and Alice. Alice Hatten. Where was she? Had she—no, certainly not. How could she overpower such a large man? But where was she? No matter. Mistress Clifford would see to all the questions.

She found Clement bending over the fire. "Oh, my dear man, you were so right. I should not have agreed to Master Frost's change in plans."

He looked up, alarmed. "What has happened?"

She shook her head, not yet ready to say the words. "God be thanked that you are able to move about this morning. I must fetch Mistress Clifford. I am setting a bench here by the door. Stay right here and guard the steps until I return with her. No one is to pass. *No one* but Mistress Clifford."

He rose stiffly and came hobbling across the rushes, reaching out to touch her cheek. "You are crying?"

Her lower lip now trembled so badly she bit it down and stomped her foot. Not now. A deep breath. "The stranger is dead. Strangled with one of the silk ropes." Tears welled up and she dashed them away with the back of her hand.

Clement groaned as he sank down onto the bench. "God help us. I *told* you. And with Lady Kirkby arriving tomorrow for a fortnight's stay . . ."

She waved him quiet. "If we are to have any hope of making this right, you must guard those steps."

"With my life, Griselde. With my life."

"Not even Master Frost."

"Not even he."

She hurried out into High Petergate.

13

3

CAGED

———⟡———

Born and raised on the northern border where she need but step out the door to find vast open spaces, Kate Clifford experienced the city of York as an openwork cage in which no matter where she paced she was watched, her movements noted and judged according to the decorum expected of a young widow of considerable means. Or such means as her late husband had led his fellow merchants to believe he had accumulated. It suited her purpose that members of his guild and fellow citizens of York continued to hold Simon Neville in high esteem. Their respect for his memory extended to her, his widow, and bought her time. But Simon's creditors knew the truth. So far she had managed to keep them quiet, satisfied with small, regular payments, but for how long? One wrong move could undo her. So could Lionel's tongue, should he see an advantage in ruining her. And now, as King Richard's troubles muddied the distinction between friend or foe, Kate had moments when she could not breathe. Or sleep.

Which was why she was stealing down the stairs in stockinged feet, trying not to wake her wards. She moved down to the hall where she lit a lantern from the embers in the hearth. Oh yes, a hearth. Simon had insisted. No fire circle in *his* hall. Such airs! He had laughed at the horror his brother expressed upon seeing the vertical loom Simon had given Kate, how he had placed it beneath the east window so she might work in the morning light. *"Fine ladies do not weave,"* Lionel had exclaimed. *"Katherine would say, 'What is that to me? I am no lady fair,'"* Simon claimed to have replied. It was all very well for him to laugh at his brother's pretentions, but in truth all the Neville family considered themselves of noble blood, and Simon's own extravagance was the cause of Kate's current financial unease. The lantern light was reflected by the polished pewter plates displayed in the wall cupboard. She could make do without them, she thought, though guests might wonder at the empty cupboard. Perhaps she might replace them with plates of lesser quality. . . .

From the cabinet at the cupboard's base she withdrew a quiver of arrows and a bow, then took a seat on one of a pair of elegantly carved high-backed chairs. As she strung the bow the wolfhounds Lille and Ghent circled her, their noses cold, their fur warm from their bed near the embers. Some time at the butt in her garden before the neighbors woke would steady her. She let the hounds out to gambol in the fresh snow while she secured her squirrel-lined cloak to give her arms the freedom to shoot, then at last stepped into her twin brother's boots, closing her eyes and imagining his smile. When her parents had purged her room of Geoff's belongings—the treasures, the memories—they had missed the boots and a few other items that had been out in the stables. She had hidden them in her trunk when she came south to York. They wanted her to let Geoff go. But he was her twin. They shared souls, life force. There could be no letting go. Not even his death could separate them.

Settling the quiver over her cloak, bow in one hand, lantern in the other, Kate stepped out into the eerie whiteness with the sky just beginning to lighten. She paused a moment beneath the eaves, taking a deep breath and remembering snowy mornings up north, doors frozen shut by the drifts. This was nothing. Trudging out to the butt, she placed the lantern on a stone where it would illuminate the target, then backed away, sensing the direction of the wind, sticking out her tongue to catch a flake and feel it melt. She called softly to Lille and Ghent, beckoning them to her side. The wolfhounds knew the mood in which she had come out into the snowy predawn garden. They knew to be still until her arrows were spent or her mood shifted. Ready now, she reached for an arrow.

Eyes on the target, Kate waited for a sudden gust of wind to subside, then let fly the first arrow. This was for her eldest brother, Walter, for rekindling the feud with the Cavertons by falling in love with their daughter Mary. The arrow hit just above center. Bow bent, arrow notched, she blinked the snow off her lashes. This was for her brother Roland for getting himself killed. She aimed, released, hit the center. A deep breath. *These are for you, Geoff, for taking on a guilt that was never yours, walking into what you knew was a deadly ambush, and deserting me.* Three arrows in succession surrounded Roland's.

Is that what I did? Then how am I still with you?

Kate shook her head to get Geoff out of it. She could not aim properly when he distracted her.

It won't work. You're wearing my boots.

Lille and Ghent whined at her feet. They sensed Geoff, especially Ghent. The wolfhounds had been their birthday presents the year before everything fell apart on the border. Lille for Kate, Ghent for Geoff.

This is for our parents for caging me in this cursed city and marrying me to a Neville. She aimed just to the right of Geoff's arrows, but hit dead center, knocking out both Roland's and Geoff's.

I applaud you, Kate.

Now for her brother-in-law's news the previous evening. Bow bent, arrow notched. This one was for King Richard for preventing Henry Bolingbroke, Duke of Hereford, and Thomas Mowbray, Duke of Norfolk, from settling their differences in a trial by combat, and exiling them instead. The arrow struck just off to the right. Another for King Richard, this one for threatening to cheat Henry Bolingbroke of the Lancastrian inheritance on his father's death. Now the king feared retaliation. If King Richard had honored his cousin Henry, he would not feel so threatened to have ordered merchant ships be searched for Lancastrian stowaways, or have his spies watch those with Lancastrian connections—including the guest Kate expected tomorrow. Dead center, splintering her parents' arrow.

I could not have done better.

She grinned. *No, you couldn't.*

And now the one to cripple the fool whose wagon crippled Matt. Reaching back, her fingers found an empty quiver. Saved by an empty quiver.

She trudged out to collect the arrows, Lille and Ghent racing out with her, their paws and their wagging tails stirring up a blizzard as they batted the arrows out of the butt, then dug for those that had been covered in new snow. She gathered them up before the hounds sank their teeth into the shafts.

The chill wind teased open her cloak, and she shivered as the church bells began ringing prime. Such a din of bells. They had kept her awake for nights on end when her mother first brought her to the city, and they still made her head pound and her temper rise. Giving each dog a good scratch behind a proffered ear, she gestured to where light and warmth spilled out the opened kitchen door. The dogs bounded toward it to break their fasts.

"Dame Katherine?" Berend the cook called to her from the doorway as she picked up the lantern and closed the shutters.

"First I must wake the children."

He nodded and withdrew with the dogs, closing the door behind him.

Back in the silvery early morning light, Kate stood a moment looking up into the spiraling snowflakes and drew a deep, easy breath. Yes. Better now. She headed to the house. Stomping some of the snow off on the slate doorstep, she slipped her feet out of her twin's boots and carried them into the hall, setting them near the hearth to dry.

On a table lay the accounts with which she'd thought to catch out her brother-in-law the previous evening. She muttered a curse as she warmed her hands at the fire. It troubled her, the king's men searching her ship. But no time for worry now. She had much to do. Lighting a lamp, she carried it up the solar stairs to where her wards slept beneath the eaves, one to either side of her bedchamber. At first nine-year-old Marie had shared Kate's bed, but her complaints murdered sleep. Kate could do nothing

17

right—the covers were too heavy, too light, the room was too warm, too cold, the pillows too hard, too soft, Kate stole the covers, she slept too hot. Enough! Another partition had gone up on the far side of her chamber.

She drew back the curtains on Marie's small bed. At rest, the child was a beautiful creature, tiny for her age, delicate, as if of fairy folk. Button nose, full lips, cleft chin, and thick dark lashes that rested so sweetly on cheeks rosy with sleep.

Neither Marie nor her brother Phillip favored their father, the man to whom Kate had been wed for three happy years. A time of innocence, before she learned all that Simon had hidden from her. Kate had imagined her husband sleeping alone since the death of his first wife, Muriel. She had ascribed his enthusiasm for bed sport to a decade-long hunger— except perchance an occasional night with a whore when the loneliness threatened to devour his soul. Such loneliness—his wife and son dead. How she had pitied him. And all the while, two bastard children about whom he had never spoken were alive and thriving in Calais, in the home of the French mistress he'd kept long past any need for consolation. He'd continued the relationship while married to Kate.

She imagined her rival, Anne, as a delicate beauty, like her daughter. Marie looked as if a strong wind would shatter her ivory skin. Both she and her brother had rich reds in their dark hair and startling blue eyes. Quite a contrast to Kate, who was sturdy, with bold features, brown eyes, and dark brown, wiry, unruly hair. Kate reminded herself that Simon had called her beautiful, and there was no doubt he'd enjoyed their bed sport and her company, laughing with her, seeking her opinion. She missed him, every day she missed him. His death had robbed her of much joy. Though once his will was read and his account books were opened to her, she had discovered she had been living in a dream.

Marie curled into her pillow with a soft sigh.

What trick of nature erased all trace of Simon from his bastards' fleshly forms? The Neville family tended to unusual height and barrel shaped trunks. Simon had been tall, fair-haired, with hazel eyes. Was this the cause of his silence regarding them? Did he doubt Marie and Phillip were his? Or had he been waiting until Kate had babies of her own before he told her about the two he had fathered with a beauty in Calais? She would never know. The only child Kate had conceived of him had been stillborn, and two years ago a fever had taken Simon from her. He'd ignored the fever for far too long, believing it would pass on its own. Had his mistress known of his death? According to the children's account, their mother died almost exactly a year after Simon. Would she have kept the news from her children?

Marie and Phillip had been grieving for both parents when Lionel deposited them on Kate's doorstep a year ago. *"Their mother is dead, two months now. Their French grandam said they are Nevilles and our family's responsibility."*

Stunned, never having guessed her husband visited a second family on his frequent travel to Calais, Kate had stared at the two small ones. Perhaps not so surprised as she might have been, had she not already learned of Simon's crippling debts and heard his will. *"Two more Nevilles—God save us all. How old?"*

"Marie is eight, Phillip eleven."

They'd reminded her of herself and her twin, Geoff, how they held hands, whispered to each other, examined her and what little of the hall they could see behind her. But she knew nothing of raising children, and she distrusted Lionel's intentions in bringing them to her.

"Add them to your *brood, Lionel. You'll never notice. Or that of one of your rich cousins."*

He'd clearly prepared a retort. *"If you insist on claiming all my dead brother's property, these are yours."*

There it was. He meant to overwhelm her so she would capitulate to one of the suitors with whom he baited her, and thus forfeit her late husband's business. In accordance with Simon's heartless will, the business would go to Lionel upon Kate's remarriage. *"How did their grandam know you were in Calais? Did you call on her? Why?"*

The boy responded before his uncle had the time to concoct a lie. *"He meant to comfort Maman and fill her with another baby she could not feed."* Phillip's English was heavily accented, but correct.

God in heaven, the children had understood every word. Kate had assumed they might understand English, but not the way it was spoken in the North. Simon had been so proud of his French, and his London

English, they might never have heard a Yorkshire accent. Too late she discovered otherwise. Now the two knew that neither she nor Lionel welcomed them.

Lionel was taking the opportunity to sneak away, but she caught his arm. He was a weak man, easily overpowered. *"Simon never acknowledged them, did he?"*

"What does it matter? You prayed to have Simon's children. Here they are."

She'd slapped him then, hard, and cursed him.

Then she had taken the children's hands and welcomed them into the hall. But the harm was done, and their hands were limp in hers.

"Time to rise, Marie." Kate gave the girl's shoulder a little shake. When the girl did not move, Kate flung back the bedclothes. "Wake up!"

The girl squeaked and flailed for the warm covers. "So cold! Your skirt is wet!"

"It is. It snowed in the night. Now dress and hurry to the kitchen. Berend will feed you before school. Jennet will brush your hair."

"*You* brush it."

"Jennet will brush it."

"You never have the time for me. Were you out in the garden with your bow?"

Tedious child. Most mornings she sullenly rejected Kate's offers to comb her hair or help her dress. Of course she was angry, because her grandmother and the Nevilles had rejected her. Kate might have had sympathy, but the girl had no fire. She whined and lay about and gave Kate no clue what might content her. "On your way down, check that your brother is awake and dressing."

Kate could not rely on them to see to each other's welfare naturally. Her first impression had been a mistake. They were nothing like she and Geoff, who had been whole only when together, naturally attuned to each other's every need. Marie and Phillip were bonded only in rejecting her; otherwise they bickered endlessly.

She moved on to wake Phillip, but his bed was made, the space tidied. Calling out to Marie that her brother was already breaking his fast and she must hurry, Kate hastened down the steps, pausing only to slip into pattens before crossing the snowy yard to the kitchen. She sighed with pleasure as the warmth of the large hearth enfolded her. Berend and Jennet glanced up from their tasks to greet her with warm benedicites. On the table were bread, cheese, and winter apples. Lille and Ghent had settled next to the fire beside Phillip, who sat hunched over a steaming bowl.

"Your aim was true this morning, Dame Katherine. Was Master Lionel your target? Father? Marie? Me?"

"Yes to all, Phillip, and more." Kate gave him a taunting grin, but it troubled her that he had slipped past without her noticing. "Hot ale?" she bent down to sniff. Hot spiced wine. "Well-watered, I hope. It is difficult to attend your grammar master if you are bleary-eyed with drink. And Hugh Grantham expects you after your classes midday to work on his accounts."

"Well-watered, Dame Katherine." Phillip ran a long-fingered hand through his curly mane.

Berend handed her a bowl of ale, her preferred morning beverage. Sipping it, she settled next to Phillip. Unlike his sister, Phillip was determined to thrive despite the abrupt, dramatic change in his life. He had offered to keep Kate's accounts—he had done so for his mother, his grandmother, and several uncles. He showed her how quickly he could add up columns of numbers.

Kate had declined his offer, having no intention of revealing his father's insolvency. The discovery of the debts had shocked not only Kate, but also his partners Thomas Holme and her cousin William Frost. She had worked hard to secure what was left, primarily property and partial interest in a ship, selling a few tenements and some land, finding lucrative uses for the rest. She tucked away what she could, in her own name, for the future. All the while, Simon's odious brother Lionel had watched for her to fail. She had disappointed him, and she meant to continue to do so. Besides, she did not as yet know whether she could trust Phillip.

Instead she was helping him develop a gift he preferred to his skill with sums, a gift his uncle had derided, seeing it as menial work, beneath a Neville—no matter that they were a minor branch of the prominent family. Phillip understood stone, and loved to work with it. A city, whether Calais or York, was to him a treasure-house of stonework, from the simple squares and rectangles that composed a wall to the intricate carvings on bosses and capitals in the churches and the minster. One touch informed him of the composition. He said stone spoke to him. She had encouraged him, giving him space for a workshop and purchasing for him some basic tools. Several of his practice pieces adorned the garden. Lionel had scoffed at her "desperate efforts to win the bastard's love." Well, she had won Phillip's gratitude, if not his love. She'd made a deal with Hugh Grantham, a merchant trader and master mason: If Phillip worked on his accounts, he might spend a few hours at the end of each day following one of the journeyman masons in Grantham's employ in the minster stoneyard. As an added incentive to quicken Phillip's journey to apprenticeship, she agreed to add Grantham to her select list of esteemed citizens of York who might rent one of the lovely bedchambers in the house on High Petergate.

Phillip was expressing his disappointment in Connor, the journeyman to whom Grantham had assigned him, when Lille began a rumbling growl and Ghent rose and moved toward the door, his ears pricked.

Jennet hastened to open it. "Sam! And Goodwife Griselde?"

Simon's former manservant assisted the elderly woman across the threshold and supported her as she eased down onto a chair Jennet had moved near the fire. "I was on my way to the house on High Petergate to discuss young Seth's responsibilities with the goodwife," Sam explained to Kate in his gravelly voice. He doffed his hat and ran a hand through his white hair, punctuating his speech with a grin, clearly pleased to prove his worth to her. She had kept him on after Simon's death to run errands, walk the dogs, and assist Jennet and Berend, fearing he was too elderly to be hired by someone new. She knew he often felt useless, so she had been glad to tell him about his new assignment of supervising Seth in helping Griselde and Clement prepare for Lady Kirkby's visit. She had impressed upon him the size of the task, as the entire guesthouse would be occupied. "I noticed her on Davygate, looking—well, as you see her. She was leaning against the pillar outside Davy Hall pressing her temples and breathing hard. When she said she was on her way here I thought it best to escort her." He leaned close to whisper, "She seemed frightened."

"Is it your husband, Griselde?" Kate asked. "Have the preparations for Lady Kirkby's stay been too much for Clement?"

Griselde shook her head. She looked a sight, her face ruddy with exertion, her hair escaping her hat and clinging damply to her cheeks, her eyes red as if she had been crying. Kate poured an unwatered cup of warm wine and placed it in Griselde's hands.

"Drink slowly," Kate said, crouching down beside the afflicted woman, silently praying that she had not been foolish in entrusting the guesthouse to Simon's former factor and his wife. So far they had done good work, but it took only one indiscretion. . . . "Take all the time you need."

But Griselde spoke after the smallest of sips. "I have failed you, Mistress Clifford. I shall"—she shook her head vigorously—"never forgive myself." Still nodding and shaking her head. "Clement—he warned me. In my pride I did not heed him."

Unease settled on Kate, to witness the stolid Griselde in such distress. "Drink a little more and take a few good, deep breaths. Phillip, go see that your sister is awake and dressing." With a whine of protest he rose and slouched out the door. When he was gone, Kate told Sam to stay near the door so he might warn her of her wards' approach. She would rather Marie and Phillip not hear of any trouble at the guesthouse. They knew nothing of the merchants who frequented it when there were no out-of-town guests.

"Now tell me all, Griselde."

"Your kinsman, William Frost—"

Last night he would have been in the best chamber on High Petergate with his wealthy mistress. "What is amiss with William?" Her mother's nephew was an ambitious man, a formidable power in the city, and, as such, could be quite the bully. And he knew about Kate's financial troubles. But Kate played to his weakness, his loveless marriage to Isabella Gisburne, his passion for the widow Drusilla Seaton. She listened now as the elderly woman described a transgression of such proportions that Kate reluctantly had to interrupt her several times asking for clarification. A stranger and Alice Hatten, a common whore? Had she not moved away? A shuttered lantern? A second stranger? Strangled with one of the silk ropes?

"How did she overpower him?" Jennet asked as she refilled the woman's bowl.

"I do not believe it was Alice who did it," Griselde said, seeming calmer now, her breath steadier. "I swear I heard another man's voice in there last night."

"Where is Alice?" Kate asked. "And the other man? Did you see him?"

"I only heard him, mistress. And this morning there was only Master Frost's guest, lying there." She pressed a hand to her lips and shook her head. "I fear I slept through it all. Two cups of Master Frost's fine wine was far too much for me. There was no sign of Alice Hatten or the second man this morning."

Kate sat down beside Griselde, stunned. Here was the crisis that would ruin her. The creditors would hear of a murder in her guesthouse and demand that she sell off everything to cover the debts, for who would stay there now? There was the manor—she might live there, leave Marie and Phillip with Lionel—or William, because this was his mess. What could she do? Had her uncle Richard Clifford, dean of York Minster, enough clout to protect her?

"My cousin William is to blame for this, Griselde. He manipulated you." Kate patted the woman's hand. "Now. Have you told anyone?"

"Clement. No one else."

"Good."

Kate's heart was pounding. *Calm yourself. This is no time to panic.* Perhaps they could see this through. If William took responsibility, all might be well, though she would be looking over her shoulder for trouble at every breath. Damn William to hell. He had shattered what little peace she had attained. Damn him. She would take him down with her—all it would take is a word with his wife, Isabella. William was beholden to his wife for his wealth and his stature in the city, and Kate knew that Isabella would not suffer an unfaithful husband. Then why had her mouth gone dry?

What would Kate's mother have done? Found another husband and let him protect her. That's what she'd done when Kate's father died. A few months of mourning and Eleanor was off to Strasbourg with Ulrich Smit, her new love. Her mother's example was clearly no help.

Kate rose. "Berend, we may be in danger. I depend on you to protect this household. I'll take the hounds with me. And Sam will stay at the guesthouse until Lady Kirkby's retainers arrive."

Berend folded his muscular arms and nodded. "The children?"

"Jennet will escort them to school and go for Marie midday. You keep her here this afternoon. As for Phillip—you've seen his knife. He protected himself on the streets of Calais. He will be safe enough on his own if trouble comes."

All three of the servants she'd hired—Jennet, Berend, Matt—had lived by their wits and skill with weapons at some point in their lives. She had felt it important. Folk wore more polished masks in York than they did up north, but Kate knew that everyone had a darkness. Everyone. She had seen to it that she felt safe in her own home.

Kate told Sam to go to William Frost. William and his ilk were already comfortable with Sam from his days as Simon's manservant. "Tell him I need him to come at once to the house on High Petergate. I will be waiting for him. And if he thinks to excuse himself, tell him—quietly, for his ears only—what Goodwife Griselde has just told us. Then come to the guesthouse."

Griselde had drained her cup and was now silently weeping.

"Jennet, see to Goodwife Griselde while I dress. And not a word while the children are in the kitchen."

Berend placed a large, comfortingly strong and warm hand on Kate's back as she moved past him toward the door. "I could go to the guesthouse right now, take care of what is there."

She thanked him, but declined the offer. "I must see it, and then see that my cousin removes it. Quietly. I leave my household in your care."

As Kate crossed the yard the hall door burst open, Phillip rushing out, calling back over his shoulder to Marie, "You will go to school hungry." He mimicked Kate's manner of speech—the pitch was wrong, but the Northern shaping of the words perfect. A talent she had not guessed. And then he tripped and fell.

Kate rushed to help him up, brushing him off.

His face was red and rigid with resentment. "I did not need your help."

Too late she realized the insult, showing off how much stronger she was than he. Of course she was. He was but twelve years old and had never trained in archery, wielded axe or sword, or even learned to ride a horse. The alleys of Calais had been his domain. But she had injured his pride.

Marie laughed as she ran past. "Stupid boy!"

Kate let them go, hurrying through the hall and up to dress, her stomach in knots once more.

4

THE DEVIL'S FACE

Dog-faced Clement Selby greeted Kate from a bench in the hall doorway, his grizzled and wrinkled visage wavering between joy to see her and worry about the circumstance that called her there. "I have let no one cross this threshold, Mistress Clifford, nor climb those steps." As if, with his lameness, he had any chance of preventing a trespass.

"Has anyone come asking to do so?"

"Not as such, mistress. There was the laundress. She knows we need fresh bedclothes by evening and she is not happy about the delay."

"She will be well paid for her patience. You heard nothing in the night?" He shook his head. "The wine—"

"Yes, my cousin's potent gift." Kate took a deep breath. "I will go up."

Clement called to Lille and Ghent, who had been sniffing the bottom steps and looking up toward the landing with worried growls. "Best leave the dogs with me, mistress." He bent to touch noses with them one at a time, something few people had the courage to do. Lille and Ghent adored Clement and settled on either side of his chair, their heads in his lap while he stroked their ears.

Kate handed him their leads, then set off up the outer stairway to see for herself the horror the goodwife had described.

She was surprised by the chill breeze when she opened the door, but one whiff had her grateful that Griselde had had the presence of mind to open the shutters. God be thanked it was as yet a subtle odor, but she must remove all trace of it before Margery Kirkby arrived. Damn William for bringing this trouble to her house. Damn him. For two years she had carefully built this delicate enterprise to pay for the masses for her late husband's soul, despite the mess he had hidden from her. His guild members knew of the request in his will and would wonder if she did not honor it. In one night her cousin had risked it all. Here, before her, lay the body of a man murdered in her place of business. A business that could survive only if the powerful in York felt the house was safe, secret.

Kate took a few steps into the room. Mother in heaven. She pressed her hands to her heart at the sight of the man's puffy, ruined face. It took her back in time to a hanging she had witnessed as a child, a vision that had haunted her sleep for years, the eyes pushed out by the swelling, the color so dark she had thought the man had been burned at the stake before hanging. The devil's face. For such a horror to lie here in this room she had furnished with such loving care . . . It sickened her. Was he a stranger to her? Might he be someone she knew, someone Griselde had not recognized? She could not tell with the face so distorted. Whoever he had been in life, and however he had come to such a fate, she wished such a death on no man. Crossing herself and whispering a prayer for his soul, she stepped outside for a deep breath of fresh air to calm herself and quiet her anger. She must clear her head and decide how to proceed, how to dispose of the body without calling attention to the activity.

Down below, Lille and Ghent began to bark excitedly, the sounds they made when a favorite human approached. A man laughed, called out to them with affection, then shushed them. William was here. God be thanked, he had come. But he must not sense her relief. He must see only her shock that he would bring such trouble into her house, and hear only her command that he remove all trace and never connect the man's death in any way with her property.

Returning to the room, she crossed it and walked round the body, trying to gauge how badly the floor had been stained. Her stomach roiled with anger. He must be removed, and soon, so that Griselde could scrub down the floor in time for it to dry before tomorrow's guest arrived. Fragrant oils in the wash water, and applewood in the brazier to both dry and sweeten the air. Perhaps first a brief fire of juniper and rosemary—their incense might mask the worst of it.

"God help us." Kate turned to see William hesitating at the threshold, resting his gloved hands against either side of the doorway as if holding it up. He was a handsome man, of medium height, slender, wearing his fine clothes with grace.

"I thank you for arriving so promptly. Now come closer, cousin. Come see the trouble you have brought me."

His first step was reluctant, and she thought he might stop there, just over the threshold, but suddenly he crossed to the body, crouched down, and touched the braided rope before turning away. "God's blood."

"We void our bowels as we die, did you not know?" she said. "How could you let this happen in my house, William? Did you expect trouble? Is that why you did not ask my permission to host this man?"

Her cousin rose slowly, staring all the while at the corpse, shaking his head. At last, tugging down on his jacket in a gesture of control, he met her eyes. "Who found him?"

That was his first thought, to wonder who had found the corpse? By the rood he would take care of this, and quickly. "Goodwife Griselde. What happened here, William? The chamber was reserved in your name. Who is this man?"

"My dear Katherine." He stepped round the body to take her hand. "I am so sorry you have witnessed this."

She shook off his gloved hand. "Why is a stranger lying dead on the floor of my house?"

"Do you think I planned this? Where is Alice?"

Kate noted his use of her first name. "Oh yes, the whore Alice Hatten. I do not know where she is. What I want to know at this moment is how she came to be in my house. You know the rules. You vowed to abide by them."

"She is a good woman who has no other means of making her way in the world." Alice had once served in his household, until he got her with child and Isabella threw her out.

"I know she is a good woman, William, no thanks to you. But we have a contract. You and Drusilla, no guests, no common prostitutes. You broke the contract. Now dispose of this body. Remove it at once!"

"She is not a common prostitute," he growled.

"You broke our contract."

He paced back and forth, eyeing the floor as if searching for something, then moved over to the bed, pulling off his hat, smoothing his hair as he studied the room. She had never seen him so agitated. "It does not look as if anyone slept here last night," he muttered, more to himself than to her. He was right—the bedclothes had not been disturbed, though the dead man wore only a linen shirt and breeches. William moved past the bed, bent to retrieve a bowl from the floor, and sniffed. "Wine." He kicked something on the floor. "The flask." Both had been tossed aside as if there had been a struggle. Whatever happened here, it had occurred before they'd withdrawn to the bed, but after the man had removed his outer clothing. His jacket and cloak were folded on the bench at the foot of the bed, and his boots were on the floor.

Kate told William that Griselde thought she had heard two men's voices. "His state of undress suggests your guest had a late, unexpected visitor." While she spoke she watched William's eyes, how he could not rest them, but kept searching the room. He was frightened. As if her gaze discomfited him, he stepped over to the window, putting his back to her. "What happened here?" he whispered, again as if to himself. "I told no one of his coming."

"Who was he, William?"

He turned to her, shaking his head. "I would never knowingly cause you such trouble, Katherine. You must believe me."

"Remove him. And say nothing of where you found him. If you involve me I'll ruin you, William. You know that I can."

"So much for familial loyalty."

"You brought this trouble on me, cousin."

He pressed his fingertips to his eyes, took a breath. "I did. Of course you are angry. Tonight, after dark, I will send someone for—"

"Before sext. By tonight the stink of the corpse will be worse. Bring something to wrap him in so that it looks as if you are carrying a tapestry, bed hangings—just remove him by midday, William. I have guests this evening in the other chamber and Lady Kirkby arriving tomorrow for a fortnight. You know how I depend on this income."

"I cannot move him so soon."

"You can, and you will. I must air the room, scrub the floor, and let it dry."

"Someone must search for Alice. She might be in danger."

"Yes, well, it is sweet that you have recovered your conscience. If she did not hate you yet, I trow she will have come to her senses."

"That was long ago—"

"*I* will look for her. And when I find her, I will tell her you are going to pay her well for her silence. Which you will do, William."

He bowed his head.

"Who was he, William? Why would someone want him dead?"

"It is better you know nothing of him."

Of course he would say that. It is what men did, endangered women by keeping them in ignorance, the bloody fools. "You will at least tell me this. Are Griselde and Clement in danger? Am I?"

He tried once more to take her hand and comfort her, but he tucked it behind him when she backed away. "I will send a retainer to guard this house." He paced over to the door. "And yours on Castlegate."

"No. Your retainers will call attention to my properties, attention I do not need."

"Are you certain, Katherine? I don't know what happened, or why. I told no one of his presence. Even Alice did not know his name."

She wondered about that. "Whores make it their business to know who is visiting the city."

"I know. That is why I sent to Beverley for Alice. She has lived there for several years." William crouched down to examine the rope round the man's neck.

"One of your men brought her here last night?" she asked. He nodded. "So another person knows she was here. And what of the visitor? Did he have a servant with him?"

"No. He was traveling alone."

"Unusual for a man of status."

"I will take care of this. Quietly. I promise you."

He was certainly being careful in his responses. Kate prayed he would be so when it mattered most. "By sext." She left him with the corpse, hurrying out onto the landing, the cold boards creaking beneath her. As she turned the corner and reached the top of the long stairway, she saw that her manservant Sam now stood sentinel at the bottom, the dogs sitting at attention to either side. Three pairs of eyes turned to watch her descent. Lille opened her mouth to bark, but stopped at Sam's command. Kate greeted the newcomer and crouched down to praise the dogs for their obedience, using it as a chance to catch her breath and frame her thoughts. When she felt steadier, she continued on into the hall.

She was surprised to find Griselde present.

"I feared the new servant might arrive. Did not want to leave him to Clement." The goodwife was ladling out a bowl of pottage for her husband, who was doing his best to pour two cups of ale while leaning on his cane. Poor soul. He had confided in Kate how useless he felt, how it shamed him to depend on his wife for the roof over their heads. He had been a proud man, Simon's factor as well as a fine carpenter. But he could no longer move about the city, much less travel. And as for the carpentry, all he could now manage were simple carvings for children—something that did not require him to lean over a workbench, and that could not be ruined too badly by his unpredictable tremors. Such items brought in little money. Despite his infirm state, and despite the money Simon had paid him to hide the extent of his financial troubles from all, including Kate, Clement had chosen not to quietly disappear. Instead he had handed over his profits to Kate so that she might keep the creditors content, and he now combed through the business accounts on the alert for discrepancies. In Kate's eyes, he had redeemed himself.

She briefly told the couple that William was to remove the body by midday, and suggested how they might clean the floor and rid the room of the odor. "Sam will stay to stand guard. He was a soldier for a short while before entering Simon's service, so he knows how to defend himself and you."

Outside, William was asking Sam to wait and serve to witness the removal of the body.

"He will remain here until Lady Kirkby arrives tomorrow," Kate said as she stepped out. She suspected that by then Seth could manage without Sam. He would have Lady Margery's servants to assist him. She took up Lille's and Ghent's leads. "The new servant should arrive soon, Sam. You know him—Seth, the Fletchers' youngest. Keep him busy until the body is gone. And tell Griselde and Clement to make up some tale about the mess in the chamber." She had forgotten to mention that to them.

"You can trust it to me, mistress."

"I know. God bless you, Sam."

Seeing that William was headed for the hall door, Kate blocked his way. "Leave them."

"I would talk to the goodwife."

"No. You are to leave them in peace. Go now. You have much to do by midday." She took him firmly by the arm and escorted him out to the street.

"I swear to you that I will take care of it all," he said. "You will hear no more of it."

"There will be consequences, William. Your guest had a visitor you had not foreseen. He has been murdered. Alice may have witnessed it. Whoever committed the crime might decide to silence her, you, Griselde, or Clement—consequences, cousin."

"Trust me, Katherine. If anything comes to light, I will make certain that your name is clear. I have influence in this city. More than you know."

His influence had not protected his guest. "The body, William. By sext."

"Ingrate woman," he muttered as he strode off to do her bidding, his breath visible as puffs of fog in the frigid morning.

He brought on such trouble and expected her to trust him, and to express gratitude? Shaking her head, Kate hurried home with Lille and Ghent, formulating a plan to send Jennet to Joan del Bek's bawdy house on Goodramgate to ask after Alice Hatten, who had lived there a few years earlier. Joan's women serviced the vicars choral living in the Bedern, the dean and chapter largely turning a blind eye to her business—anything to keep the vicars out of the taverns and off the streets. Unfortunately, Joan guessed the flavor of Kate's little business and considered her a threat to her trade. So Kate could hardly expect to learn anything from the woman. Nor did she want to begin rumors of a connection to such a house. She would dress Jennet such that no one would recognize her as Kate's servant. Yes. Satisfied with her plan, she hummed to herself to lift her mood so that she might manage to nod and smile to acquaintances along Stonegate, down Coney Street, and on to Castlegate. But Lille and Ghent, alert to every unusual noise, were not fooled by her false cheer. Some folk gave her a wide berth.

Once back in her own kitchen, Kate could not disguise her heavy heart. A man was dead. Someone who waited for him would wait and wait, perhaps never knowing what had become of him. So many times up on the borders in Northumberland she and her mother had sat huddled by the fire late into the night, waiting for her father and her brothers to return. Generations of enmity between families loyal to the Scots crown versus the English crown had created the habit of violence. A stray lamb crossing the invisible border became a call to arms, and, far too often, the death of at least one son beloved of his family. One night it had been her brother Roland, whom the men brought home draped across his horse. Roland, whose fingers had flown along the harp he loved so well, whose voice was that of an angel, who could charm the devil himself.

But it was his battle-axe that was valued. He'd perished in a bloody altercation over who owned the wool in a cart overturned by a rockfall—at least, that was the immediate provocation. Kate, too, wielded an axe with skill, trained to aim for the backs of the knees or the groin if a neck was out of reach, and to finish it with a blow to the neck when her opponent had toppled. All those from the wrong side of the border were enemies, not human beings.

And then one night it had been Geoff.

No matter how long it had been since she sat and waited for news, Kate could still remember that icy dread in her stomach, how she had known, the dark hole spreading in her mind.

She prayed that the dead man had no kin awaiting his return. But surely he did. Perhaps she could tease a name from William and find a way to get word to the dead man's kin without bringing trouble on herself or her cousin. Perhaps she had the courage to do that.

As soon as Jennet returned with Marie, Kate took Jennet up to her bedchamber to fit her out in an old gown she had begun to cut down for her young ward. "A few stitches and the hem will be right."

"It will need more adjustment, for weapons," said Jennet when Kate stepped away, satisfied. "But for now . . ." She twirled round. "Am I sufficiently disguised to pay a visit to the brothel?"

Kate smiled at the transformation. "Joan will not know you."

"She'd best not offer me work." Jennet laughed as she departed in a swirl of skirts.

Kate was sitting in the kitchen with Marie and Berend when Jennet returned awhile later, accompanied by a scowling Phillip.

Kate had expected him to be gone until late afternoon. "You did not go on to the stoneyard to observe Connor?"

"Connor did not show up for work. So when I finished the accounts, Master Hugh sent me home. I don't think he's serious about making me an apprentice, pairing me with that lazy journeyman."

"You called Connor gifted."

Phillip gave a reluctant nod. "He is. When he handles the stone, I swear it breathes. But he's hardly ever there of late."

"I must see Hugh Grantham about some business this afternoon. I'll ask him about Connor." Phillip looked uneasy. "I promise I will neither embarrass you nor irritate your employer," Kate assured him.

Berend set out bowls of stew for the latecomers, then stood back, rubbing the scar where an ear used to be with his three-fingered hand. He was a former soldier, missing fingers, a few toes, an ear, but a remarkable cook. With his strength and formidable appearance he was a reassuring and helpful presence in the household. And fiercely loyal to Kate. Which was why she felt she could do without William's retainers. At the moment Berend was worried about her safety. She sensed it in how he hovered.

"Why is Jennet wearing your old gown?" Marie demanded of Kate. "You were cutting that down for me."

"And so I was, but you declared it hideous. Have you decided otherwise now that you see it on Jennet?"

Marie made a face and returned to her stew, asking Berend questions about the spices and the vegetables. At a very young age she had been trained to cook for the household in Calais, alongside a mute serving man who did the kneading, stirring, reaching, and lifting that she was too young to handle. Kate had noted Marie's interest when she arrived and had quietly asked Berend to befriend the girl. Marie now often assisted him in the kitchen, quite ably according to Berend. At least she showed an interest in something.

Kate motioned to Jennet to step outside with her.

Out in the cold, Kate smiled at how lovely her maidservant looked. Jennet might attract a suitor wearing that gown to church on a Sunday. But she was so proud, she was not likely to accept it as a gift. "What did you discover?"

"Alice was not at the bawdy house. And I heard nothing on the streets, no gossip. About *her*. But I did hear a woman on High Petergate commenting to her companion as they passed your house that all the bustle must be readying for Lady Kirkby's visit."

"All the bustle, you said. So you saw someone removing the—item—from the solar?"

"That had already been moved, and one of Master Frost's men was carrying a bucket down the steps for Goodwife Griselde. She told me the item had been loaded into a cart that headed off toward Bootham Bar."

So William had the body. Kate had wondered how he would dispose of it without sparking his wife's disapproving curiosity. A cart toward Bootham Bar. Would he take it into the Forest of Galtres, burying the body somewhere deep in the woods? Or might he weight it with stones and send it to the depths of the River Ouse? She wondered what it was like, knowingly depriving an acquaintance of the last rites, a burial in consecrated ground. Would William sleep tonight? Would she?

"Mistress Clifford?" Jennet touched Kate's hand.

She shook herself out of her thoughts. "I did not realize that Lady Kirkby's visit was common knowledge." Perhaps the archbishop had mentioned it to someone? Kate sensed that her uncle, the dean of York Minster, was not a close confidant of the Archbishop of York, Richard Scrope. He might not have felt comfortable telling him of Kate's request for discretion. If Scrope had spoken of it, might the murder have anything to do with it? Kate could not know that yet, so she pushed the thought aside. What mattered was that there was much work to do to prepare. Margery Kirkby was expected midmorning on the morrow, and would bide for a fortnight in the large chamber on High Petergate, her retinue in the hall below. And the smaller chamber needed freshening for tonight's guests, in fact, so the larger chamber could be aired after cleaning. Those were her priorities at present.

"I should see that the laundress has collected the bedclothes, mistress, and help Goodwife Griselde," said Jennet.

"When you've eaten. I will join you at the guesthouse after I see Hugh Grantham."

In the kitchen, Kate had a word with Berend about protecting her wards. Fingering a meat cleaver, he assured her she had nothing to fear. "We will work on a meat pie. That will keep them in the kitchen until your return."

Simon had laughed at her choice of cook, predicting that Berend would desert their kitchen as soon as someone noticed him at market and offered him a job as a retainer. But she had stood her ground, and Berend had rewarded her confidence with five years of loyalty, and a willingness to step outside the kitchen when she needed his strength or comfort or advice when she fought inner demons. She had grown to think of him as her guardian. Marie and Phillip would be safe with him.

To compensate them for having their morning routine disrupted, Kate took Lille and Ghent across Castlegate and let them off leash so they might run through Thomas Holme's extensive gardens to the river. A generous swathe of his property across Castlegate was given over to a park, a number of small gardens, and a wild band of underbrush and trees that Lille and Ghent loved to explore. Their enjoyment of the area was part of Thomas's payment for his use of the guesthouse with his mistress. Kate's kitchen also enjoyed the bounty of the herb and vegetable gardens, but that was an arrangement she had made with her cousin and Thomas's second wife, Catherine Frost—a young woman with her own secrets to keep.

Midday the grounds were a quiet refuge within the city, the calls of songbirds and waterfowl, wind in the trees, the rushing river all masking the usual street sounds. No matter the weather, Kate often used the peace of the place to restore her sense of balance before heading back out into the fray.

By the time she, Jennet, and the dogs set out for their afternoon appointments, the morning's snow flurries were replaced by an icy sleet. But Kate's squirrel-lined cloak and hood were warm, her rabbit-lined boots kept out the damp, and she counted her blessings.

In Stonegate, Jennet went on to the guesthouse while Kate stopped at a goldsmith's shop to see whether a brooch she had brought for repair was ready. As she left the shop, tucking the small pouch in the purse she wore at her waist, she heard her cousin William greeting someone. His expression was so uncommonly grim that the mercer who had called out to him hurried away as if grateful to have escaped his bad humor. Kate hooked her arm in William's and drew him into the shadow beneath an overhanging story. The dogs stood sentinel to either side of her.

"Have you disposed of it?"

"Can't you smell it on me?"

"No." She pressed his arm. "Are we safe? You know I have an important guest arriving for a fortnight."

"God help me, Katherine, is that all you can think of? Your trade?"

Glancing nervously about, he tried to push her aside, but she widened her stance and stood firm.

"If you would tell me who he was, I might be able to judge for myself what precautions I should take."

"And I might be able to judge that as well, if I knew who had murdered him. But I was not there." He kept his voice low and watched the street.

"You are in trouble, cousin, I can see that. I have a right to know what it is."

"Have you found Alice?"

Telling, that he should ignore her demand. "No. You might send one of your retainers to Beverley, eh? Find out whether she returned on her own?

37

I am worried for her. And for Griselde, if the murderer heard her out on the steps. Was the man from King Richard? A messenger? Or from the exiled Duke of Lancaster? Are you in the middle of that?"

"I'll send one of my men to Beverley."

So he would not comment on that, either, though she guessed he was aware of the rumored escalation in the conflict. She would remember his reluctance to reveal his loyalty, king or duke. For now, she said simply, "Thank you."

"Why is Lady Kirkby biding with you?"

"My uncle Richard arranged it. She is on a mission for her husband, raising support for a peaceful reconciliation between the king and his cousin."

"The dean of York is a confidant of Lord Kirkby? I would look to your uncle then for news of the king or the duke."

Clearly he had no intention of confiding in her. "Thank you for doing as I asked, William."

He bowed and bid her good day. "I am off to the York Tavern for several ales to wash away the taste of death."

She caught his arm. "You sent a cask of wine to the guesthouse yesterday?"

"I did."

"For Alice and your guest?"

He frowned. "Why do you ask?"

"Griselde and Clement partook of it. They found it uncommonly strong."

"That will teach them," he muttered. "Is that all?"

"For now."

He moved on, but after a few steps, he turned to say, "Have a care, Katherine. Go nowhere without the hounds."

"I will not."

He nodded and set off again, this time continuing down Stonegate.

As if she understood, Lille leaned against Kate's hip, earning an absentminded ear rub, which inspired Ghent to lean against the other hip. Such canine affection would usually warrant a laugh, but Kate was not even smiling when she motioned them to move on. As she crossed to

Grantham's house the burdens of the day weighed Kate down. Had she known when she woke what troubles this day would bring . . . Added to her worries was a new, nagging question—had her cousin arranged the murder? His belated concern had not dislodged that idea. She did her best to push that aside as she knocked on Grantham's door. Hugh's servant welcomed her into the hall.

Kate apologized for intruding, seeing that Grantham was still at his dinner with his family. But Hugh rose from the table at once, assuring her it was high time he returned to work. His wife Martha asked after Marie, and commented on what a fine young man Phillip was. Her kindness was a welcome distraction from Kate's troubles.

Hugh continued in the same vein as his wife while leading the way to his office in a separate building behind the house. "I must commend you on your gifted ward. My factor is mightily pleased with him. He says he has never felt so at ease handing over the account books. Very satisfied with young Phillip's work, very satisfied."

"It is about Phillip I wished to speak to you, Hugh. And your journeyman Connor. Phillip tells me Connor is often absent, and he worries about having so little instruction. I am determined that he should be accepted as apprentice in the minster stoneyard. He needs some basic instruction, for there are plenty young men with the same dream. If you cannot provide that, I must find another place for him."

Hugh fussed with a chisel he was using to anchor a stack of parchment. "I am sorry about Connor. It's the drink, you see. He has no sense of when he has had enough. No doubt that is why he did not come today. I have spoken with him about this problem, and he has expressed remorse, promised to reform. I thought having Phillip depending on him might give him a reason to keep his word. But the devil has him in his grip and will not let go."

"I am sorry to hear of this. To be frank, it makes me even more determined to find another journeyman for my stepson's purpose."

"Not so hasty, Katherine." Hugh patted her arm. "I don't overstate the case regarding Phillip's value to me in keeping the accounts. I don't want to lose him. What if I were to work with him here, in my workshop, on the carvings I have undertaken to finish? I have promised Sir Ranulf that we will complete his family's chantry chapel before Easter, so I have taken up the chisel and hammer once more."

She placed her hand on his, nodding. "That is a generous offer, Hugh. I shall present it to Phillip."

"Surely he could hope for nothing better than what I offer, to study with a master?"

"No, I cannot imagine so. But Simon's children would rather be contrary than wise."

Hugh nodded. "I've children of my own. I understand."

"There is another matter to discuss. I have a guest arriving tomorrow for a fortnight's stay in the house on High Petergate. She travels with a not-so-small retinue, enough that we have much to prepare. So that we might not disturb you, tonight, you will be entertaining in the smaller chamber."

"Katherine . . ."

"It is a lovely room, the bed almost as large and just as elegantly appointed. You are the last of my York customers to stay there until she departs." She saw his expression soften to know others would be far more inconvenienced. *I've got him now.*

"We shall be quite comfortable, I am sure."

—⁖⁖—

At sunset, a mere erasing of the slight contrast between the sleet-heavy clouds and the gray sky, Kate and Jennet hastened back across the city along the slushy streets. They hurried to reach Castlegate before the deepening chill froze the slush into dangerous ruts and ridges, the dogs straining at their leads. The two women had worked hard to bring order to the house after the events of the morning, and now, weary in bodies and spirits, they moved along in focused silence.

Kate had left instructions for young Seth, the new manservant eager to win her approval, to tend the fragrant fire in the large bedchamber throughout the night in order to hasten the drying of the scrubbed floor. She wanted no trace of the tragedy lingering to greet Lady Kirkby on the morrow.

Berend welcomed them back with a spicy meat pie and mulled wine. Kate tried to relax beside the crackling fire in the hall hearth, assuring herself that she had done all that she could, though she imbibed slightly more wine than she usually permitted herself. Phillip and Marie tried to trap her into revealing what had so upset Griselde, and she derived some enjoyment from disappointing them. They were even more curious to hear that Jennet was sharing Kate's bedchamber.

"A lady's maid often shares her mistress's bed." Kate laughed at their protests that she was no lady, though she was not so lighthearted as she pretended. She thought it prudent to have Jennet near in case the dogs woke them in the night, to help her defend her wards. Jennet's lodging in the small house between Kate's home and the street felt too far away that evening.

When at last Kate readied for bed, it was with a prayer that she might sleep soundly.

As she closed the shutters against the cold, she noticed that it was snowing again. Big, lazy flakes. But the beauty of a snowy night held far less appeal for Kate than the soft, warm bed. Jennet was already snoring as Kate pulled closed the curtains and slipped beneath the bedclothes, head and all. Soon the warmth drew her down, her body growing heavy, her prayers confused.

5

A TRAVELER'S PACK

———⌑⌘⌑———

Kate sat before the kitchen fire wrapped in Berend's blanket, sipping watered wine and watching him knead bread. Just being in his presence comforted her. His strength was not only in his powerful body, but also his quiet clarity.

She had come out to the kitchen after a panoply of nightmares involving hangings and unmarked graves—Jennet's presence had not been enough to calm her. She had stoked the fire, hoping not to wake Berend, wanting simply to be here and know he was just beyond the carved wooden screen; but he had sensed her presence, and her need, and asked what was on her mind.

"That man, whoever he was, unshriven, buried without prayers—"

"Your cousin may have said a prayer over him." Berend had risen, taken her damp cloak, and put it near the fire to dry, wrapping her in a blanket warmed by his body.

"His praying over the dead man is not the same as a priest's doing so. And someone surely waits for him. They will wait and wait."

Berend had added a few logs to the fire and warmed some wine, spiced it, poured them each a cup. After kneading the rising bread dough he'd begun before retiring, he settled down beside her. Wearily she leaned against him. Though he wore only his linen tunic and leggings, he radiated warmth.

"This trouble between King Richard and his cousin Henry, how did it become our trouble?" she asked into the silence.

A log shifted, giving off a shower of sparks as it settled.

"Our king's quicksilver moods worry both the nobles and the merchants, eh? He is unpredictable. No one feels safe."

"If Duke Henry returns to claim the throne, will the nobles side with him?"

"I pray he has the wisdom to return to help his cousin, not overthrow him. Such an act would unsettle the kingdom for generations."

"I fear you waste your prayers," said Kate. "Duke Henry knows his cousin will take advice as treason. He will not make that mistake twice."

"Apparently Lord Kirkby hopes that he will. But I fear you are right." Berend stroked Kate's hair. "And I fear I've been small comfort. Forgive me."

"I prefer truth, Berend. That is why I trust you over all men."

So this was how it would be, factions circling each other, everyone suspect. For generations. As it had been up on the border. Well, she had been trained for it. That was a blessing. Kate rose now and opened the shutters on the window that overlooked the yard. "It is almost dawn."

Berend glanced up, nodded. "And a busy day for you. Will you invite Margery Kirkby to dine with you while she is in York?"

"Are you asking whether you will have the opportunity to prepare a feast? I hope so."

Berend grinned, and as he rose and returned to kneading the dough, he began to hum.

The draft from the window awakened Lille and Ghent, who had been sleeping beneath the table where Berend was working. Strange how the thump of the dough in the bowl did not wake them, but the draft did, despite all their fur. They stretched and padded over to the door in expectation. Kate stepped into Geoff's boots, picked up her cloak, and opened the door. "Bless you, Berend. Thank you." She stepped out onto the snow, her booted feet breaking the top layer of ice. Gingerly she made her way across the garden in Geoff's too-large boots.

"You're right, you know, just like on the border. Be vigilant, Kate."

"I am, Geoff."

In the hall, Jennet glanced up from the hearth, where she was stoking the fire.

"Bad dreams?"

Kate nodded. "I've left Lille and Ghent outside. Fetch some ale for both of us before you come to dress me. And let them back into the kitchen to break their fast."

Back up in her bedchamber Kate threw open the shutters. The soft light of dawn spread across the sky, silver tinged with rose, gradually reddening. She stood there long enough to witness the sun rising over the snowy rooftops and the bulk of York Castle to the east, setting the wintry city aglow. Even the bare branches wore sparkling coats of white.

"Do you think the snowfall will delay Lady Margery?" Jennet asked from the doorway.

"I doubt it. If her mission is important enough to bring her north in winter, she will be impatient with anyone or anything that threatens to delay her." Kate smiled to think of Margery Kirkby. She had been so preoccupied with her immediate troubles she had forgotten how much she had enjoyed the woman's company on her previous visit. "I should wear something bright today."

Jennet grinned. "Your red wool gown with the dark gold surcoat."

While they fussed over Kate's dress, Marie woke and stomped through the room to close the shutters. "I'm freezing. Is that what you want? What is *wrong* with you? Come dress me, Jennet."

Kate glanced over her shoulder at the petulant girl. "Perhaps I should sprinkle angelica on my threshold to protect myself from demons."

Marie made a face.

"Jennet will assist you when she is finished here, and not a moment sooner."

"Witch." Marie stomped her foot, then crawled into Kate's bed, burrowing down beneath the bedclothes.

"You let her speak to you in that way, she will be a shrew all her life."

"So be it." Kate had no time to dance the dance with Marie. She let her lie there and stew until Jennet had teased out the last tangle in Kate's hair and gathered it into a gold and silver crispinette. "Come out now," Kate called to Marie. "Time to dress." She lifted the covers to discover the girl softly snoring.

"I will see them to school and then join you at the guesthouse."

"Bless you, Jennet."

Despite the crisp beauty of the morning, Kate moved through the city preoccupied with questions and uneasy with secrets and worry, grateful that Lille and Ghent tugged on their leads now and then, reminding her to glance up and smile at passersby. It would not do to start rumors with her dour expression. No one must guess that her thoughts were out beyond Bootham Bar with the corpse of a man unshriven, wondering what had happened and what trouble was yet to come. And whether her neighbor's warning had anything to do with the death in the guesthouse.

As she crossed Castlegate with Lille and Ghent for their morning run, Kate was hailed by her neighbor and partner, Thomas Holme.

"We had trespassers in the night, Dame Katherine. One of my servants saw a pair trying the doors of my outbuildings. He said they came down the alleyway. I mean to keep a lit lantern there for a while, to discourage them."

"Lille and Ghent have been edgy several mornings. I thought it nothing, but now I wonder. Did your servant see them well enough to recognize them again?"

"No. He'd gone out to the midden without a light, the daft one. He guesses that one was a man and the other either a small woman or a child."

That description suggested poor wayfarers seeking a warm place in which to sleep, nothing to do with her trouble. But Kate thanked Thomas for the warning, and for thinking of the lantern in the alley.

At the guesthouse on High Petergate she found Griselde anxiously discussing with her husband a fresh discovery: outside damage to one of the shutters in the window of the main bedchamber, and a piece of cloth caught in the splintered wood that she believed to be from the dress Alice had been wearing. Had Alice managed to escape out the window onto the landing? Or had there been a struggle out there?

"I slept through it all, Mistress Clifford. I cannot be trusted."

"Beating your breast is of no help to me, Griselde. Now *you* understand why I have such clear rules. And *I* know that you require a manservant under your roof at night at all times."

Griselde tucked a few loose strands of hair back in her white kerchief and smoothed down the skirt of her simple gown. "Yes, Mistress Clifford." The housekeeper glanced over at her husband. "We both owe you everything."

Kate knew Griselde was thinking of Clement's part in hiding Simon's financial troubles. But Kate had come to value both of them; indeed, it was Clement who had noticed the missing shipment of cinnamon. "I am not going to cast you out, Griselde. But I expect you to adhere to the rules of the house from now on unless *I* tell you to bend them." She glanced round the hall. "What else? Surely we have more stools?"

Griselde sighed. "I meant to fetch the other two."

Only two. "Send a few of Lady Kirkby's servants with a cart to Castlegate when they arrive. I can part with a few benches for a fortnight. For now, I'll collect what we have."

"I will show you where they are, mistress," said Sam from the hall door, curling his left hand as if catching something. Their signal.

While Griselde protested that it was her place to fetch the stools, Kate crossed the hall to her serving man.

"The stools are stacked just inside the lean-to behind the kitchen," he said quietly. "But you will want to check the farther shed near the privy. Beneath the wheelbarrow. I left everything as I found it."

Waving Griselde silent, Kate plucked her cloak from the bench near the door and followed the path young Seth had cleared out past the kitchen to the privy. Fortunately, he had cleared side paths to the kitchen, the lean-to, and the far shed as well; neither she nor Sam would leave an obvious trail. Within, she found the wheelbarrow upended, and beneath it a leather traveling pack. She shone the lantern round the room to see whether anything else seemed out of place. All but the barrow and a corner of a shelf near the door was silvered with frost. She pulled the pack out from beneath the barrow and set it down on top. Fine leather with a shiny brass buckle to secure the flap, at present opened. Inside, a man's linen shirt, soiled, but of good quality, a pair of travel-stained breeches, a comb, a pair of dice in a small pouch, a pot of unguent, a pair of barely worn shoes, and a small pack that was a miniature of the larger one. This pack's buckle was also undone, and it was empty but for a letter carrying the seal of the Duke of Lancaster—the title the exiled Henry claimed, which his cousin King Richard denied him. She held her breath as she brought the lantern close to read it. It was a letter of credence introducing a Hubert Bale as the duke's envoy. An envoy. For what? Returning with an army to wrest his inheritance from his cousin the king? Or to take the throne? The letter was beginning to wear at the folds. A busy man, this Hubert.

Did this pack and the letter belong to her cousin's guest, or to the murderer? Hubert Bale. Was he the dead man? She held up the breeches—they might have fit the man who had lain on the floor in the guest chamber. But so might they fit many men she knew.

An envoy would travel with money. But there was none in the pack. That might be why it had been unbuckled—someone had stolen the money. Alice? Certainly someone who did not appreciate the importance of the letter, someone who did not recognize the seal. Or they had left it as evidence. Perhaps the man had carried his money on his person, but Griselde had not mentioned a scrip that would hold money. Kate did not think the woman would be so bold as to keep it from her, not when she was already worried she had jeopardized her post.

Except for the letter, which Kate tucked into her own scrip, she left everything as she had found it. As she lifted the lantern, something on the ground near the door caught the light. A silver coin. Spilled from the pack, perhaps. Hers now. It joined the letter. She opened the door slowly, peering out, half expecting to find someone spying on her. But all was clear. Pulling the door shut behind her, she picked her way back along the swept path, taking deep breaths to steady herself. A man murdered in her guesthouse, either he or his murderer a traitor to the crown. *Damn cousin William to hell for all eternity if he brings me down with his treachery.* By the time she collected the pair of stools and returned to the hall, she had decided to put young Seth at the door and send Sam home with the letter.

"Find young Seth, then take this to Berend," she quietly ordered Sam as she bent to shift the letter from her scrip to his boot. "And don't let it get wet!"

Jennet had arrived, bringing order to the last bits of preparation. Kate took the opportunity to sit down with Griselde and Clement to discuss the night of the murder before they forgot some of the details. "Was Alice Hatten brought here by one of my cousin's men?"

"She was," said Clement. "We heard someone on the steps. Griselde found Master Frost's man Roger, Alice Hatten, and Master Frost's guest halfway up the steps."

Griselde nodded. "I called to Master Frost's man to come within so that we might review with him the rules. He told the other two to wait for him on the landing up above."

"You recognized my cousin's man?"

"*I* did," said Clement. "I would know him anywhere, with that pale pate and those strange eyes."

Roger was her cousin's most trusted retainer, a former soldier. "Could it have been Roger you heard upstairs later in the evening, Griselde?"

"I do not believe so. No. Roger has a wheeze in his voice. This man spoke sharply. I am sorry I heard only the tone, not the matter, Mistress Clifford."

"When did my cousin come to you with this arrangement?"

"We were cleaning up after the midday meal," Griselde said, looking to her husband for confirmation. He nodded. "I would have sent Matt to you, but that was well after his accident, past midday."

"That very day William sent word?"

Griselde nodded.

"And the stranger . . . Roger did not name him, or give you any other information?"

Griselde shook her head. "Master Frost had told us it would be so."

The more she heard, the more uncomfortable Kate was with her cousin's part in this. But there was no more time for questions. A shout from Seth alerted them of Lady Kirkby's arrival.

Margery Kirkby entered the hall on the arm of Kate's uncle, Richard Clifford, dean of York Minster, his somber robes providing a contrast to her Lincoln green cloak lined in pale gray rabbit fur. She slipped her arm from his to hurry to Kate, enfolding her in a heavily scented embrace.

"Benedicite, dear Katherine." She kissed Kate's cheek, then stood back to look her up and down. "It gladdens my heart to see you looking so well, and out of mourning." Margery kissed the other cheek, then stepped aside for Kate to introduce her to Clement, Griselde, and young Seth. Margery, in turn, introduced the small crowd pooling in the hall doorway. Two maidservants, a manservant, and four retainers. "And my two grooms will be along soon with the dogs. You must bring Lille and Ghent over every day to play with Troilus and Criseyde, dear Katherine. Have you heard Geoffrey Chaucer's poem about the two lovers? Oh, you must. Perhaps we might have evenings of reading it aloud while I am here."

Her banter continued up the stairs into the main bedchamber, which she declared perfect before asking her maidservants to leave them in peace for a moment.

Without an audience, Margery Kirkby turned to business. "I pray the rumors about my Thomas going over to the Lancastrian side are not going to cause trouble for you, Katherine."

Of course they would. Hence the high fee for a fortnight's stay. "A little more trouble will hardly be noticed," Kate lied, being the gracious hostess she was. "But my uncle has promised his support."

"My husband is not a traitor to King Richard, I want you to know, and I hope that by the time I depart all will know that he has gone to the continent to broker an agreement that will allow the exiled duke to return in peace and take up his position as Duke of Lancaster."

"I do not hold out much hope for his success."

Margery shrugged. "Thomas felt the need to try."

"Then I hope you can bring the gossipmongers round to admiring his courage."

"Bless you for saying that, Katherine. It is my hope that I will find supporters here who might use their influence on the king. And financial support for my husband's efforts."

"I pray my uncle has warned you how the citizens of York treasure and protect the autonomy King Richard granted them. Not that they worship him. He has taken advantage of their gratitude, extorting large loans and fines. But they protect themselves first." *And are wary of such foolish gambits,* Kate added silently.

"He has warned me to tread softly."

"Have you had much luck elsewhere?"

Margery bowed her head. "No. His Grace King Richard has alienated men of property. Not all. But those who still support him believe he can be safe only so long as Henry Bolingbroke remains in exile and deprived of the wealth and power of the duchy of Lancaster."

Hence the rumored alienation of the Lancastrian inheritance. How unfortunate that Kate and Berend were so right in their assessment.

"What of your late husband's family, the Nevilles?" Margery asked. "Might they be persuaded of the benefits of peace?"

A small laugh escaped Kate. "Only if it might win them more power, more land."

"Ah." Margery met Kate's honesty with a wry smile. "Well, I can but try. I hope I will see much of you while I am here."

"As much as you like."

"And your wards. I should love to meet them. I miss my children. Marie and Phillip, I believe? Your uncle tells me they are most fortunate in their guardian."

"That is kind of him. Marie will adore you. Now, I imagine you would like to refresh yourself after your journey?"

Once Kate and her uncle were out on the landing, she invited him into the second chamber and dismissed the servants who were filling it with traveling trunks. She had decided she was duty-bound to inform him of the murder. Richard Clifford listened without comment, his expression unreadable. When she was finished, she apologized for not telling him sooner.

"It would not have changed my plans, Katherine." He fiddled with his sleeve. "What is William Frost up to?" He sighed. "My poor Katherine, you are cursed in your kinsmen. We bring you nothing but trouble. I can at least discreetly inquire about the woman. She may have sought sanctuary close by in the minster."

"That would be helpful. And if you might, give my servant Sam a letter of introduction to the chapter at Beverley for their help in learning what he can about Alice Hatten?"

"Of course. He can come for it tomorrow morning."

"Will you tell Margery of this?"

The dean walked over to the window, staring out for a long while. He rubbed his fingertips with his thumb on his right hand while he considered, the only outward sign of his concern. Kate glanced round at the trunks while she waited, wondering at the number. *For a fortnight in York?*

Finally her uncle turned. "I chided Margery for traveling with four retainers, but now I am glad of it. I think it best I do not mention what happened here. The fewer who know of it the better. I shall trust that her retainers will be on the alert. But what of you? Are you safe?"

"I have Berend, Jennet, Sam, and the hounds."

The dean nodded. "You choose your servants as your father taught you. Good."

"What of Archbishop Scrope? Are his spies likely to be sniffing about? Should I be worried they might discover my secret?"

"I do not believe so. His mentor was the exiled Archbishop Arundel— former archbishop, I should say—known to be advising Duke Henry, so Scrope is quite certain King Richard has a spy in his household. He dare not raise any alarms. Now, will you come dine at the deanery when Margery is dressed?"

Kate had been expecting the invitation, and accepted with the hope that she might hear more about King Richard's plans and what Duke Henry was doing on the continent. Her uncle was not only dean of York Minster, but also King Richard's Lord Privy Seal and, until recently, Keeper of the Wardrobe as well. His choice to come to York himself rather than name a proxy to the post suggested he was not in the king's best graces at the moment. Or perhaps it was he who wished to distance himself from the king. Or, considering what he'd said about the archbishop, perhaps he was here to observe Scrope. That was a new twist.

In the event, she learned little that she had not already heard. Her uncle was maddeningly discreet, but at least she was clearer about the lay of the land, so that she might better separate wild rumors from those with some foundation in truth. None of it cheered her. King Richard had indeed decided to split up much of the Lancastrian holdings among those he trusted.

As they made their way back across the city, Kate told Jennet all that she had learned about the incident in the guesthouse, and of the pack and its letter.

"Whatever happened, Alice is in danger, Jennet. William expressed concern for her, but you know he and whoever else is involved will consider her expendable if they fear she might expose them. It's up to us to help her." Over time, Kate and her three servants—Berend, Jennet, and Matt—had honed their skills as a team investigating the backgrounds of landlords whose property she'd considered acquiring, inquiries requiring discretion and thoroughness. It was not always obvious who actually held the deed to a property. Kate was confident they could put those same skills to good use in searching for Alice.

"I will go a-hunting," said Jennet. "This time I think I should be a lad. That way I can easily slip about." With her slender frame and round, freckled face, Jennet could easily pass as a boy. As long as no one pulled off her hat. "I'll see what I might discover about Alice's habits and haunts, where she might seek sanctuary when in trouble. And I'll keep my ears pricked for any mention of Hubert Bale."

"For my part, I will call on William's mistress in the morning. She might slip with some information."

"Drusilla Seaton slip?" Jennet chuckled. "I would fain be present to witness that."

"Miracles do happen."

At the house, Berend greeted Kate with concern in his voice. "The letter—I have encountered this man, Hubert Bale."

"But that is good!"

He shook his head. "When our paths crossed he was a cutthroat for hire. Unless he is much changed, he is not here seeking a peaceful solution."

"Would you recognize him?"

Berend touched the scarred hole that now served as an ear. "We were of a kind. He might be much changed."

"Would he recognize you?"

A nod. "That is the good news. If he is alive, he will avoid me at all cost. And you, I pray."

"God guided my heart the day I approached you, Berend." She took a deep breath. "We will want to find the fresh grave and see just who William buried. Will you see to that?"

"I will see what I can do, Dame Katherine. Sam knows the servant who accompanied your cousin and his man Roger out into the Forest of Galtres. And if your cousin simply weighted the body down in the River Ouse?"

"I've grown soft and stupid in the city. I should have had Sam follow William, not guard the guesthouse."

"Such regret is unhelpful."

"I needed to say it aloud to spur myself forward. Let us pray William did not resort to the river. Meanwhile, Sam will return the letter to the pack. We have the information we need. Whoever tucked the pack beneath the barrow may return. Jennet and I will watch the next few nights. Can you describe what Bale looked like when you last saw him?"

"Why Jennet? Why not Sam? Or me?" Berend searched her face. "You and your twin itch to be the one to catch the murderer."

Kate averted her eyes. "*I* do. So. Describe Bale for me."

6

TRUANT

———⌖———

At first Kate blamed the clatter of a loose shutter banging against the house for her agitation upon waking. But after Jennet rose to secure it, Kate still could not settle, going over and over all the missed opportunities of the previous days. It was not merely her failure to have Sam follow William when he disposed of the corpse, but she'd also neglected to examine the body for additional wounds or identifying marks, or search the man's belongings. They had the pack now, but had he anything on him, something now in William's possession, or, even worse, something buried with the body? She should have taken Berend or Jennet with her. Since when had protecting her investments and her reputation blinded her to matters of actual survival? She disappointed herself.

And now the silence felt rife with menace.

Jennet groaned and sat up, listening. "Hubert Bale has become a specter of the night. He might be anywhere."

As if she had not been thinking the same thing, Kate reminded Jennet that Sam and the dogs were below in the hall. "They will warn us. And we don't even know that Hubert Bale survived."

"Berend would be surprised if he had not."

It was true. Berend doubted that the man strangled in the guesthouse had been Hubert Bale, the best assassin he had ever encountered, unless he had been attacked by an equally skilled assassin.

"Such as?" Kate had asked him.

"Someone from King Richard's own network of spies. His Grace might have learned of Bale's mission, and, knowing his reputation, sent someone to prevent Bale from murdering royal supporters."

She'd argued that the situation was all the worse because the identity and motive of the murderer were as yet a mystery. "We must find Alice and protect her, discover who was murdered, and by whom, and why. Your mission is to identify the dead man. Exhume him or wrest a description out of the servant who helped bury him. That is our focus."

"As you wish," said Berend. "As long as you appreciate the danger."

She assured him that she did. Of course it bothered her that, according to Berend, Hubert Bale was a man so ordinary in appearance—height, weight, coloring, features—that he moved through crowds unnoticed. Even those he attacked struggled for a description of any aspect, even clothing, that would assist identification. "He left survivors? I thought he was an assassin."

"Some of his missions were to maim—intimidation, not execution."

"God help us."

Kate had hoped for a clearer image of the man who might count her partly or wholly responsible for an attack in her guesthouse. They could not rely on recognizing a face, but must mark behavior.

Jennet was right. If Bale was the murderer on the loose, he could be anywhere. As Kate lay in bed she tensed at every gust of wind, each creak of the house, and cursed William for endangering her and all she held dear.

"I feel some satisfaction thinking how frightened your cousin must be," said Jennet. "Either his guest or a stranger murdered, and Master Frost put Bale there that night."

Kate sighed into the darkness. Despite his betrayal, she did not wish harm to her cousin.

Don't be soft, Geoff growled in her head. She felt him brush her cheek with his lips. She must still be half asleep. *Glad you have such a loyal maidservant. Sharing a bed with our brothers and our servant Tuck was comforting only for the heat. If we lay awake worried or tensed for trouble, we never admitted it to each other.*

What are you doing here, Geoff? But she knew. When she was in danger, he was there.

Jennet abruptly sat up. "I surrender. I cannot sleep. I will begin my search." She slipped out from beneath the pile of bedclothes.

"It is still dark."

"I do my best work in the dark, remember?"

Before she came to work for Kate, Jennet had used her tailoring skills to create clothing in which she might squirrel away valuables lifted from houses she slipped into at night. That was how they had first met, when Kate came upon Jennet emptying the shelves in the hall into the roomy pouches of her clothing. Simon had slept through the incident, and by the time Sam appeared Kate had invited Jennet out to the kitchen for a chat—with Berend as backup in case the young woman was not as interested in "honest employment" as she claimed.

Smiling at the memory, Kate rose as well. It was a relief to dress and then help Jennet transform herself into a young lad, all in silence so as not to wake Phillip and Marie.

For her present purposes Jennet had removed most of the bulky compartments from the tunic and breeches. Nowadays the compartments she inserted in her own and Kate's clothing were for weapons, and the tailoring for ease of movement. Kate blessed the night Jennet had attempted to rob her. "Three knives, Jennet?"

A soft laugh. "Never too many."

"No. Not for us," Kate agreed. She never let down her guard, never. When the last strand of hair was tucked into Jennet's roomy hat, Kate checked the landing. "It's clear."

Jennet strode to the door, already in character.

"Trust no one," Kate whispered.

"Only you, Dame Katherine."

"And Berend."

A cocky shrug, a curt nod. "He's kept quiet about me, it's true."

"Be back before sunset. We have a watch on Petergate."

Jennet nodded, then slipped onto the landing, down the stairs, and out the door.

How Kate yearned to tuck her own wild hair in a hat, don Geoff's breeches and shirt, and rush off after Jennet. How free she was. No eyes watched Jennet for missteps in propriety. Secrecy weighed Kate down, pinned her in place. Outside—all the gossips. Inside—her wards. And through it all she must emulate the ideal of the virtuous widow. She itched for some practice at the butt in the garden, but with Jennet gone Kate must see to her wards.

Women may be better at comforting each other, but men are so free, Geoff.

Free to die. Or haven't you noticed?

"Who was that?"

Kate's heart leapt as Marie padded out onto the landing squinting and yawning, swaddled in a blanket.

"Jennet. I sent her off on an early errand."

A whine. "Who will dress me?"

"Curl up on my bed while I fetch something warm to drink. Then I'll dress you."

The girl shuffled past and managed to climb onto the bed without unwrapping herself, rolling to the center, facedown.

Kate slipped a sheathed dagger into a slot in the front of her gown, then moved the scrip attached to the elegant leather and silver girdle on her hips to doubly conceal it. Not enough protection. Glancing back to check that Marie was not looking, Kate pushed aside a chest and peeled back a section of floorboard to reveal the little casket in which she kept the small battle-axe—a third the size of a soldier's, but efficient and deadly—that her father had given her on her twelfth birthday. She kept it sharpened and ready, in the fine leather pouch that was small enough to slip into the compartment in the right side of her skirt. She would prefer a larger weapon, but even this was difficult enough to hide. No voluminous skirts for her; the less fabric the better. With the axe, the dagger, and the wolf-hounds, she was as ready for trouble as she could be.

Marie began to snore.

Kate took a deep breath, preparing for another day of pretending all was as it should be in her world. She had grown so skilled in duplicity she thought that if all fell apart around her she might run away with a company of players and do quite well for herself. Turning that possibility over in her mind, she stepped out onto the landing, closing the door behind her.

Phillip shuffled out to join her, his face flushed from sleep, his buttons awry on his jacket. He yawned in her face as she reached to redo his buttoning.

"Mother of God, put your hand over your mouth when you yawn, Phillip. And chew some anise on your way to school."

"I can button my own jacket," he growled, turning away from her and bounding down the steps with the grace of a deer in the forest. Down below Lille and Ghent barked as Phillip rushed past their bed in front of the hearth. He ran out the rear door, but they waited until Kate gave them a nod before they dashed out with him. She saw that Sam had already put away his sleeping pallet. He had grumbled about the privacy he lacked when sleeping in the hall, having grown accustomed to his room in the front house. But he had agreed. So all were up early this morning.

On another snowy morning seven years ago, she had awakened from a dark dream to discover all the men and the hunting and guard dogs gone from her father's hall, only the pups Lille and Ghent left behind. She had run up to her brothers' chamber and found them gone as well. It was no surprise, but she'd wanted to see for herself. It was then that she'd heard the muffled sobs. Followed the sounds through the hall, past the buttery and pantry. More than one woman wept. *Oh God, please, not one of my brothers.* She'd hesitated in the kitchen doorway, crossed herself, stepped through. Her mother and her maidservant were bathing a body. Her brother, her sweet brother Roland.

Stop it! she ordered herself.

It's worse seeing it through you. I'd been so angry I didn't really see his body.

You're too much in my head this morning, brother.

She stepped into Geoff's boots and out onto the crusty snow. So cold, God help her, tonight she must wear several more layers to stand watch behind the guesthouse. She could not afford to be too stiff with cold to move and wield a weapon. She and Geoff had stood watch as children when an attack was imminent, serving as runners to warn the elders as the marauders appeared. Always the Scots were tagged as the attackers, even when her family or another English household had stirred the embers of the ongoing feuds. In winter, in snow, she and Geoff would huddle with the dogs beneath layers of skins that had to be shaken now and then to relieve the weight of the snow drifting over the lookouts cut into hillsides. The pack of dogs had been well trained, never making a sound.

Lille and Ghent bounded up to her now, shaking off the snow in a spray that chilled her unprotected face. She laughed and rubbed their backs with her gloved hands. "Hungry?" She signaled permission to go on along the cleared path to the kitchen door—bless Berend or Sam for shoveling it. The dogs trotted a few paces, then stopped before turning toward the alleyway to the street, alert, ears pricked. Lille growled.

An intruder. Hah! Kate withdrew beneath the eaves, slipping her axe from its sheath as she crept down the path to the alley, taking care to avoid the light spilling into the narrow space from Thomas Holme's lanterns. She saw no shadow. Perhaps she was wrong about an intruder. Would one be so foolish as to choose a lamp-lit alley? Lille and Ghent, trained to respond when she drew her weapon, squeezed past on either side to take the lead. They came to a standstill as someone in the alley stepped onto ice-encrusted snow, the noise loud in the predawn hush. Another mistake suggesting this was no threat, stealth not the stranger's intent. Yet Ghent growled.

Kate raised the axe and leaned to peer round the corner. It was Sam, the white hair sticking out of his hat and catching the lamplight.

"God save me," he said, shielding his eyes.

Behind him she noticed a slight movement. Ghent and Lille would not growl at Sam's approach, nor that of anyone else in the household. Someone was shadowing him.

"Drop to your knees, Sam," Kate whispered as she stepped away from the corner, aimed, let fly the axe. In the charged silence she heard the weapon spinning round and round, landing with a solid, satisfying thud. A curse, a tearing sound, a flicker of movement.

"Stay!" she commanded Lille and Ghent—they were trained to kill once she had used a weapon. She rushed down the alley. Nothing. The street was deserted but for a peddler pushing a cart, and a neighbor gossiping with her best friend. Kate cursed herself for being too cautious, calling off her hounds. She was out of practice.

Back in the alley, she pulled the axe from the wooden archway separating the yard of the small street-front building from her own larger house. A piece of cloth came away with the blade. Wool with a fur lining. No wonder the curse rather than a cry or groan; she had caught the edge of the shadow's clothing. A cloak, it would seem. Gratifying. Her senses had not entirely dulled with city living. She bent down to the dogs, let them sniff. "Find." She followed them out to the middle of the street, where they lost the scent. She asked her neighbor whether she had seen anyone running from the alleyway.

"I did. He followed your serving man into the alley, then came running out. He threw his cloak in the rag cart, then hurried off toward the castle. Such an odd thing to do in this cold. Is there trouble?"

So that was why they'd lost the scent—the cart. "Bless you, no. Nothing for you to worry about." Kate called over her shoulder as she picked her way along the crusty snow to the ragman's cart, Lille and Ghent trotting alongside.

To her surprise the person pushing the cart was neither a ragpicker nor a man. Kate motioned Lille and Ghent to her side. "They will not harm you," she assured the woman.

"I see they are well trained. I commend you on that." The woman pushed back her hood and studied Kate. "I do not believe I've had the pleasure of your acquaintance. Jocasta Sharp." She extended a gloved hand. "And you, with your fine hunting dogs. You must be Katherine Clifford."

Jocasta Sharp, the wife of one of Kate's customers at the guesthouse, with a fine house by All Saints Church. Kate took her hand. "The women back there thought you were a ragpicker."

Jocasta opened her arms to show off her simple but well-cut garb. "*You* see with your eyes, without prejudice, unlike those women who saw me as a ragpicker. My husband calls it a humiliation that his wife sees to the poor. My devotion to Christian duty shames him." She tapped the heavy cloth covering her load. "You want the fine cloak the thief tossed in my cart, I'll warrant. Tuppence to redeem it. For the poor of the parish."

"I'll gladly give you that and more if I might take it now and come to your house later today with the money and more clothes."

The woman tilted her head. "You did not take the Neville name. A Clifford born and a Clifford you remain, and your mother a Frost." She nodded. "As you are your own woman, I believe I can trust you. Your offer is more than fair, Katherine Clifford. God watches over the poor of our parish." She handed Kate the cloak, bid her a good morning.

"Did you get a good look at the thief?" She saw no point in correcting Jocasta's assumption that he'd stolen the cloak.

"I saw but the back of him, and he wore a hat that quite covered his hair. Queer that he stole the cloak. The clothes he wore beneath were just as fine."

"So you did not see him approach my house?"

"No. He startled me out of my prayers when he tossed the cloak on my cart. Sudden hard times, I would guess. Fortune's wheel claims us all eventually. I suppose he might have lost his own cloak. Or sold it. May God watch over you, Dame Katherine." Jocasta moved on, the wagon's wooden wheels clattering on the cobbles.

Kate draped the cloak over her shoulder to free her hands. "Come, Lille, Ghent." They headed back to the house.

In the alley, Sam was pacing. "What happened? What do you think you saw?"

"Someone slipped into the alleyway behind you. Ghent and Lille sensed danger. The neighbors said he was indeed following you."

"Oh. Yes. I do recall there was someone walking near me. I thought he meant to ask the way, but he never spoke."

"That is all, you say? You cried out, Sam. Lille and Ghent were growling. My dogs know you. They don't growl at you. He was behind you. My axe caught a bit of his cloak. The dogs caught the scent and helped me retrieve the rest." She handed him the piece of cloak that had caught on the archway.

Sam held it at arm's length as if it might burn him, shook his head, quickly handed it back to her. "Why would the knave follow me into the alley?"

"That is the question, isn't it? How long did he follow you?"

"I don't know. He never spoke. I should have challenged him."

He grows too old. Just a manservant now, Geoff whispered in her mind. *He's older than Simon would be, were he still alive.*

Kate wondered. Sam was the only one of Simon's original servants she had retained. She'd never had cause to complain about him. Too old? Perhaps. And embarrassed to have led the man to the house.

"Where had you been so early in the morning, Sam?"

"At the guesthouse. I rose early to return the letter to the pack in the shed. I thought if I returned it before dawn . . . But I found the barrow righted, the pack gone." He drew the letter from his scrip and handed it to her. "I blame myself for not going last night."

"I had not thought of it, either. But I expected you to be alert to who was around you. Didn't Berend impress on you how dangerous our adversary might be?"

"He did, God help me, and now I see he did not overstate this man's stealth."

Poor man, he was shivering now. She told him to go get warm in the kitchen.

"Should I talk to Master Frost's man Roger before I leave for Beverley?" Sam asked.

"No, we will not bother Master Frost's household." Kate no longer expected William to weaken the protection around himself and his family by sending any of his men to Beverley. Alice was nothing to him, or worse, a liability. Nor would she send Sam to Beverley now that he was either marked or caught in a lie. As Berend opened the door to Lille's and Ghent's barks and bowed all four in, Kate told Sam she was postponing his journey. "I want to know more before I send you."

—⚬⚬⚬—

Later, when Marie was dressed and loudly arguing with her brother in the kitchen and Sam was busy shifting more of the firewood from the shed to the hall, Kate took Berend aside to tell him of Sam's discovery at the guesthouse, and what had happened as he returned home.

Berend's expression was grim as he took the letter for safekeeping. "If Bale is alive, he will want this. That is a fact."

"Then hide it well. What of the cloak—is it something Bale would wear?"

"I never knew him to wear fur. He did not pamper himself. I need to see the corpse."

"I fault myself—"

Berend put a finger to her lips. "We move forward. I have some good news. I paid a visit to Matt early this morning on my way to the baker. Already he is moving about with the aid of a crutch. His injuries were not as dire as we feared."

That was a bit of good news. This would be a good time to switch him to her household and Sam to the guesthouse. Sam and Seth. "Griselde and Clement will be happy to hear he is doing so well. Does he recall anything about the accident?"

"It happened so quickly he remembers only turning to leap out of the way and falling beneath the oncoming wagon. Sometimes just as he's falling asleep he glimpses a man behind the wagon. He cannot describe him."

"Do you think it was Bale?"

"I am merely reporting what he said, not what I think."

"Has Matt received any unexpected visitors?"

"No, but he's armed at all times. The memory troubles him."

"It should."

Berend tucked the letter in his shirt. "I will hide this well. So Sam will not be going to Beverley. Perhaps I could slip away."

"I need you here, discovering who William buried, and where."

"I will think about what we might do."

Kate turned as a draft hit her. Marie was now alone at the table. "Where is Phillip?"

"He said he had an errand on his way to school." Marie wrinkled her nose at the roll she had just bitten into. "Soft cheese? *Merde*." She tossed it aside, considered her sticky hands, and bent toward Ghent.

Kate rushed forward, grabbing the girl's wrists. "What did I say I would do the next time I found food in their fur?"

A sulky lower lip. "Pour the chamber pots over my head."

"I do not make idle threats, Marie. I will do it."

Squirming. A whispered, "Sorry."

Church bells. "Time for school. Fetch your boots. I will help you with them."

Berend winked at the girl as she flounced past him. He was rewarded with a trembling smile. Kate thought to scold him, but to what end? The girl would be angry until it suited her to notice she had landed in a safe, secure, welcoming home. Until then, Kate must be patient. But she would not allow the girl to abuse any member of the household. There were limits.

As they walked, they leaned into the wind, scarves pulled up over their mouths and noses so they might breathe without swallowing blowing snow. Kate kept an eye on Marie, who had insisted on holding the dogs' leads. How cold it was out on the streets. Where could Alice Hatten have gone? Jennet and Sam both confirmed that the woman had moved away from York several years ago. No one seemed to know where she now lived, though they knew it could not be far, for she had come to York once to see old friends, looking well, even prosperous. That had been over a year ago. People repeated rumors of a rich lover or a business in a nearby town, but they were only ideas without firm details to support them. So Alice's home in Beverley was a secret. William's secret? He certainly had known Alice's whereabouts and was able to communicate with her. What hold did he have over her? She had been a young and innocent maidservant in his house, and he had seduced her. When his wife Isabella noticed that Alice was with child, William had meekly bowed his head and done nothing to protect her. Turned out on the street, she had been taken in by the bawd Joan del Bek. Of course. Pretty and fresh, Alice would bring in business. And now William had put her in the path of danger. Kate stopped in her tracks. What had become of the child? He or she was not in William's household.

"Dame Katherine?" It was Marie and Phillip's schoolmaster. She had not even noticed they had arrived at the school in the yard of St. Michael le Belfry on High Petergate. "Is Phillip not with you?" he asked.

"Phillip is not here? He left before us."

"No, nor was he here yesterday. I sent Marie home with a note. She did not deliver it?"

Marie was already in her place, whispering to two other girls.

"No, she did not." The little vixen. "Has he had trouble here?"

"Nothing I'm aware of, Dame Katherine. He's a good student when he cares to be. As is Marie."

"I will find him and talk to him. As he's not here, would you make certain Marie does not leave until my maidservant Jennet arrives for her?"

"Of course, Dame Katherine."

Before turning toward the widow Seaton's house, Kate went to the minster stoneyard to ask whether anyone had seen Phillip. Not this morning, but one of them had noticed him yesterday. With Connor. For a while.

"Then the bloody man stomped off in one of his moods, and the lad went after him. Then he returned to try to finish the work." The mason showed her what Phillip had done. "He has skill," the man noted.

No doubt about it, Phillip showed promise. But where was he?

Hugh Grantham appeared as she was leaving the yard.

"I've wondered about the boy. He's not come to me for instruction—still shadowing Connor."

"Clearly he needs to give him up. If you see Phillip or hear anything, would you leave word at the guesthouse?"

He promised to do that, reassuring her that Phillip was a clever lad, resourceful. "Wherever he is, I trust he is safe."

Kate knew better than to be so sure.

7

SLY SYMPATHIES

William Frost's mistress Drusilla Seaton lived with her son and his family on Stonegate, inhabiting a suite of rooms with its own entryway, in the part of the house that extended into the garden. Welcomed warmly, Kate settled beside the fire to warm herself, Lille and Ghent beside her, while her hostess fussed with the maidservant over the wine she was mulling.

"Just back from market with new spices. I believe they're from your warehouse, Kate. I have a new recipe you must taste!"

"It is a day for hot spiced wine," Kate said, pretending interest. Lille and Ghent made noises about a dog outside the window, scratching in the frozen turf. So cold. Had Phillip dressed warmly? She fretted that she wasted time here. She should be out searching for her ward.

"Is something wrong, my dear?" Drusilla inquired, leaning forward and resting a lavender-scented hand on Kate's shoulder.

"The usual worries about Phillip and Marie, whether I am doing what is best for them. William does not approve of Phillip's work for Hugh Grantham."

Drusilla Seaton wrinkled her nose. "Your cousin is too influenced by his wife's prejudices. The woman sees everyone as a threat to her own interests, just as her father did before her. You are a capable young woman. Do not doubt yourself. You are giving Phillip a profoundly generous and wise gift in allowing him to find out for himself what will give him the most satisfaction." The widow sipped her wine, her clear blue eyes watchful over the edge of the cup. "Margery Kirkby is fortunate to be hosted by you and the incomparable Goodwife Griselde, my dear Kate, her every comfort seen to so seamlessly. I do pray she is not tempted by your welcome to extend her stay. For all his faults, three weeks without William seems an eternity."

"A fortnight, not three weeks, Drusilla."

"Three weeks for me. I did question the wisdom of your giving up revenue for a week prior to her stay so that you might prepare. She is not so fine as all that. But I suspect it was Goodwife Griselde who persuaded you. Clement's illness . . ."

Kate had stopped listening. So William had never intended to stay that night with Drusilla. The stranger's evening there had been planned in advance, and William had waited until Griselde had little time to warn her. Why did this make her heart race when she'd already guessed he dissembled with her?

Realizing that her hostess awaited a response, Kate said, "I am quite fond of Margery. But it was my uncle Clifford who insisted I treat her as an honored guest." She could see by the widow's expression that she had not guessed correctly what the unheard question had been, but she could hardly ask Drusilla what she had missed. Something about Griselde and Clement. "As for Griselde, I've hired young Seth Fletcher to help her," said Kate. "Some brawn about the house."

Drusilla chuckled. "Well, the lad's better than nothing, I suppose. But what of Matt? Oh—I'd forgotten. The runaway wagon. Will he walk again, do you think?"

Kate did not answer, thinking about what Matt had told Berend, a vague memory of a man behind the wagon. Perhaps the murderer—or William?—had disabled Matt so that he might not interfere that night at the guesthouse. It seemed far too much of a coincidence.

"My, you are preoccupied this morning, Katherine."

"Forgive me. Poor Matt. I should pay him a visit and see how he fares."
No need to let people know how quickly Matt was recovering.

"Such a tragedy for him. And for you at such a time." Drusilla shook
her head. "A man of Richard Clifford's stature—well, he might be your
uncle, but you could not have denied him this. He will not be dean of
York Minster for long, I hear. A bishop's miter is in his future. Though
with King Richard planning an expedition to Ireland there may be more
of a delay than your uncle might like."

Kate felt a twinge of regret. She enjoyed her uncle's company, and the
added security of his presence in the city. But she was not surprised he
would soon be promoted. "Yes, that branch of my family is well-placed
at court, and particularly my uncle—privy seal, wardrobe. They are also
well liked by the Lancastrians, if it should come to that. As for my mother's
kin—the Frosts are ever the opportunists, like the Nevilles. William has
not spoken of the king of late. Is he still in his favor?"

"Is that what this visit is about? You want to know whether William
sympathizes with King Richard or the Duke of Hereford?"

Of course Kate's purpose was to learn what was more likely, that
William's secret guest was King Richard's man or an envoy from the
Lancastrians. An unknown, or Hubert Bale. She had no idea how far she
might trust Drusilla. "I cannot deny that I wonder where he stands, but
no more so than I do about anyone of stature in York. King Richard gave
us our charter as a self-governing city, and William was very much a part
of that. But to exile the Duke of Lancaster's heir—"

"And that he might confiscate his property. I know."

They both shook their heads.

"William has been quiet about the affair," said Drusilla. "Perhaps he
and Isabella disagree about which side to support, if it comes to that. And
considering the power and wealth of the Lancastrian affinity, I expect
Duke Henry might well return with an army."

Yet another who saw it as the most likely result.

Drusilla glanced out the window. "Oh, my dear, you cannot see the
garden for the falling snow. Will this winter never end? You must stay to
dine with me."

Cursed weather. "I should see to my wards."

"I pray you, wait here until the storm passes, Katherine. Stay and break bread with me. See? My maidservant is already bringing the food. And I have a fine wine."

Perhaps over a meal and some wine Drusilla might forget herself and confide something useful. Kate agreed it was best to wait out the worst of the storm, so she took Lille and Ghent out into the wintry garden while Drusilla's servant set the table for the meal. Wrapping her fur-lined cloak tightly round her, Kate stood beneath the eaves while the wolfhounds hesitantly explored the sheltered space, Ghent snuffling out in the wind, Lille pressing into the corners. Despite the sheltering overhang, she was buffeted by the gusts that caught her skirts. The blowing snow stung her face. Where was Phillip?

She forced her thoughts to the task at hand. Drusilla was being as cagey as William. Kate did not believe that her cousin had not discussed the tension between the king and the duke with Drusilla; he valued his mistress's insight into the state of the realm and civic issues, seeking her counsel in such matters.

She felt more and more certain that the meeting in the bedchamber had not been an accidental encounter. As for Matt's injuries and Griselde's "few cups of wine" that made her sleep so soundly through what must have been a noisy brawl—they fit with a planned ambush. Even Clement, who often lay awake through the night, had slept through the event. It was all too tidy.

If this was William's doing, Drusilla was likely involved. Or had it gone wrong because William had not taken her counsel?

Had it gone wrong? William seemed frightened. But so might he be after executing a daring plan, for he was not by habit a man of action, prizing comfort over courage.

She must have a care in talking to Drusilla. She valued the woman's friendship, appreciating her clear-eyed outlook, her curiosity, and her sense of humor. But Drusilla loved William, risking her reputation to be with him.

No one could be trusted.

When the serving woman stepped out to say the meal was ready, she held out a thick cloth to dry the dogs. "I dare not try to wipe them myself, mistress."

Kate laughed. No, they would not tolerate such handling by a stranger. Calling Lille and Ghent to her side, Kate dried them off as best she could before they reentered the parlor. Drusilla fussed over Kate, offering her a pair of soft leather slippers to warm her feet while her boots dried.

"I should have forbidden you to stay out so long, my dear. You had only just recovered from your journey here—though I suspect you had not come directly from home—you and your hounds were so wet and cold when you arrived. What drew you out early on such a morning? I did not see you at the market." Drusilla's blue gaze expressed both concern and affection, her hand warm on Kate's.

"My household is busy with so many biding at the guesthouse and young Seth being so new. I took the dogs for their run in the gardens across Castlegate and then walked Marie to school. This snow is nothing to me, growing up on the northern border."

A nod and a pat on the hand, and Drusilla launched into questions about Margery Kirkby. "Tell me all about her wardrobe. How many chests? Still the bright henna in her hair?"

Kate went on at length about all she had observed of Margery's gowns, boots, slippers, and jewelry, hoping to exhaust her hostess so that she might forget herself and voice some opinion regarding Margery's mission. But by the time Kate grew hoarse and the stew tepid, Drusilla had not yet uttered a wayward word. No wonder William trusted her.

"I pray Lady Kirkby is able to convince those with influence of her husband's sincere wish for peace," said Drusilla.

Ah. Now? "What of William? Should I suggest that she invite him to dine with her?"

A chuckle. "As I said, William looks to his wife, the imperious Isabella, in such matters. I have little insight into the woman married to the man I love. Faith, I try not to think of her. After all, I intrude on her marriage."

Defeated, Kate complimented Drusilla on the delicate spicing of the stew and the remarkable wine she was serving.

"The wine—yes, it is exceptional, is it not? A gift from William. I should have thought he would share some with you. His factor made a clever deal with a vintner who found himself short on funds in Calais. Which reminds me, how are you faring with Lionel as your factor?"

Kate groaned.

Drusilla laughed and took Kate's hand. "Something clearly troubles you, Kate. I believe your trade is doing well, both the guesthouse and your shipping, yes? So it is Lionel Neville who troubles you?"

"Not just Lionel." She told her about the king's men searching the ship.

"Oh, my dear, that is troubling. Perhaps it is time you remarried. The Nevilles are clearly not protecting you sufficiently."

"I am better off on my own. You know the terms of Simon's will." Kate fought to keep her tone light, teasing.

"From what I've heard, not one of those who have approached William for his consent is worth less than Simon."

It would not take much to be worth more than Simon. But it infuriated Kate that William took it upon himself to advise her to remarry. "My cousin should not jeopardize friendships with offers he's no right to make."

"Katherine, your mother, my dear friend, asked William to watch over you. Any one of the men he's chosen for you would make you a good husband. And save you from the clutches of the Nevilles."

"I will decide whether or not to wed again. And, if I do, I will make my own choice. William should see to his own. What has he done for Alice Hatten? Did he help *her* make a new beginning?"

Drusilla flushed. "Alice Hatten. Another woman I choose not to think about. You might have simply told me to mind my own business. You did not need to bring her up. But as you did, I know nothing of her fate. He never speaks of Alice."

That had been clumsy. "Forgive me, Drusilla. Clearly the wine has gone to my head, and it is time I left." Kate rose. Was this the same wine that William had sent to the guesthouse? It *was* strong. But not so unusual, not enough to topple the sturdy Griselde with two cups.

Drusilla hurried round the table to embrace Kate and apologize for bringing up the subject of marriage.

Kate forced a laugh. "I trust you to advise William to inform potential suitors that he has no say in my affairs." She glanced out the glazed window. The snow had stopped, though the wind was still blowing the already fallen snow into drifts. Kate thanked Drusilla for the meal and the companionship before stepping out once more into the blustery weather.

Lille and Ghent set their muzzles to the wind and pranced up Stonegate and across High Petergate, clearly glad to be out and about. Kate was headed to the deanery to tell her uncle that she had changed her mind about Sam going to Beverley, so she would not need the letter of introduction from him. But her uncle was not at home. His secretary, Alf, informed her that Dean Richard was dining at the guesthouse with Lady Margery. He did not expect him back until evening.

As she headed back toward Stonegate, trying to decide how she might best use what was left of the afternoon, she was surprised to find the dean striding toward her. That was not a good sign; Lady Margery's dinners usually lasted through the afternoon. Kate hailed him. "I came to tell you I've changed my mind about sending Sam to Beverley."

"Too late, Katherine. Your servant came for the letter of introduction this morning. He hoped to be on the road before the storm."

"But I had told him—" Kate closed her eyes against the self-blame. How could she know Sam would suddenly decide to go against her wishes? But it was disturbing news. "How did he seem to you? Anxious?"

"I do not know him well enough to say. Do you not trust him?"

"I told him to wait until the snow passed. He's not a young man."

"He is not an old man." Richard Clifford put his gloved hands on Kate's shoulders and gave her a long look. "You carry such a weight, Katherine. I pray you, let me help. Tell me what I can do."

She nodded, knowing she could trust him. Perhaps in telling him all that was on her mind, she would see the way forward. "Come. Let us take shelter for a moment in St. Michael's." Once settled on a bench set beneath a window in the corner of the nave, she recounted the incident with Sam.

"Who do you think followed him?" the dean asked.

"Whoever murdered William's guest? Or perhaps it was merely someone who hoped to follow him into the house and steal the pewter plates. The cloak was old, the wool threadbare in places, much of the fur matted. It had been fine at one time. A servant wearing his master's old clothes? A thief, as Jocasta Sharp assumed? Someone disguised as lesser than he is?"

"You know more about the murder than you told me, don't you?"

She told him about the pack, the letter, and Berend's description of Hubert Bale.

72

"That is a worry. How might I help? Should I send my groom after your servant? He loves nothing better than an excuse to ride out. He might at least find Sam if he's been waylaid, help him home."

"No, uncle, I will not have two frozen corpses on my conscience." She squeezed his hand. "But thank you."

"There is more?"

"Phillip is truant from school today. Yesterday as well. Did you see a messenger from Hugh Grantham while at the guesthouse?"

"Is the lad daft? Does he not understand the danger?"

"Neither he nor his sister know of the murder."

A frown. "Is that wise? Perhaps if they knew . . ." Richard shook his head. "Forgive me. I am not a parent. I trust you have good reason to keep it from them."

"Nor am I their mother. We exist in an uneasy truce."

"The Nevilles should have claimed them. You might petition the earl—"

"Too late, uncle. To my surprise I have grown fond of them."

A grunt. "Again, forgive my blundering advice. Do you have any idea why he's truant?"

"I wish I knew. He seems to care overmuch for the stoneworker who was guiding him, who now rarely shows up to work. It seems Connor is a drinker. I pray Phillip is not in a tavern with him."

"Surely most innkeepers in the city know better than to serve your young ward. You mentioned Jocasta Sharp. I suggest that you talk to her about Phillip's wanderings when you next see her. She will have her people watch out for him."

"Her people?"

"The poor. She is a patron saint to them. They will do anything for her. Under her guidance the poor of York are learning to support one another, and to be guardians to others in the city. Many have found work in service through their good deeds—returning a lost scrip, rescuing stray animals." He patted her hand. "I believe I see the hand of the Divine in your encounter with Jocasta this morning."

Her uncle rarely invoked the divine. Indeed, it was easy to forget he was a priest, so seldom did he reference his calling. "I will ask her. And thank you, uncle. I feel better to have shared my burden." She kissed his cheek. "So. I was surprised to see you away from Lady Kirkby's dinner table so early in the afternoon. Did the mayor attend?"

"He did, as did several other aldermen and their wives. But your cousin William Frost declined the invitation, and they all took that as a sign not to support her."

"And said so?"

He bowed his head. "They did. Leaving no one in the mood to linger. Lady Margery went up to bed with a pounding head."

Her cousin had much to answer for of late. "I was not aware she had invited William. Had I known that was her intent I would have dissuaded her. I cannot imagine his feeling easy in that house just now. But of course his fellows would not know why."

"Perhaps we should have told her all that happened?"

"Not yet, uncle. Right now I need to talk to Griselde and Clement, then stop at the school to make sure Jennet fetched Marie. And consult with Jocasta Sharp."

"If I hear anything of your ward I will send you word at once."

He drew her up and kissed her on each cheek. "May God watch over you and your household, Katherine." As Lille and Ghent rose, Richard Clifford bent to pet them. "And you, my regal friends, I entrust my niece to your protection in these troubling times."

⁓⊚⁓

For once it was Kate urging Lille and Ghent to hurry along the snowy streets. As she negotiated the drifts and frozen ruts she whispered a prayer that she would find Phillip safe at home. Her relief that Jennet had collected Marie at the school had been dampened by the schoolmaster's shake of the head—no, Phillip had never shown up.

But she found only Berend and Marie in the kitchen. Jennet had gone back out.

Marie glanced up from her stirring to inform Kate that she must have a word with her maidservant when she returned. "When she arrived at the school she had dressed with such haste she had missed a button and her gown was askew. Her slovenly appearance embarrassed me."

74

"You are one to throw stones. You did not give me the note your school-master entrusted to you. That is far worse than a missed button." Kate held out her hand. "I would see it now."

A shrug. "I lost it." Marie returned to her stirring.

Kate grabbed the spoon from the girl's hand and pushed the bowl aside. "Find it. Now."

With a sniff, the girl tossed aside her apron and pulled off the cloths protecting her long sleeves, narrowly missing the bowl as she tossed them onto the table. As she flounced out the door, Lionel Neville entered.

From bad to worse. "Dear Lionel. To what do I owe the honor of your visit?"

"I would have a word."

Kate had passed through the hall on her return to collect her bow and a quiver of arrows for some time at the butt. Scooping them up she stepped across the threshold, glancing back to invite him to follow. "We will talk out in the fresh air."

His look was pained. That pleased her. And it interested her that Lille and Ghent fell to sniffing intently at him as he stepped into the yard.

"Would you at least do me the courtesy of keeping them away from me?"

Agreeing that it was enough to make the man stand out in the cold with her, she shooed the dogs into the hall where they could happily nap by the fire, and alert her to any unexpected activity. That settled, she knocked the snow and ice off the straw-stuffed butt and turned it so that the wan winter sunlight was behind her. Then she notched an arrow, aimed. A superstitious thought arose as she let it fly—*If it lands in the center, Phillip will come home safe and sound.* It landed ever so slightly off center. She silently cursed herself.

"So? Speak, Lionel." She reached for a second arrow.

"I ask you to introduce me to Lady Kirkby."

She laughed. "If she wishes to confer with a Neville, it would not be you she would call on."

Most people would have rosy cheeks out in the snow, but his narrow face was pinched and pale though there was some spark in his eyes. "It was my cousin the earl who suggested it."

"If he writes a letter, I promise to deliver it." She aimed. Dead center. "He doubts Lady Kirkby's professed mission?"

"King Richard did not send Lord Kirkby to the continent to make peace with his cousin Bolingbroke. In whose name, then, might he sue for peace? Why would Bolingbroke trust Kirkby with his fate?" Lionel stomped and blew on his gloved hands. "Are you impervious to cold?" He tucked his hands inside his cloak.

"I find it refreshing. As to your questions, I of course cannot answer for Lady Kirkby. All I can say is that if she wishes to invite a member of the Neville family to dine with her, she would confer with your powerful cousin the Earl of Westmoreland as to whom he would care to have represent him. And as the earl does not reside in York, I doubt she has him on her list for this visit." Kate turned back to the butt and notched another arrow.

A brief silence ensued. She shot several arrows before he spoke again, startling her.

"I understand you are concerned about Phillip, that he has been absent from school for two days and you have no idea where he goes instead."

She lowered the bow and turned to him, the arrow still notched. "Have you information?"

"In fact, I do. He's been seen at the bawdy houses round the Bedern, and in a tavern with a drunk stonecutter. My nephew. A Neville. Disgraceful!"

She took a step toward him. "Where? Take me there."

"Gone now. I will bring him to you next time I catch him—in exchange for a meeting with Lady Kirkby."

Hah! She could not imagine him dragging Phillip away from Connor. She watched Lionel for a moment, how his face tensed and relaxed as he studied something off in the distance. He was scheming, as usual. What she could not make out was whether it was as he said, that he wanted to trade information for an introduction, or whether there was more. His nervous eye movements would suggest more.

"I will consider your proposed trade and let you know what I decide." She turned back to the butt, raised the arrow, and hit dead center. First she would talk to Phillip. She hoped.

Lionel cleared his throat.

"Still here, are you?" She glanced at him.

He grimaced, apparently an attempt at a smile. "I wondered where I might find your man Sam. I have something of Simon's I meant to give him. I think he would appreciate it."

God only knew where Sam was. Frozen in a snowdrift on the road to Beverley? Lying wounded on the ice in a ditch beside the road? "He is on an errand for me. You can leave the item here. I will see that he knows it is your gift to him."

"I would prefer to present it to him myself. When will he return?"

She pulled another arrow from her quiver, notched, aimed. A little off to the right.

Why does he bother you so? Geoff wondered.

It's Sam's journey to Beverley that troubles me.

"Katherine?"

"I gave him leave to attend to some personal business as well, Lionel. He might not return tonight."

"Oh."

The worry in that one syllable caught Kate's attention, but when she turned to see Lionel's expression, he was gone. It left her wondering what he meant to give Sam. She looked down at the bow in her hands. The practice had not relaxed her. She had wasted it, using it to irritate Lionel. Gathering the arrows from the butt, she tucked them in the quiver and withdrew to the hall, where she found Marie sitting by the fire, combing Lille.

"Have you met Connor, the stonemason your brother admires?"

A pouty shrug, then a vigorous shake of the head that set her dark curls dancing. "Phillip said I would only insult him, so he would not introduce me. I have seen him, though, drunkenly tottering down Low Petergate, his torn and tattered clothes filthy with stone dust and who knows what else." She wrinkled her nose.

"Has Phillip been with Connor the past few days?"

"He will not say. Even after I hid the schoolmaster's letter to you he would not say." Marie reached down, picked up a soggy piece of parchment and offered it to Kate. "So here. Here is the letter. Phillip does not deserve my loyalty."

"Thank you for combing Lille."

"I'm not a bad person, Dame Katherine."

Kate bit back a smile. "No. No, you are not, Marie." She wished she knew how to cheer the girl.

And why Phillip was following Connor about to bawdy houses and taverns.

8

IN THE REEDS

—◦◦◦—

Stepping out onto the street in the last light of the afternoon, Kate paused, sensing a change in the weather—more than the hint of weak winter sun that had graced her time at the butts, and a hint of green in the scent of the air. The snow oozed underfoot, already melting. God be thanked. It had been a long winter in the confines of a city, where the freeze and thaw on cobbles required one to keep eyes to the ground. She readjusted the clothes draped over her arm so that she might more comfortably hold the dogs' leashes as she struck out for the Sharp house. As she turned onto Coppergate she collided with a lad.

"Steady now, young man. Oh. Jennet." She whispered the last word, catching her maidservant as she stumbled. Kate guided her off to the side, beneath the eaves of the corner house. Lille and Ghent sniffed Jennet with great interest to see where she had been.

Red-faced and short of breath, still dressed as a lad, Jennet bent forward, hands to thighs, catching her breath. When at last she straightened, her expression prepared Kate for bad news.

"What we have most feared has come to pass, Dame Katherine. Alice Hatten was found floating in the reeds at the edge of the King's Fishpond."

"Drowned? Merciful Mother."

Jennet was shaking her head. "She did not drown. Her tongue was cut out, then she was beaten and discarded in the water."

Kate crossed herself against evil. "What devil moves among us? Her tongue was cut out? Are you certain? It was not the fish?"

"Her jaw was broken, hanging open, so the men who pulled her out could see clearly that the cut was too straight for fish to have nibbled it." Jennet closed her eyes. "I pushed through the crowd and saw it myself." She pressed her hands to her face and bowed her head, an unusual gesture for Jennet.

Kate sagged against the building, searching for what she might have done differently, how she might have prevented this. But it was William's doing, hidden from Kate until disaster struck. "God grant her peace," she whispered.

"Amen." Jennet fingered the clothes on Kate's arm. "Where are you going with these?"

"To Jocasta Sharp."

"Shall I come?"

"No. Tell Berend about Alice, if you will."

Jennet nodded.

"You saw her, then?"

"I did. I am sorry I did."

"You know where I hide the brandywine."

A little smile. "Thank you."

Ghent growled as Jennet headed on down Castlegate. Kate gave his leash a little tug to reprimand him for wanting to follow Jennet home, but then noticed he was looking at the dark space between two houses. Lille joined him. Holding tight to their leashes, Kate commanded them to continue on down Coppergate. Just past All Saints Church the dogs calmed, though they kept glancing round as if expecting to find danger following.

So like that day, many years before. Still being trained to track, Lille and Ghent had led Kate and Geoff to the fresh corpse of Maud, their neighbor's daughter and Kate's best friend, in a field. The pups went mad with the smell of blood. It soaked Maud's gown, her hair, the ground beneath her. It was only later, as the women cleaned the young woman's body, that they discovered the source of the copious bleeding: Her tongue had been cut out. All knew why. Maud had told her father that she had been raped by the Caverton brothers, and they had warned her she would die if she told.

Her mother had brought Kate south to York, for her safety. Useless effort.

She was so afraid for Phillip. Damn William. Damn him for bringing this terror on her household. And for putting Alice in such danger. Had he not done enough, abandoning her when Isabella had learned of his lust for her?

Holy Mary, Mother of God, gather Alice in your loving arms and hold her close, Kate prayed.

Ghent suddenly shied away from an alley. His ears back, he let out a low growl. Kate crouched down to the dogs. Lille was sniffing the air, her upper lip curled back. Ghent shook his head and went quiet at Kate's touch. She peered into the darkness, saw nothing. An acquaintance stopped to ask her whether she needed help.

Brushing the snow from her cloak and stomping it from her boots, Kate assured him that all was well—though of course it was anything but. Someone shadowed her. But the merchant, born and raised in the city, was hardly the person to help her. He would suggest she report her concern to one of the sheriffs, who would doubtless pat her hand and suggest her hounds had been spooked by a cunning cat. It was up to Kate to make the sheriffs sit up and take notice of the violence done Alice Hatten. She urged Lille and Ghent forward, arriving at Jocasta's doorstep with a chill at her back that had nothing to do with the melting snow. She paused and took note of her surroundings to steady herself.

The house looked narrow from the street, but it was clearly a long structure set solidly on a stone undercroft for the storage of Edmund Sharp's merchandise, wine and spices. The one window facing the street was glazed, subject to a costly tax. She urged the dogs through a wide archway into a cobbled courtyard and up to a hefty oaken door, polished to a soft sheen. It opened upon her knock, and a young male servant appeared, bowing and asking her business in a respectful manner. Well trained. When she explained her mission, he nodded.

"My mistress said you might come. She is away at the moment, but should be back shortly." As he spoke, he was upstaged by a small terrier who rushed out between the young man's legs and proceeded to sniff at Lille and Ghent. The two giants nudged her gently with their muzzles while wagging their tails.

"Ah. As Lady Gray seems quite happy to welcome your dogs, I am able to invite you within to wait for my mistress. When Dame Jocasta stepped out, she told me to take Lady Gray's guidance as to whether your grand hounds might wait comfortably in the hall, or whether they would be more at ease in the kitchen. My mistress puts great store in Lady Gray's discernment."

Kate found the servant as intriguing as his mistress—his serious expression, his treatment of the dog, the exaggerated courtesy with which he invited her to sit and inquired as to whether she would prefer wine, brandywine, or ale. She requested brandywine.

"How long ago was your mistress called away?"

"Long enough that we expect her anytime now." He bowed to her and slipped away to fetch her refreshment.

Her amusement regarding this odd welcome was a blessing, easing her sense of danger, allowing her to relax muscles already stiffened from the strain of worry as well as the cold. When the young manservant returned, Kate proffered him the clothes she had brought for the poor. He carried them with courteous ceremony to a large, leather-bound trunk near the service doorway, where he arranged the items with care. She guessed that this young man was a recipient of Jocasta's charity, and thus carried out his duties with a grave sense of the wonder of life. As she sipped the brandywine in a delicate Italian glass goblet, Kate watched the petite Lady Gray shepherd Lille and Ghent to a long cushion near the fire, where they settled in a jumble of gray, white, and black. But once the dogs had settled, Kate's thoughts returned to Alice's grisly death.

I am sorry you were reminded of that awful discovery, Kate, Geoff whispered in her mind.

Peace, Geoff. This has nothing to do with you.

Kate drew out her ebony and ivory rosary beads and distracted herself with prayer until Jocasta should return. But the warmth of the fire, the ease of her dogs, and the strength of the brandywine lulled her into a doze. She was awakened by a soft touch on her forearm and the young servant's announcement that he heard his mistress's cart in the courtyard.

Kate followed him, standing to one side as he opened the door. Winter dusk had settled, the courtyard lit by several hanging lanterns. A procession of women, some of them carrying lanterns, escorted Jocasta and her cart. Lying atop the covering was a woman's body. Alice Hatten. Kate crossed herself.

As Jocasta guided the cart into the courtyard, her companions fanned out, then flowed through the archway. Jocasta stepped away from the cart, and, turning to the women, lifted her arms and her voice in a hymn of evening and departures. The women joined in, singing as they lifted Alice Hatten's body and carried her past Kate and the servant into the hall and through to the buttery, where they lay her on a stone table. Jocasta nodded to Kate as she followed. A few quiet orders and two serving maids hurried off. Still singing, Jocasta lit candles round the room. When the servants returned with herbs, oils, a sewing basket, a comb, and clean linens, Jocasta plucked a pair of scissors from the basket and began to cut at the hem of Alice's sodden, bloodstained gown.

Kate stepped closer, watching as one of the other women took a comb and began to work on the tangles and debris in Alice's pale hair. The dead woman's face was badly bruised and her jaw hung open to reveal the horrible emptiness within.

—◦⊙◦—

A memory. Kate hiding in one of the stable stalls, listening to her brothers speaking in hushed voices about the mutilation of her friend Maud.

"Can you imagine the pain of someone forcing open your mouth until your jaw breaks?" Roland's voice broke.

"Why'd they do that?" Geoff. It was Geoff asking, the little brother, his voice shaky.

"So they could use the scissors or the sharp knife to cut out her tongue. How do you think they managed that otherwise?" said Walter. Kate guessed that Geoff must be getting sick imagining it. "They had to pull her tongue out as far as possible, you see." Walter, trying to sound like a wise eldest brother.

"How she must have suffered," Roland sobbed. "Damn the Cavertons. Damn them all to hell."

Solemnly the brothers swore to avenge Maud's rape, torture, and murder.

"They must be shown they cannot commit such acts and live," said Walter.

—◦◦◦—

I did not get sick.

No, you did not, Geoff. But Walter need not have spoken so.

It was to stir us to action.

Kate could still feel her fear, how her heart had raced. She had feared she might be next.

She shook off the memory, forcing her attention back to her concern for Phillip. Where was he? Was he in danger?

"Dame Katherine, come, sit by the fire." Jocasta took Kate's arm and escorted her back to the cushioned chair near the fire. The young servant appeared at his mistress's elbow to pour brandywine. "Take a sip of your wine, my dear. You are white as the snow."

Kate realized she still held her prayer beads. "May God receive her into his loving embrace." She crossed herself and slipped the beads into her scrip so she might drink.

"It was difficult for you to watch?" Jocasta asked. "Forgive me, I had not thought how it might affect you."

"No, it is not that. I have seen mutilated bodies before. It is my ward. He is out on the streets, somewhere. I fear for him."

"My dear. Tell me. Perhaps I can help."

The concern in the woman's expression eased Kate's sense of guilt for interrupting her preparations for Alice's burial. She told Jocasta about

Phillip's disappearances, and Lionel's report. "And now, seeing that poor woman, knowing he is out on the streets somewhere . . ."

"I will have my friends watch out for him and keep him from harm, Katherine. You have my word. You say this stonemason's name is Connor?"

"Yes. Do you know him?"

Jocasta looked into the fire. "A slip of memory. Gone now. Perhaps as we talk it will return."

"How did you learn of Alice's death?"

"From one of the men to whom I have given aid. Well, he is still begging, and sometimes tries to poach from the King's Fishpond. As he was doing when he noticed Alice in the reeds, raised the hue and cry, and then came to me. Word spread. By the time the sheriffs' men had arrived to pull Alice's body from the water several women from Joan del Bek's were there, offering to prepare her body for burial and keep the vigil."

"How did the beggar know to come to you?"

"I take care of the women no one claims. See that they are prayed over, watched over. So naturally he brought her here, though he did not know what she meant to me." Jocasta closed her eyes.

"You knew Alice Hatten well?"

"She was like a daughter to me. But I did not know she was here in the city. What drew her from Beverley with the roads so treacherous I have no idea. Was she here to seek my help, but never made it so far?" Jocasta's proud face twisted in grief. She bowed her head and was quiet a long while, until Lady Gray scrambled up onto her lap, nudging her chin. "Dear one," Jocasta whispered, stroking the terrier's back until she settled.

Kate asked if she would prefer to be alone.

"Not at all. Did you know Alice?"

Kate shook her head. In truth she had known her only as William and Isabella's victim. "I know that she once served in my cousin's household. William Frost."

"She did indeed. I took Alice in when your cousin's wife Isabella put her out on the street. I assisted at the birth of her son, and arranged for his adoption by her married sister."

85

"A son." Kate sat up. William and Isabella had only a daughter, Hazel, an invalid. Her cousin was devoted to his daughter, but yearned for a son. "I did not know of your part in her story."

"No one knew I cared for her here. I put out a rumor that Joan del Bek had taken Alice in. It is what everyone wanted to believe, and so they did. Alice served me for several years. She was a good companion for my youngest daughter. I thought she had put the past behind her. Not so. Eventually her heart betrayed her. She let William know she was still here, and that he had a son."

Kate wondered whether Dean Richard had known what she might learn here. "How is it that William did not adopt the boy?"

"I made certain he could not, not without going to great expense, which would alert his wife. He would not want that. Even if he did wish to pursue custody, Alice's sister, Tessa, swears he will never win it."

Had this something to do with all that had happened?

"I am sorry if I sound as if I blame your cousin," Jocasta said. "He has done much good for the city. In his relationship with Alice he was no different from many other men."

Kate did not trust herself to speak wisely about her cousin at the moment. "God smiled on Alice to provide you as her protector."

"God guided me in this. I take no credit for it." Jocasta gestured to the servant to refill their goblets. She noticed Kate put a hand over hers. "You are wise. Have you any knowledge of how it was between Alice and William of late? Might he have summoned her to the city?"

God forgive me for my lies and silences with this good woman. "I had not realized they were still entangled. He did not speak of her to me. I assumed it was William who provided her with the house in Beverley. But was it you?"

"No, it was your cousin's largesse, an attempt to ease his guilt. And, I believe, he hoped that he might visit his son there."

"That is where her sister lives?"

"No. They live just downriver from Bishopthorpe. A cousin lives in Beverley, so Alice had a connection with the community. And it is my understanding that the child often visits her on market day, with her sister."

"Someone must tell Tessa and the cousin of Alice's death."

"I shall speak with one of the friars who assists me in my work. I think he will be willing to take word to Alice's sister and her cousin. And I will see to her burial, of course. Her kin might bide with me to attend the requiem."

"They will come?"

"If the snow continues, I doubt the cousin will, but her sister will come if her husband agrees to it."

"He was not fond of Alice?"

"He considered her an embarrassment to the family. As so many who manage to climb to some level of comfort, he is fiercely protective of his respectability. He worked hard to afford a small holding and fears that a connection with a fallen woman will cause him to lose everything." Jocasta excused herself, rising to address the women now filing out of the buttery. "Go to the kitchen, where there is ale and food for you. I leave it for you to decide among yourselves who will sit with Alice tonight." As she turned back, she passed the leather-bound trunk holding the clothing Kate had brought. Lifting the items one by one, she fingered the cloth, shook out the clothes to examine the tailoring. Returning, she smiled and kissed Kate's hand. "Bless you. I know several men who will benefit from those fine garments. They are your late husband's clothes?"

"Some. The ones I hid from his brother Lionel. There are other pieces I will save for Phillip, things that can be cut down to fit his smaller frame."

"The Nevilles. I have little to do with them. But your late husband was not quite like the rest of his family. He was generous to the poor, and was often at church. My husband was fond of him. As of course you know." Her glance was suddenly sly.

By that Kate guessed her hostess meant to acknowledge that her husband patronized the guesthouse on High Petergate. Kate felt suddenly awkward, unsure how to respond.

Jocasta leaned to touch Kate's cheek. "Forgive me, I did not mean to cause you discomfort. When God called me to this life of ministry, I assured Edmund that he was free to see to his needs, asking only that his affairs be ones of mutual consent, with widows of his own class, if possible. I did not wish him to harm a young woman, as did your cousin."

"We are alike in that." Kate put aside the brandywine. So much to take in, so much to consider. "I will inform my cousin about Alice's murder," she said, meeting Jocasta's steady gaze. "And I will attend the requiem."

"Oh, my lovely Katherine, yes, I welcome your company. God put us in each other's path for a reason today."

Kate rose. "I should be at home in case anyone has news of Phillip."

"My people will watch out for him, Katherine. I pray he will soon be returned to you, safe and sound."

As Jocasta rose to embrace Kate, the courtyard door opened, spilling in cold air.

"My dear Jocasta, is it true? Has that poor unfortunate Hatten woman been murdered?" Edmund took a step back as Kate and Jocasta separated.

Jocasta nodded gravely. "Alice has come back to us for burial, husband. You know Katherine Clifford, I think?"

He nodded gruffly, searching Kate's face.

"I brought some of Simon's warm clothes for the poor," Kate explained. "And now I must hurry away and see to my household."

"Ah." Hand to heart, he bowed to her. "My wife will see that they are given to those in need, Dame Katherine. You are most generous."

"She is," said Jocasta.

"The sun has set," Edmund added. "Do you need an escort?"

Kate thanked him for his concern, but she assured him that Lille and Ghent would be sufficient escorts for so short a journey.

"I prefer to see you safely home. It will be my pleasure."

The portly man, already red-faced from the walk from his warehouse near the river, clearly imagined her a helpless woman. As she called to Lille and Ghent and secured their leashes, Kate smiled to herself, imagining Sharp's surprise if he witnessed her drawing out her axe to defend herself against an assailant. She guessed she was far more able to defend herself than he was. But she appreciated the gesture, and guessed that it had more to do with wanting to ask her just what she had told his wife about the guesthouse.

Jocasta accompanied them out onto the cobbles, embracing Kate in farewell. As soon as Kate stepped away, Lille and Ghent each barked once, straining at their leashes. Familiar barks. She searched the twilight until she spotted Berend leaning against the small gateway into the courtyard.

"It seems I have an escort." She indicated Berend to assure Edmund he had nothing to worry about.

"Ah," he nodded, flustered. "Well then, God go with you, Dame Katherine."

"And with you, Master Sharp."

The night sky was clear, the stars coming sharply into focus. No snow for now, but the cold penetrated Kate's thick leather boots. "You might have come within to get warm," she said as she joined Berend.

He shrugged as he leaned down to greet the dogs.

"Has Phillip come home?"

As he straightened, the light from the lantern illuminated the worry etched on Berend's scarred face, answering for him. She told him what Jocasta had promised.

"That is good news. Such a wide net might just catch Phillip before he falls." Berend proffered Kate his arm as she stepped out onto the street. "I understand Alice was brought here."

Kate nodded.

"You saw her?" Berend whispered.

Another nod.

"Phillip's disappearance likely has nothing to do with Alice's murder, Dame Katherine."

"We cannot know that until we find him."

"I know."

"Somewhere there is a great deal of blood," Kate said, remembering how Maud's blood soaked the ground. "Perhaps someone will notice. We must keep our ears pricked for such news."

"You can be certain that whoever murdered her did not do so where he is sheltering."

"No, but we might find something there, or someone might have seen someone enter."

Berend nodded.

"Any other news?"

"None. I stayed out here in case Bale came to see where his prey had been taken. No sign of him."

As they headed down past All Saints Church, Kate told Berend of Lille and Ghent's behavior when she approached the Sharp residence.

"You are armed?"

"Well armed," she assured him.

They fell silent, watchful. The earlier melt had refrozen. She kept a tight rein on Lille and Ghent so they did not unbalance her. They pulled on their leashes to follow Berend as he stepped aside to investigate any movement in the shadows. Each time he returned she glanced up to see him shake his head. Nothing.

As they turned into Castlegate, a night watchman hailed them from several houses away, ordering them to take the dogs off the street as night fell. When he grew close and recognized Kate he apologized. "Forgive me, Dame Katherine. I know your hounds are trained well. We are all overcautious after seeing what someone did to Alice Hatten."

"All the more reason for a woman to have her dogs to guard her when caught away from home after dark," she noted. "But we are almost there now, and I will have a care to keep them on my property tonight, ever watchful."

"Be assured we will be walking the streets, mistress, keeping you safe." He bobbed his head and moved on.

"Useless clerks, the watchmen," Berend muttered. "Have they ever caught a miscreant in the act?"

"Other than escorting drunkards to their homes? If so, I have not heard about it. But folk find them reassuring."

As they neared the house Kate returned to praying that Phillip had dressed warmly, that he had kept his wits about him, that he was among people who would look out for him. His truancy made her question her decision to encourage his interest in stonemasonry. She resolved to insist that he work only under Hugh Grantham's guidance from now on. *Please, God, let there be a from now on.*

In the hall, she halted in confusion as Matt rose from a seat by the fire to come take her cloak and offer her something warm to drink. He looked well, though he steadied himself with a crutch tucked beneath one arm.

"Forgive me, mistress," Berend hastened to explain. "I brought Matt here to sleep in the hall, for protection. We do not know when Sam will return."

"Good. I am glad you thought of it, Berend." Kate greeted Matt warmly as she handed Berend her cloak. "Are you in any pain?" She boldly lifted the hair that fell over his forehead, exclaiming at the dark bruise.

"It looks far worse than it feels," Matt assured her. "Same for the other cuts and scrapes. I am ready to work. I thought I might go mad sitting about."

She relieved him of the cup of mulled wine he had been holding in his free hand, though she set it aside after one sip to pull off her boots and stand near the hearth to warm her toes and dry the hem of her skirt. Sam. She had forgotten about him, going off to Beverley after she had told him to wait.

"I will find someone to send a message to Jocasta in the morning, asking the friar who is taking word to Alice's sister to watch out for Sam on the road." She saw the doubt in Berend's expression. "I know how unlikely it is that he will happen upon Sam, but what if he does?" She told the two of them she would like them all to eat in the hall. She would welcome the company.

They were a quiet gathering round the table, Marie making no note of Matt's presence or his injuries, clearly worried into silence by her brother's disappearance on the same day that a woman's mutilated body had been found in the King's Fishpond. When she noticed Marie fighting sleep, Kate suggested she share her bed that night.

"Jennet is going out after the meal to listen for news of Phillip. You will want to be in the room when she returns, eh?"

Marie whispered a *merci* and gave Kate a peck on the cheek. It was her first kiss from either of her wards. She averted her eyes to hide her sudden tears. A first step.

As Kate coached Matt in cohabiting with Lille and Ghent for the night, Jennet helped Marie settle up in the solar, then left with her pack of boy's clothes.

‑‑⊙⊙⊚‑‑

While Kate lay awake worrying, Marie tossed and turned, fell heavily asleep for a while, then tossed and turned some more. The girl's unsettled humors produced so much heat, Kate turned down some of her blankets, much as she had as a child when her cat slept with her. Mite would tumble and romp beneath the covers, then curl up atop Kate and warm her so effectively that her nurse found her with her feet hanging out of the covers in the morning. Kate smiled to herself, remembering Mite. She had been the terror of the household, lording it over all the other cats, as well as the hunting hounds. Kate's mother would tsk and moan when the gray cat streaked across the parlor and dove into sewing baskets, tangling herself in silk thread, batting at the threads dangling from the women's embroidery. Lille and Ghent would have disapproved. But they never had the chance. Mite had died a warrior's death long before they were whelped. Tears wet Kate's temples as she stared at the ceiling. Try as she might to stay with happy memories of Mite, and of Lille and Ghent as puppies, her thoughts perversely returned to Alice Hatten's mutilated body, and the memories of the summer of Maud's rape and murder—her brother Roland's terrible grief and her own conflicting emotions, mourning Maud's loss and fearing she would suffer the same violent death.

At last she heard Jennet let herself in down below, Matt's startled challenge, Lille and Ghent's joyous greetings. The voices hummed for a little while, long enough that Kate grew impatient and considered extricating herself from beneath Marie's slender limbs, remarkably heavy in sleep, so she might join them. But now she heard Jennet on the steps, and Marie sat up. As soon as Jennet stepped through the door, Marie anxiously asked if there was news of her brother. Kate relaxed to see Jennet's smile in the light of the oil lamp.

"Phillip was seen in a tavern in early evening with the stonemason, Connor, and some of his fellows. When the news came about Alice Hatten, Connor, well, he was deep in his cups and went quite mad. Broke a bench and some pottery before several of his fellows escorted him out. They took him home and Phillip stayed with him."

"Alice?"

Jennet nodded. "Apparently they had once meant to marry. Before her troubles."

That was why Jocasta recognized the name. Kate was relieved to have news of her ward that suggested he himself was unharmed, but she was troubled, very troubled by Connor's connection to Alice.

"Is it true?" Marie asked. "Is he there?"

"I went to Connor's lodging and listened at the door. I could hear Phillip softly singing to Connor in a steady voice. I thought to leave them in peace until morning."

"God be thanked," Kate said, but she would not have left him there, not after hearing the connection. For once, she feared Jennet had used poor judgment. Kate would go to him first thing in the morning.

"I was so afraid for him," Marie sobbed, throwing her arms round Kate and burying her head in her shoulder.

A miracle. Kate rocked the girl as she wept. For her part, she was more afraid for Phillip than ever.

9

ABOVE THE CHAPTER HOUSE

———⚬☙☙⚬———

Despite her worry, Kate must have slipped into a deep slumber. When a loud knocking on her chamber door wakened her, she was confused for a moment by the tangle of arms, legs, and hair trapping her in the soft feather bed. Ah. Marie.

Matt called through the door that she was summoned by her uncle, Dean Richard. Gently disentangling herself from Marie, Kate slipped out of bed, shivering as her sweaty flesh met the predawn chill of the bedchamber. She wrapped herself in a blanket that had slipped to the floor and opened the door to Matt, who stood on the landing with an oil lamp in hand, leaning heavily on his crutch.

"My uncle the dean summoned me? But it is not yet dawn, is it?"

"No, not yet, but Dean Richard's secretary waits at the threshold. Lille and Ghent will not let him cross it. I did not know the command for them to stand down. He says you must come as soon as you can. To the minster yard. It is your ward, Phillip. He found the stonemason hanging from the rafters of the chapter house."

Marie wailed from the bed. "Phillip? My brother is dead?"

"No, Marie. Phillip found—someone in trouble." Kate nodded to Matt. "I will dress quickly. Do you need help going down?"

"I need the practice."

"Come, Matt." Already dressed, Jennet slipped out in front of Kate. "I will go first, and if you need to, use my back to steady yourself." Over her shoulder she told Kate that she would wake Berend and tell him where they would be.

Pulling on her clothes from the previous day, still heavy with weaponry, Kate was out the door before Marie crawled out of bed. When she reached the hall she found the dogs calmly standing to either side of Matt, keeping a close watch on her uncle's secretary, Alf, who bent toward the fire, warming his hands.

"Connor? Was the stonemason's name Connor?" she asked.

Alf straightened and gave Kate a little bow. He was an earnest man, his brows always knit together over his pug nose as if to ensure all that he was reliable. "Yes, that was the name, Mistress Clifford. Can you come?"

"At once. Matt, when Marie comes downstairs, she will be in a fury that we left without her. Do not let her out of your sight. Take her to the kitchen. Berend is good with her. Tell him there will be no school for her today because I cannot trust her not to run off in search of her brother." She felt for Matt, seeing the anxiety in his dark eyes. "I am sorry to burden you with her, but it cannot be helped."

"I am here to serve, Dame Katherine. Perhaps I can charm her with my smile."

He did have a winning smile. One of the reasons Kate had stationed him at the guesthouse rather than her own home was that smile, and the rest of his quite pleasing person. As a young widow, she had quickly registered the danger and kept him across the city. Seeing his smile at this early hour cheered her, but her worry quickly reinstated itself.

"You may find Marie far less susceptible to your winning ways than most females, Matt. I pray you, do not despair. Berend will busy her with something in the kitchen." Kate called the dogs to her, slipped their leashes through their collars, and nodded to Alf. "Lead the way." They collected Jennet in the yard.

"What about dressing Marie?"

"She is perfectly capable of dressing herself, Jennet. At least for a morning in the kitchen."

The snow glistened with a crust of ice that had formed in the night. Kate appreciated the substantial lantern Alf carried. Even so, she stepped with care. They saw few citizens other than a watchman on his rounds, who hailed them to ask if they needed assistance. Kate thanked him and sent him on his way, though she noticed him following them at a distance. A watchman rarely paid for his ale, trading the stories gathered on his watch for drink. Kate did not begrudge him, though she hoped he gave a true account of whatever he witnessed.

Torches and lanterns made pools of light in the snowy yard, casting shadows against the dark mass of the minster and upon the small building that sheltered the stonemasons' workshop from the weather. As they entered the yard, Kate asked Alf to stop a moment. She needed to compose herself. The minster filled her with unease. Stone should not soar into the heavens; it should be stacked solidly on the earth. She disliked the lifelike statues painted bright colors and adorned in silver gilt, ever watching with their shifty eyes. She hated the feeling of being watched, judged. It was worse at night. She hurried past trying not to look toward it.

Her uncle was pacing at the door of the unfinished east end, casting an eerie shadow on the decorated stone as he moved in and out of the lantern light. Kate focused her eyes on him as she approached. It helped that her uncle caught sight of her and hurried forward to embrace her, kissing her forehead, filling her vision.

"Katherine, God be thanked."

"Where is Phillip?"

"He is still inside with the body, in the roof of the chapter house. Even after I gave Connor the last rites your ward refused to leave his side. Lady Margery is with him."

"Lady Margery? Why?"

"Her men alerted her."

That was no answer, but Kate did not pursue it, concerned about her ward. "Is Phillip hurt?"

"Only his heart. Perhaps his pride."

"What happened?"

"All I know is that he tried to cut the man down, but could not reach the rope."

"Of course he could not, he is but a child." But she knew the frustration he must feel, how he would blame himself. "How did you find out?"

"A scrubwoman came for me, saying Dame Jocasta Sharp had put out the word to watch for Phillip Neville. When she heard a commotion at the stonemason's shelter, she overheard Phillip's name. I hurried here fearing the lad was the one hanging." He wiped his brow. "I thanked God when I saw Phillip. But Connor—from all accounts he was a gifted stonecutter. Clearly he had won your ward's allegiance."

"I can stay with the dogs while you go in, Dame Katherine," Jennet offered.

"No. I would prefer you beside me, noting things." And keeping her safe. Jennet would strike out at anything that leapt out in the yawning cavern of the minster. "Alf, would you wait with Lille and Ghent, perhaps walk them back and forth? Can you do that? They know you now."

He nodded. "I am happy to walk them if they will permit me."

She knelt to tell Lille and Ghent they must wait for her with their new friend. Alf crouched beside her, gently patting their backs.

"I had a dog at home."

"What was his name?"

"Nosewise."

"Was he—"

"Oh, yes. Quite a tracker."

"Lille and Ghent are named for Flemish cities my parents' friend spoke of as places of wonder." She rose once she sensed the three were at ease.

Dean Richard picked up a lantern and led the way into the incomplete east end of the minster.

Kate shivered as the door closed behind her. Such immense darkness, only slightly illuminated by her uncle's lantern. Their footsteps whispered on the stone and tile floors, and faraway voices echoed eerily beneath the massive stone vaulting. She tried to focus on the patterned tiles beneath her feet as her uncle led them past the choir, his light picking out the silver gilt on statues, the shadows seeming alive. It shamed and troubled her to be overwhelmed by fear of marble, stone, and painted plaster—something that no one else counted a threat. Some night she should come sit in the dark and make her peace with it. That is how her father had broken her fear of the cave to which they retreated when the Scots came en masse, burning their barns and stealing their livestock.

She was relieved when they came to the far transept, to the warren of booths in which lawyers would be conducting church business later that day. The crowded area felt more like a human habitat. Richard Clifford paused before a small door that stood ajar. "Have a care, the steps are shallow, uneven, and narrow. I will lead."

"How did Phillip know of these?" Kate wondered aloud as she climbed. The steps were carved into the thickness of the stone walls, the stairway like a catacomb.

"The masons use these daily. They have workrooms up above the chapter house."

So it was no mystery how Phillip knew of these steps. "But he could not have simply happened on Connor. He must have been following on the man's heels. Did he witness what happened?"

"I have not been able to make much sense of his story."

Quiet voices echoed along the steps, and soon Kate emerged into a space dominated by huge wooden beams angling up into the darkness.

"These immense rafters support the chapter house without a central pillar," Richard said in a hushed, reverent tone. Lanterns hung in regular intervals from the thick beams.

"How could anyone climb up to hang themselves so high?" she asked.

"Over there." He led her about ten steps farther, to a board balanced on trestles, a stool providing a step up. "The men say it's always placed over here and moved about as they hang the lanterns, but someone had taken the board and hidden it in one of the rooms. This is where Connor was, and this the noose." He lifted the thick rope, nodded to where several men stood with heads bowed by something on the floor. "The broken nose, split lip, and the fresh wound on the back of Connor's head were noted before they cut him down. None of it the result of their rough handling. They swear to it. He was one of their own."

Kate crossed herself and nodded.

Near the men sat Lady Margery, her legs curled up beneath her. She was offering a wineskin to Phillip, who sat cross-legged, rocking back and forth and wringing his long-fingered hands as he gazed at the body, ignoring her. Someone had kindly covered the dead man's head with a jacket.

As Kate crouched down in front of Phillip, Lady Margery touched her arm. "Dear Katherine, I am so glad you are here."

"And I you. Thank you for staying with him." The boy's fine eyes were swollen, his nose red. "Phillip?" Kate cupped his ice-cold hands in hers, stilling them. Someone had brought him a fur-lined mantle, but he had let it drop behind him. He wore his favorite jacket, not nearly warm enough for the weather. She draped the mantle across his slender shoulders.

"I could not save him," he whispered. "Not tall enough, not strong enough, too late." Phillip did not look at her, but down and to one side, numbly staring at the draped body.

Kate took the wineskin from Lady Margery and tried to put it in the boy's hands, but he would not grasp it. "Drink some of the wine, Phillip. Drink."

He shook his head. "They would not listen to me."

She smoothed the hair from his face, kissed his forehead. "Who? What did you want them to hear, Phillip?"

"Too late, now."

"Drink some wine. When you are calm, you can tell me everything. I will listen. I promise you we will do what needs to be done."

At last he took the wineskin, lifted it to his mouth.

While he drank, Kate asked Lady Kirkby how she came to be there.

"My men alerted me to all the lights and the shouting in the minster yard. After that, I could not go back to sleep. I found Richard here, with this poor boy—your ward, he said. Such a sad meeting. I saw my own sons in him. If I can help in any way, I pray you, come to me." Margery rose. "Here, this is your place." She went over to stand by Dean Richard and Jennet, who were talking to the workers.

"Do you mind if I look at Connor?" Kate asked Phillip.

He shook his head.

She lifted the jacket covering Connor's head, steeling herself for a face like the one she had encountered in the guesthouse bedchamber days before. But Connor had not been dead so long, nor had the noose remained round his neck. His features were not so distorted as the stranger's. She bent closer—a split lip, dried blood from that and his nose, which looked broken. Curious, she lifted his head, felt behind, and came away with blood. A fresh wound, as the dean had said. A badly injured man climbed onto a platform on trestles and managed to hang himself from those high beams? Of course not. With such wounds, was this a third murder? Stranger, Alice, Connor. Victim, witness, and the witness's confidant? Kate closed her eyes, fighting down fresh rage. Pointless at the moment, when William was not here to receive it. When she had composed herself, Kate covered Connor's head once more and returned to Phillip. Was he now on the murderer's list, another witness?

"What did you see, Phillip? Did he struggle with his attacker before the hanging?"

Phillip looked her in the eye as he wiped his mouth. "You see it? That he did not kill himself?" His expression broke her heart, the grief, the hope, the gratitude.

"Yes. What did you witness, Phillip?"

"By the time I found him, he was hanging. Will they believe me?"

"My uncle is a reasonable man. I will ask him to examine Connor's wounds. I believe he will agree to bury Connor in sacred ground."

Phillip handed her the wineskin.

A sip emptied it. Good. She hoped it had numbed his grief. She held out her hand. "Lille and Ghent are down below, in the yard. Shall we go down to them? Perhaps we could walk them to the deanery where we might all warm ourselves and break our fasts. What do you think? Jennet can go home to fetch a change of clothes for you and let Marie and Berend know you are safe. They have been praying for you."

Phillip wiped his nose on his sleeve. "No one prayed for Connor."

"You did," Kate reminded him. "And you stayed with him in his grief. You did all that you could, Phillip. You eased his pain, I am certain. It is no small thing to have a friend such as you near."

Phillip bowed his head and said nothing.

"Should we send for Marie?" Kate asked him.

"No. Keep her from all this."

Dean Richard grunted as he crouched down to speak to Phillip. "Connor's body will be cleaned and prepared for burial by my own trusted servants. You can rest at the deanery and I will bring you to him later, when you are ready to sit the vigil."

Phillip nodded. "Thank you, Dean Richard."

For a second time in as many days Kate's heart warmed to her uncle's regard for the strong bond of family.

—◦◦◦—

Though it was a short walk across the yard and beyond the stonemasons' hut, by the time they reached the deanery Phillip's knees were buckling beneath him. Alf called for a serving man to set up a cot in the warm kitchen, screened off so that Phillip might rest undisturbed. The boy fell asleep before Kate tucked a second blanket round him. She kissed his forehead and left him in peace.

She, her uncle, and Lady Kirkby retired to the dean's parlor where a brazier warmed them. A servant brought mulled wine. They were a quiet trio, absorbing the events of the early hours—the horrible death, the boy's grief.

"Such desecration of a sacred space," the dean muttered, breaking the silence.

Margery set aside her cup and rose. "I sense that you have much to discuss, but it is not for my ears."

"My lady—"

"No, Richard, you need not apologize. I hope that when you are both more at ease with me you will let me help, if I can. Katherine, I pray you send word if there is anything I can do."

"Thank you for staying with Phillip, comforting him," said Kate.

"You would have done the same."

"Perhaps it is time to take her into our confidence," Kate said when Lady Margery had departed.

Her uncle sighed as he settled back in his chair. His face was drawn, his eyes shadowed, the lines more etched than usual. "We shall see. Tell me what you noticed, eh?"

"Connor's broken nose and split lip might be from the incident in the alehouse, but not the injury to the back of his head."

"The alehouse?"

She recounted what Jennet had learned about Connor's reaction to the news of Alice's murder.

He nodded. "As I mentioned, the men who cut Connor down noted the injuries as well."

"You agree it was murder?"

"I do. And as he died in the minster liberty, I have the authority to decide what is to be done. Connor will be buried as one murdered, not as one who committed the sin of taking his own life. If asked, I will say that in my judgment a man so injured could not have managed such a hanging. But I will ask all to be circumspect with the news, to neither confirm nor deny the rumors, so that we might have a better chance of flushing out the murderer."

Kate nodded, agreeing. "But we will not be able to keep this quiet."

"Of course not. The rumor will spread, connecting Connor's death to Alice Hatten's murder. A lovers' quarrel ended in tragedy. Perhaps that is not a bad thing. His fellows know of his wounds, and how he could not have hanged himself. They have sworn to say nothing."

"So Connor will not be buried as an apostate?"

"No. I would not so rob him of salvation. I will be criticized for that, but no matter. I gladly absorb the blame in order to shield you, Katherine. For I cannot help but think it is your favor to me, welcoming Lady Kirkby to your guesthouse, that has brought on this triple tragedy."

"You believe this is all connected to Margery's arrival?"

"If not, it is an extraordinary coincidence."

"Hence your hesitation to speak in her presence."

"Hm . . . Yes. I confess I had misgivings about her visit. Archbishop Scrope was too keen for me to arrange it. I find it difficult to trust Scrope, with his mentor Arundel in exile with Bolingbroke. I feared her mission might not be so innocent, though she might be unaware she is being manipulated."

"I do not believe much slips past Lady Margery, uncle." But it was good to know her uncle was not at ease with the archbishop. Friction between the dean and chapter of York Minster and the archbishop was to be expected—they presided over the cathedral and its operations, yet it was the seat of the archbishop's authority. But this was about Scrope's personal, not his professional, integrity. "What did you learn from the workers?"

"Your serving maid asked them whether the rope would have been out near the platform. Good question. The men said it would have been stored in one of the rooms up there."

"So the murderer was familiar with much about the minster."

"Too familiar. The workers were stealing glances at their fellows, worried that the murderer is among them." He leaned forward, forearms on his thighs, shaking his head. "I fear that your trust in Lady Margery might be misguided, and that I have been foolish in supporting her husband. Stealing away as he did has colored his actions in men's minds. Some call him a traitor to King Richard, others suspect the king has sent him to assassinate Duke Henry."

"Perhaps I am too close to these tragedies, uncle, but I find it difficult to see them as part of the rift between the royal cousins."

"Did you feel so about the unrest in the borders where you grew up, Katherine? That, too, was born of the wars begun by our king's great-great-grandfather."

"I did. Our feuds grew out of the fields soaked in our family's blood."

"And that began with King Edward leading his army into Scotland."

"Providing the opportunity to resume a feud under cover of war." Kate rose. "I would like to see Connor's body before I go comfort Marie. I will return in a while to wake Phillip, so that he might tell us all he knows."

—◦⟨⊙⟩◦—

In late morning Dean Richard had moved Phillip to his own bedroom so that work might resume in the kitchen. In thanks for preparing Connor's body, the lay sisters from St. Leonard's Hospital deserved a warm meal.

Now the boy blinked in the soft midafternoon sunlight as Kate opened the shutters. She stood a moment looking out at the minster, watching water coursing out the downspouts. The thaw had begun and the world, so quiet in snow, was loud with water dripping, sloshing in the street. People cursed as their boots sank into the ooze.

Remember the stink of the spring thaw? All that had frozen in the snow, rotting corpses of birds, rats, squirrels, mice. All the dung and piss from the horses and cattle.

A city is worse yet, Geoff. Now go. I need to speak with Phillip.

She sat down at the edge of the bed. "Marie picked out fresh clothes for you. Dean Richard's serving man will help you dress."

"I dress myself."

"Let them fuss over you. They all feel helpless."

Phillip sat up. She handed him a cup of honeyed milk, his favorite. "Sleep well?"

"I remember someone carrying me here. But even that did not wake me." A sigh. "I feel guilty. I should be praying."

"Self-abuse will not bring back the dead. I know. I have tried it."

"Your twin?"

"Yes."

He finished the milk, setting the cup aside and swinging his legs out of the bed. "Soft," he said as he stepped onto a bearskin.

"My uncle enjoys his comforts." The walls were hung with hunting tapestries, small tables held pewter lamps and candlesticks, and a bench and a chair were piled with cushions embroidered in jewel colors.

Phillip gazed round the room, but his expression was grim as he turned to Kate. "I know about the murder in the guesthouse. And now Alice Hatten, and Connor."

God in heaven. "How do you know about the guesthouse?"

"I will explain. But the dean will want to hear as well."

"Of course. Would you prefer to talk in here, or in his parlor?"

"The parlor. You can call the serving man to come dress me." He still looked weary.

"Would you eat something first?"

"I can eat while we talk. I mean to sit the vigil."

Before she closed the door behind her she asked, "Does Marie know of the earlier murder?"

He shook his head. "And she must not, not until the killer is found and put away."

Kate intended a swifter, more satisfying end, but she simply nodded.

10

PHILLIP'S TALE

Kate found herself alone in her uncle's parlor. She welcomed the quiet as a respite, at first. Everywhere she had gone this day she had heard talk of the death at the minster. She hastened to assure those who offered their condolences, mistakenly believing it was Phillip who had been found hanging, that he was very much alive, though in mourning for the stonemason who had been his teacher. Most of the gossip swirled round the rumor that Connor hanged himself in remorse for murdering Alice. *That woman brought such trouble upon herself,* many said. Kate did not bother to answer them. They would twist any retort to their purposes, the rumor too sensational to discard. William was named the catalyst for the tragedy by many, a detail that would worry her had they hinted of the murder in the guesthouse, but it was his transgression leading to her banishment from his service that had been resurrected for their entertainment. Pampered city folk with loose tongues and too much idle time. Only at the Sharp residence, where she had the opportunity to talk to the friar before he departed for his sad journey to Alice's sister and cousin in Beverley, did she feel the sorrow of the past week held in appropriate respect and solemnity.

Still chilled, she warmed her hands at the brazier in her uncle's parlor, but she could not reach the true cause of her tremors, a chill deeper than any fire could dispel. Any sense of safety she had once felt being in York, away from the northern border, had been undermined by the events of the past week. The delicate balance she had achieved between meeting Simon's debts and saving for a future she might choose for herself was threatened, the safe haven she had created for Phillip and Marie invaded. She wanted to find the murderer and end this. She wanted his blood. But at the moment, she had only the name of someone possibly connected to all this, Hubert Bale, and a vague connection to Henry Bolingbroke, Duke of Lancaster. Something did not feel right about that. The deaths seemed far too personal to have been arranged by a noble in exile. She knew she would not sleep soundly until she had eliminated the danger.

So much for a quiet respite. By the time her uncle escorted Phillip into the room, Kate welcomed the distraction from her own uneasy heart.

She smiled at the elegant outfit Marie had chosen for her brother. Phillip wore a dark red velvet jacket, deep brown leggings, and red leather boots. Elegant. But the clothes hung loosely, revealing a loss of heft since Jennet had fitted him months ago. Kate wondered what he had eaten the past few days.

A servant brought food and wine, then withdrew. Kate urged Phillip to eat. He tore some bread, smoothed soft cheese on it, and nibbled at it.

Dean Richard smiled. "My favorite cheese."

Phillip nodded. "I like it. Marie would hate it."

They ate in silence for a few minutes.

"Tell us how you found him, Phillip," Kate began. "You said you witnessed nothing, but then how did you happen to be there? I know you stayed the night in Connor's lodgings."

"How do you know that?"

"Jennet learned where you were, and made certain you were safe." Not safe enough. "Go on, I pray you."

"I think it was the sound of the street door closing that woke me. The door to the room was open, and Connor was gone. I pushed open the shutters, saw him hurrying in the direction of the minster yard. He was with another man."

"Was he following the man, or walking with him?"

"With him."

She nodded for Phillip to continue.

"I tried to catch up, but by the time I put on my boots they had disappeared. I thought it must be one of his fellows who had come for him, so I went on to the minster yard, hoping to catch them there. But the yard was dark, and there was no one yet in the masons' lodge. I didn't know what to do." His voice broke. He wiped his eyes on his velvet sleeve. Foolish Marie.

"How were you able to see him down in the street?" Kate asked softly.

"A lantern. The stranger carried a lantern."

"Why were you with Connor last night?" the dean asked.

"He went mad in the tavern when he heard that Alice Hatten had been pulled from the King's Fishpond, and what had been done to her, how she died. I feared he would hurt himself when he sobered up."

"They were lovers?" Kate asked.

"I think so. At least that's what I guessed when I saw them together the morning after she witnessed the man murdered in your guesthouse."

"You know of that?" the dean asked.

Phillip shrugged, averting his eyes. "I heard them talk about it, and he told me more." For a moment, it seemed the boy's weariness took over. He slumped into himself, bowed his head.

"Phillip, do you need more rest?" Kate asked.

He straightened and rubbed his cheeks. "I heard you complain to Berend that my father kept things from you that you would have been better off knowing, as all men did, thinking to protect you. But you do it too. If I had known . . ." His voice broke again.

"You might have prevented Connor's death? No, Phillip. We knew of it, but we've not spoken to anyone who was there in the room that night. We do not yet know what happened. But we will find out. And we will avenge these deaths."

"Katherine," the dean warned, "this is not the border country."

"We will argue that point once we know more. For now, we need to hear all that you know, Phillip. Something you heard or witnessed might hold the key. You saw them the morning after the murder in the guesthouse?"

His slender face solemn, his voice soft, he began to spin out the sad tale of Connor's last days. Phillip skipped school one morning. Master Grantham had said he would be away, so the boy hoped he might catch Connor at his work and convince him to straighten up so that they could work together. He found Connor working on a corner fit. At first he invited Phillip to watch him at the task, telling him he could then try a corner himself. He had set aside a flawed piece of stone for Phillip to work on—so no worry if it split, no one would care, there were plenty more on the pile. As he watched Connor work, Phillip told him about Grantham's offer to train him himself, and his own preference to work with Connor.

"He said nothing until he was finished. Then he said maybe the master was right. He had lost the gift. I argued that he had not.

"Connor blew on the piece of stone to judge his progress. He fit the chisel into the edge of the cut, then looked sidewise at me, shaking his head. 'A master is guided by the beauty in his head, a vision. I've lost that. I thought myself a good man, a man who would never balk at doing the right thing. Most of all for those I love. But last night . . . I succumbed to my demon. I went first to the tavern, arrived late. . . . Damned I am. Had I been there—' Then Connor brought down the hammer with such force the chisel sank deep into the stone, splitting it in an explosion of fine particles. With a curse, he dropped his tool. 'You have promise, lad. Take Grantham's offer. You will learn precious little from the likes of me,' he said, then stormed off, shedding his smock as he headed toward the minster gate.

"I picked up the hammer and ran after him. I tried to tell him he was a good man, I knew he was, but he just told me to leave him be, to work with the master and leave him to hell."

Phillip pressed his hands to his face, bowed his head.

Kate and her uncle exchanged a look. Perhaps it was too much too soon. She was about to suggest that Phillip rest awhile when he sat up with a huff.

"You see? I was right all along. Connor was not a drunkard, he was sad. He believed he had failed someone. I followed him, to see if I could help."

He found Connor behind his lodgings, holding a woman by the arm. "Alice. I know that now. She was trying to break away, he was begging her to stay. She was crying. Her clothes were crumpled and her hair all undone. She looked frightened. He was telling her they had to go away on their own, they could not wait for everything to be readied, it never would be now. She kept saying she would go to her son's father, he would make it right. And Connor kept saying he was the one who had put her in danger. They were both angry and frightened. I was afraid he would hit her, but she got away from him and told him that he was better off without her. He turned away and marched to the nearest alewife."

Phillip tried to follow him, but Connor shooed him away. After that Phillip stole away from school when he could. Usually he found Connor in one of the taverns near the Bedern or near Joan del Bek's bawdy house, where the mason would ask after Alice. No one had seen her. They seemed surprised to hear she had been in the city. After a while he would go back to a tavern and drink.

"For two days all he did was drink and search for her. He pretended to ignore me. I guess he hoped I would give up and leave him be. Yesterday I asked some of the other stoneworkers to come with me, to help me convince him to eat something. We almost succeeded. But then someone came with the news about a body found in the King's Fishpond, a woman named Alice Hatten. Connor wanted to go to her, to warm her, to save her, and the man told him it was too late, her tongue had been cut out before she was thrown in the pond. She was long dead. Connor started to shout *no no no no* and throw things."

Kate was angry that Connor had not seen what he was doing to Phillip, a boy who admired him to such an extent he would do anything to protect him.

"Have some more food?" the dean suggested.

Phillip shook his head. "This morning that man must have come for him, or maybe Connor saw him passing. If I had been quicker—"

"He was not your responsibility, my son," Richard said.

"Why did he go with him?" Kate wondered aloud. "Why would he?"

"I wish I knew why he left, why he did not wake me."

The dean poured more wine, watered his own and Phillip's. Kate set hers aside. "Do you wish to continue, Phillip?"

A nod. "Just as I was cursing myself for assuming they'd headed to the minster, one of the apprentices came with a lantern to light the fire in the stonemasons' lodge. I saw fresh prints where someone had broken through the frozen crust atop the snow. I had been following them all along. I think I frightened the apprentice, and he let me borrow the lantern so that I would leave. I think I was crying." Phillip ran his slender fingers through his hair. "Please say nothing of any of this to Marie. I never let her see me cry."

Kate promised she would repeat none of it to Marie without his permission.

"Once inside the minster I heard raised voices. A long way in, and up above me. I started running. The voices got louder and louder, and then stopped. The silence frightened me and I stumbled and fell. I lost time."

Kate moved beside Phillip, put her arm round him. He did not push her away.

"Just before the lawyer's stalls I heard someone running at me, then saw the lantern light, swinging wildly. It confused me. He rushed right into me. I think he meant to. I fell backward, and he ran on. I scrambled for my lantern and started to chase after him. I was angry. Then I remembered Connor. More time lost." Tears streamed down his cheeks. "I prayed Connor was just hurt. Or spent from a fight. But I kept thinking of Alice Hatten, what they said happened to her. The door to the steps leading up above the chapter house was open. I climbed up, calling Connor's name. Up the steps and—he was hanging there, the rope creaking. God help me. The board to stand on had been cast aside. I struggled to get it back onto both trestles. And I still could not reach him. I could not save him."

"It is far more difficult to cut a man down than it is to hang him," the dean whispered. "I could not manage it by myself."

Phillip shrugged out of Kate's embrace, wiping his eyes. "I want to go to Connor now, Dean Richard."

"Of course. I will take you to him." As her uncle rose, he asked Kate to stay. They should talk.

"I will just see whether Helen minds Lille and Ghent being underfoot in her kitchen awhile longer," said Kate.

It felt good to escape the parlor for a while, to stretch her legs. In the kitchen, the dogs drowsed by the fire, despite the proximity of Richard's cat, Claws, who napped with one eye open on a stool just above Lille and Ghent.

Helen, Richard's longtime cook, bustled over to give her a welcoming hug. "Bless you for bringing Lille and Ghent with you. When they are here, Claws stays put, and I have some peace. Most days she's in everything, and I live in fear the dean's guests will find her fur in their stew."

"Perhaps it is time you brought a dog into your household."

Helen wrinkled her nose. "Your uncle would have the dog in his bed-chamber, tracking mud and heaven knows what else onto those beautiful skins on which he likes to walk barefoot."

And Helen as well, Kate guessed. She had long suspected Helen and Richard were far more to each other than master and cook. She thanked Helen for taking such good care of her hounds and her ward.

"He is a sweet lad, Phillip. Let him bide here awhile and I'll do my best to fatten him. Perhaps your Berend's cooking is not to his taste. Some men cook too fancy, eh?"

The suggestion gave Kate pause. Phillip might be safer here than in her home. The deanery was a hive of activity from early morning until late evening. Someone would always be there to watch him. For now, Phillip would be close to Connor, and, after the burial, close to Grantham's house if he felt ready to return to work. "What a kind suggestion, Helen. I will consult my uncle about the possibility." Not that Kate believed for a moment that Phillip would prefer Helen's food over Berend's. He was simply a light eater. But it would free Kate, Jennet, and Berend to investigate. Only Marie posed a problem, being far more inquisitive than her brother. Might she stay as well?

When Kate returned to her uncle's parlor she found him pacing the length of the small chamber, from the shuttered window to the prie-dieu that served as a small altar, his expression one of grave concern. She settled in a high-backed chair near the brazier, leaning back to gaze at the dark oak beam above.

"Much to ponder in Phillip's tale," said Richard as he handed her a cup. "My best brandywine. A bit of comfort after our harrowing morning."

He sighed as he eased himself down across from her. He was a handsome man, dark hair and brows, light eyes, more gray than blue, with a strong jaw and an air of command. She still wondered about his not naming a proxy to handle his duties at the minster but rather taking up residence for a few months now, going so far as to bring along Helen. As King Richard's Lord Privy Seal he might be summoned by the king at any moment. Perhaps she should not burden him with her wards.

He leaned forward, interrupting her reverie. "Alice Hatten expected Connor to join her at the guesthouse that night. Did I hear that right?"

"That was my impression, that Connor had stopped at the tavern and arrived late." Kate paused, wondering whether to continue. Had King Richard sent her uncle to spy on Lady Kirkby? Or to help her? Either way, could she trust him? Nonsense. He had gone out of his way to be kind to Phillip, and to her. She must trust someone. "Arrived to what, I wonder? Was Connor the other man Griselde heard? Did he and Alice witness a murder? Is that why they are both dead? Or do we have it all wrong?" She shook her head. "No, I don't believe Connor was a murderer. But what do we truly know?"

The dean shook his head. "If I believed the man to be a murderer I would not give him a Christian burial, eh? But after Connor's burial we might ask Phillip whether the stonecutter confided any more to him."

"After he has satisfied what he sees as his duty to his friend."

"He is an admirable lad."

"I confess I had not guessed him to be so steadfast in his loyalties."

"He had not yet been tested. What do you think of the brandywine?"

Kate tasted it. Smooth, warm, soothing. "Quite a luxury. You are well compensated for your duties at court and in the church."

"I should be. My life is not my own."

No. It was not. He served two lords, God and King Richard. She wished she knew which held precedence.

"It is curious that Connor was expected at the guesthouse," her uncle was saying. "And the following morning, Alice saying her son's father would fix it. I did not know she had a child."

Kate had not had the opportunity to tell him what she had learned from Jocasta the previous afternoon. Now, questioning why he was lingering in York, she wondered whether she should.

When she did not answer, the dean added, "And Connor blamed him for the trouble. William Frost? They were lovers. That is why she lost her position in his household, is that not true?"

Pointless to dissemble when he already guessed the truth. She told him what Jocasta had done for Alice.

"Ah. I told you God had put her in your path for a reason." A satisfied grin. "Your cousin has much to answer for."

"He does." She was angry with herself for wasting her time with Drusilla Seaton the previous day. She should have seen William. Had she known of the connection between Connor and Alice . . . But had William known? "I wonder whether Alice went to William that morning. And why. I need to talk to him."

"Hm." Her uncle nodded as he began to settle back, then suddenly shifted forward again. "If the coroner should come to you with a complaint about not sending for him, direct him to me, Katherine. Or if he should demand the fine from you as Phillip's guardian, responsible for keeping him here as a witness. Any matters regarding the incident, I claim responsibility. Send them to me. The minster is my domain."

"The archbishop might disagree."

"If he cared. Richard Scrope has expressed no interest in interfering in minster business."

"And if he does, you will put his nose out of joint?" she teased.

A chuckle. "We are Cliffords. We know our worth." He sighed and shook his head. "You have much to do, Katherine. I wondered—might it not be best if Phillip bides here until we have apprehended those responsible for this nightmare? I do not question your ability to keep him safe, but if you must take action, will he not be in the way?"

So much for doubting her uncle's loyalty. Family came first, even her late husband's bastards. "I was about to ask if he might stay. And his sister Marie? She will hate being away from her brother so long."

The dean grunted. "She is a prickly child."

"I do not deny it. But she finds solace in the kitchen. Helen might be just the person to reach her."

"Helen is a wonder." He poured himself more brandywine, settled back to consider the proposal. Kate waited, silently praying his generosity might extend to the girl. "I certainly have the room. The servants might prepare two guest chambers as easily as one." He shook his head. "Why am I hesitating? Of course. As long as Phillip agrees."

Perfect. She would have freedom of movement for a little while, at least until Lady Kirkby departed. Surely her uncle would remain in York through Margery's visit. "You are a blessing, uncle." Kate was already in motion, eager to consult her ward. "I will tell Phillip what we propose, ask whether he is willing."

"You will be careful, Katherine? You will not do anything rash?"

"With Phillip?"

"You know what I mean. We are not on the borders."

"Berend and Jennet will see to it that I do nothing rash, uncle."

He did not look reassured. "That question you asked Phillip. About whether Connor was following the man, or accompanying him. What was the significance?"

"A man bent on taking his life does not bring along a companion."

"You were thinking of your twin Geoffrey?"

"My mother shared that with you?"

"Actually, your father."

She was surprised. Her father had said little after Geoff's death. "Yes, Geoff."

"And you?"

She shrugged. "That was a long time ago. I have responsibilities now."

"And here I was worried about all you carry on your shoulders."

"Bless you, uncle."

But it was he who blessed her as she took her leave.

Father talked to him about me?

I know. I find it strange as well. Perhaps we were wrong about Father.

No. I will never believe that.

Quiet now, Geoff. I need to think through my conversation with William.

11

WHO CAN BE TRUSTED?

———◦◦◦◦———

Above, the rooftops glistened and steamed, below, puddles in the narrow streets shimmered darkly. Kate kept her gaze low, ensuring that Lille and Ghent did not lead her through the deepest streams flowing between the cobbles. There were fewer puddles in the center of the street, but she stayed well to the side, beneath the eaves, where it was quieter and away from the rooftop runoff. Darker, but drier overhead and better for thinking.

Sifting through all the revelations of the day, Kate felt as if the earth were shifting and reforming beneath her feet. Suddenly her usual worries seemed such simple issues, minor problems that threatened neither life nor limb. She would give anything to have her greatest worries be how to accommodate as many important couples as possible, how to tuck away a goodly amount of money while remaining choosy enough for her customers to feel special, or how to keep the business a secret from the rest of the city and her wards. She was dizzy juggling all she had learned and what she suspected while staying alert to her surroundings, straining for subtle changes in the street sounds. Time and again she turned, certain someone was following close behind. She started at the gentlest greeting, eyeing everyone with suspicion. Lille and Ghent began to pick up her mood and shy at sudden movements.

Despite her efforts to focus on her own thoughts, snippets of the conversations swirling round her began to coalesce and form a story. People believed that Connor had murdered his mistress, Alice Hatten, then taken his own life. She halted in midstride, to the great confusion of Lille and Ghent, who barked in unison then came close to sniff her hands.

"Dame Katherine?"

She shook her head at the neighbor eyeing her with concern. "Lost in my thoughts, Peter. How are Ann and the baby?" His wife had delivered two days earlier, their first child, long-prayed-for. Peter's blue eyes twinkled. "Ann is happier than I have ever seen her, and our son is thriving. I swear he's done a week's worth of growing in two days."

They laughed, nodded, blessed each other's households, parted.

Matilda Baker slipped into step beside Kate, asking after Phillip, poor lad, finding the stonecutter who had hanged himself. Kate forced herself not to correct the woman. The rumor might be all for the best, as her uncle had suggested. She assured the woman that Phillip was in good hands, thanked her, wished her a good day. God be thanked, the woman nodded and moved on before Kate lost control and chided her for heedlessly believing rumors.

The early start to the day and all the emotion began to take its toll. Noticing she was rushing, Kate slowed down. She dreaded the prospect of another trip to the deanery and back home again before sunset. If only the long-term tenant in the house next to the guesthouse would move on—or die, she thought, then quickly crossed herself—but if Odo Marsden would agree to move she might bide closer to the heart of the city. Twice she had asked him to consider one of her other properties, and once she had simply offered money; but he would not budge. He was an elderly man, set in his ways, but his family was—unfortunately for her—long-lived. Once he was gone she might sell or lease the Castlegate house, bringing in welcome income to tuck away for the future. High Petergate felt closer to the heart of York. She might be far more comfortable there, close to the guesthouse.

Or perhaps it was better to keep her distance. She let it be. For now the house on Castlegate was home, and she pushed on, fighting the sense of urgency that might cause her to slip in a puddle and make matters worse.

Phillip had said he would like Marie's company at the deanery. So as soon as Kate arranged a meeting with William, she would return to the deanery with Marie, taking along sufficient clothing for both wards for a week. She hoped they need bide there no longer than that. Surely with the help of Berend and Jennet she could catch a murderer in a week.

As she and the dogs made their way round a peddler's cart in St. Helen's Square, she noticed both dogs glancing back behind her, their ears signaling alert. Looking round, she saw her cousin's man Roger hurrying toward her.

He bowed curtly. "Master Frost wishes to talk to you, Mistress Clifford. When shall I tell him you will call?"

There was something about his raspy voice that set her teeth on edge. "Tell him that I can receive him at my house within the hour."

The man continued to pace her, self-important cur.

She refused to be bullied by him. "You have your answer," she said. "Deliver it."

"Mistress—"

She shook her head and moved on through the square and up Coney Street, her mind already turned to wondering about the archbishop's purpose in welcoming Lady Kirkby to York. He was not the king's man. Did King Richard welcome Thomas Kirkby's peace efforts? Or did he want her uncle to observe and report back? Or was her uncle in York out of disaffection with the crown? Her uncle's ambivalence toward Archbishop Richard Scrope interested her. He said the archbishop was too devoted to his predecessor as Archbishop of York, Thomas Arundel, who was also his mentor. Not one of King Richard's favorites by any means, for the king had executed his brother Richard, Earl of Arundel. Who might be interested in peace? The king or the duke? And to whom was her uncle most loyal? Could she trust him not to have had some hand in her troubles? She shoved that thought aside. Again. For good.

As she crossed Ousegate she prepared herself for Marie's onslaught—she would want a full report of the day's activities. Kate smiled in anticipation of Marie's delight when she told her of the proposed stay at the deanery. She would save it for the end.

The bells of St. Mary's Church were ringing nones by the time Kate unbuckled Lille's and Ghent's leads, and she let them rush down the alleyway to the kitchen. By the time she caught up with them, Berend stood in the open doorway laughing at their hopeful barks.

"Do not be fooled. They spent the morning in Helen's kitchen. No one walks out of that kitchen hungry." She patted his forearm as she stepped past him into the warm kitchen. "Phillip is unharmed. Sad and weary, but with a few days of rest he should be home."

"God be thanked," Berend murmured.

Her back to Kate, Marie mumbled a greeting without a pause from her work, kneading dough.

"My boots are soaked through," Kate moaned as she settled on a bench by the fire to wrestle them off. "Did you hear, Marie? Your brother is uninjured."

"I know. Jennet told me." The girl pretended disinterest.

So that is how it would be. Where was Jennet? No matter. First things first. "Then you know that Connor is dead."

A sniff and a nod. Kate waited. At last Marie turned from her work, wiping her floury hands on a rag. Her eyes were red and swollen, her voice shaky. "I will help you with your boots." She dropped to her knees and began to tug. "You should have worn pattens."

"I was not thinking of myself when I dressed this morning," Kate muttered.

"No," the girl whispered.

Kate leaned back, surrendering to the child's struggle to separate the soaked leather boots from the swollen feet, her expression one of fierce determination.

"Your brother is eager to tell you all that happened, so that you understand," said Kate.

Marie fell backward with the right boot in hand. "Your feet stink."

"How kind of you to tell me." The child made it difficult to love her.

Marie sat on the floor considering Kate, the damp, muddy boot forgotten and soiling her apron. "You said a few days of rest. Here? Or at the deanery?" she finally asked.

"At the deanery is best."

Tears welled in the girl's eyes, and her bottom lip quivered.

Kate could not bring herself to torment the child. "That is why he asked that you stay there as well. If you care to do so. Dean Richard is happy to have you both there."

"Phillip asked?" Her eyes widened, a smile teasing at the corners of her mouth.

"Yes. He misses you. Will you go to him? I can take you there before sunset." Or she could if William showed up soon. Perhaps she might send Marie with Jennet. Ah, excellent thought. Except if she learned something from William . . .

A knock, then Matt hobbled in.

"No need to knock, Matt, you are a member of the household," said Kate.

Berend quickly fetched him a chair, but Matt shook his head. "I cannot stay. There is a guest in the hall, Dame Katherine. Master Frost?"

Good. He had come. Kate pressed her hands to her eyes, took a deep breath, then remembered her barely thawed feet, the soggy hose.

Marie jumped up. "I will fetch shoes and pattens for you, Dame Katherine."

The girl was right about pattens. They made far more sense than her riding boots when navigating the waterways of the street. "On your way, tell my cousin I will be with him as soon as I have dry shoes."

Marie nodded and was out the door before Kate could thank her.

"What happened to sweeten her mood?" Berend wondered aloud.

Kate told him about the invitation to bide with her brother at the deanery.

"Ah." He smiled. "Good lad."

"Where is Jennet?"

"She is out listening to the gossip about the deaths," said Matt.

"Well done. We might learn something to our advantage." She noticed how Matt leaned on his cane. "I would like you to stay here with Marie, keep her company and ensure that she does not wander off. Berend will bring wine and stay to witness my discussion with Master Frost."

She saw that Berend understood. Make William uneasy. He rummaged in a corner and produced the cloak. Kate draped it over her arm.

Matt hobbled over to the fire, taking the seat Kate had vacated.

Berend poured him an ale and told him to ask Marie for some food. "Keep her busy."

With a laugh, Matt said, "I am quite able to do that. She reminds me of my youngest brother, deep down a wounded sparrow."

Kate liked Matt more and more.

As soon as Marie returned with dry shoes and pattens, and, bless the girl, dry hose, Kate had her hold up the cloak to screen her from view while she changed her hose. "Would you do me yet another favor? Will you keep Matt company here in the kitchen while Berend and I are talking to my cousin in the hall?" Marie quickly nodded, earnest in obedience so that her invitation to stay with her brother at the deanery was not rescinded. Kate felt a pang of sympathy for the child. "I will miss you while you are there," she whispered.

Marie responded with a quick hug.

Kate was smiling as she called to Lille and Ghent, who were reluctant to give up their warm spaces by the fire.

William wore a fine squirrel-lined cloak and a matching fur hat. The hand that touched Kate's face as he kissed her cheek in greeting was gloved in softest leather. "May God watch over all our loved ones," he said. "I do not have much time, Katherine. I have an engagement in an hour." He nodded toward the cloak draped across her arm. "You as well?"

"You have one foot out the door before we even begin, yet it was you who wished to speak to me."

"I did wish to talk. At my home."

She stifled a retort. "Come, have a seat by the fire. Berend has brought us brandywine." She gestured to a high-backed chair. "I pray you, sit, cousin."

Apparently mollified by her courtesy, the foolish man, William smiled as he removed his cloak and draped it across the back of the chair. Beneath he wore velvet and silk. "And you, Katherine?" He reached for the other high-backed chair.

THE SERVICE OF THE DEAD

She pulled up a backless stool. "I prefer this." For freedom of movement— she imagined lunging for him of a sudden and strangling him. But of course she would not do that. At least she did not intend to do so. She draped the intruder's cloak on a bench within easy reach, then signaled Lille and Ghent to either side of her cousin. It was an arrangement her father had taught her, a dog sitting so close on either side that the person found it difficult to move. And the dogs would shift to restrict his movement if he tried to rise. She found it satisfying to make use of their affection for him.

Berend set a small table at Kate's side, poured the brandywine, handed a goblet to William, one to Kate, and then moved to stand behind their guest. Now her cousin was surrounded.

"I presume you want to hear what I learned about Alice Hatten, how her body was found floating in the King's Fishpond, how she was murdered?" said Kate.

William's smile dimmed. "How quickly you come to the point."

"Is that not what you wished?"

Her cousin glanced back at Berend with a little frown. He had never trusted her cook. "Roger told me you were at the Sharp house last night, where Alice was taken."

"Yes. I happened to have business with Jocasta, but when I arrived I learned of her sad mission."

As on the morning in the guesthouse, William could not focus on any one thing but kept looking this way and that, restive, fearful, clearly uneasy. "I do not know what happened, Katherine. I never would have asked Alice—"

She waved him silent. "I do not care to hear your excuses, cousin. I want facts."

"I thought you—you want facts from me? How would I know? Do you think I killed her, Katherine? Do you accuse me of drowning Alice? I loved her."

"Did you?" She shrugged. "Then it was a timorous love. You could not bring yourself to defend her against your wife's angry dismissal."

"I grant you that. But I could never take Alice's life."

"I know that, William. I am not accusing you. But you are responsible for putting Alice in danger."

"I had no way of knowing she would be in danger." He gave her a look that suggested he had put the tragedy behind him, and so should she.

His smugness put her on the offensive. She wanted to shake him, wake him to the suffering he had caused. She took a deep breath, and then, in a quiet voice, described Alice's mutilation, her broken jaw, her bruised face. "Can you imagine the pain of having your jaw broken as someone forces open your mouth, William?" He squirmed. Good. "You see, her assailant needed to do that in order to use the scissors or the sharp knife to cut out her tongue." She paused to let that image sink in. "How do you think he managed that? Did he pull on her tongue to draw it out as far as possible—she would gag I should think, and then—one cut? Or several? Do you think she heard her torturer cursing with the effort? Or had she already, mercifully, fainted with the pain and the fear?"

"There is a darkness to you sometimes, cousin. . . ." William growled and tried to rise as an answering low rumble came from the dogs' throats. They leaned in, and Berend put a hand on William's shoulder to stay him.

Seeing the agony in her cousin's eyes, Kate relented. "I pray you, sit. I have had a long, trying day, wakened early by Dean Richard's servant."

William shrugged Berend off and resettled. Lille and Ghent relaxed. "I had heard that young Phillip found the stonemason in the minster," he said. "How is the lad?"

"Heartbroken. And weighed down by guilt that he could not cut him down in time. He admired Connor."

"I am sorry for the lad. He has suffered so much loss. On the street they are saying the stonemason murdered Alice, then took his own life. Might it be true?"

"Knowing what you know, how can you ask that, William?"

"Passion can twist into hate." He shrugged, but he looked embarrassed, averting his eyes while he took a long drink. He clutched the goblet with both hands as if he feared his hands would tremble.

"Three deaths, William. I need your help to catch the murderer. You can start by telling me who the dead man was, why he was there, and what Alice and Connor had to do with him."

"Connor?"

"Do not try my patience, cousin. The stonemason murdered this morning. He was expected to join Alice at the guesthouse that night."

"Murdered? I did not realize he had been murdered."

"My uncle the dean rightly advised we keep that quiet so we might catch the murderer."

"Hence the rumor. But of course she would have . . ." William ran a gloved hand down his face. "I gave her no time to let him know," he whispered, as if to himself.

"Go on."

"Perhaps it is still best I tell you as little as possible—"

"No, William. I need to know all that you know, or guess, if you want to help catch Alice's murderer." She waited to see whether she needed to remind him that he actually had no choice, that she could ruin him with one visit to Isabella. It need not even be a visit. She could greet her at market and whisper the name *Drusilla Seaton*. She had no doubt Isabella would jump to the correct conclusion. She found it difficult to trust. She had brought so much to the marriage. Her father's elegant house, his money, his influence. Even his enemies? That was a possibility Kate had not considered. "Have John Gisburne's enemies become your enemies, William?"

"It is a long story, Katherine."

"Then it is best to begin."

"Perhaps tomorrow. My engagement—"

"Alice bled to death, William. In agony from her jaw, then the cutting of the tongue, she bled to death in the presence of her executioner. Or alone. Perhaps he tossed her on the floor, or the ground, and left her to die. In the dark, alone, unshriven. Then he returned to bundle her up and carry her to the pond, tossing her in like a butchered animal. Imagine that, William. I want you to appreciate how her life ended."

The bastards threatened to do that to you, Geoff said in her head. *That was why—*

Not now, she warned him.

"I did not mean for this to happen." William's voice broke.

"You put it in motion, as you did Alice's earlier humiliation. For her sake I will not make it easy for you to forget that."

"Why do you care so?"

Maud. It is Maud you are avenging, Geoff guessed.

"I cannot believe you need to ask. Is she any less precious in the eyes of God because she is not wealthy?"

William winced. "When did he—they—whoever did this—when did they take her?" he asked.

"Phillip saw her with Connor the morning after the murder in the guesthouse. And then it seems he was searching for her until he heard that she had been found."

"How frightened she must have been."

"Yes. A cruel death. And for what, William? What did she die for?"

William's shoulders drooped in resignation. "Might I at least send my servant—" The young man who had accompanied William had been sent out to the kitchen.

"I will tell him to go on ahead," Jennet said from the doorway.

Kate had felt the draft as the door opened and guessed, from Berend's and the dogs' lack of reaction, who it was. "Thank you, Jennet. Tell him to say a family matter delays his master."

"Katherine, I pray you," said William.

Kate nodded for Jennet to go on. Turning back to William, she asked how he had arranged to lure Alice to her death.

"I did nothing of the sort. I had no idea. He was just to—" He sucked in his breath, looked down as if thinking how to take back the words.

"This 'he,' what was his name?"

"Underhill. Jon Underhill."

"He was just to do what?"

"It is a long story, Katherine."

"As you said. But whoever is expecting you undoubtedly knows that your cousin's ward found Connor in the chapter house this morning. By now all the city knows. He or she will understand and approve of your kindness to me. Now. From the beginning." She smiled sweetly. "More brandywine?"

He sighed and held up his goblet. "Whose cloak is that, if I might inquire?"

"We will come to that." She poured wine for both of them.

He took a sip. "I never imagined she would be in danger, Katherine, you must believe me. Underhill was just to set up Griselde and Clement as his spies for the king. They would inform him about Lady Kirkby's guests, to whom she spoke, what she said, what they agreed. That was all."

"That was all. You were setting up my servants as spies? In my guest-house? Spying on my guest? That was all? William!" As Kate's voice rose, Lille barked, Ghent growled.

"Mistress . . ." Berend whispered.

She took a deep breath, calmed the dogs. "No more outbursts. Go on, William. Tell me all of it. Why did you need Alice?"

His hands shook as he wiped the sweat from his forehead. "She was there to make it look as if I were offering Underhill some entertainment." William had the decency to wince at the detail. "He did not share with me how he hoped to accomplish his plan, how he would coerce Griselde and Clement. God help me." He began to rise, felt Berend's hand on his shoulder, and cursed as he settled back down on his seat. He drained his goblet. "Something went wrong that night, very wrong. The man is dead, and now Alice. And Connor?"

The dogs suddenly sat up, ears pricked, their attention on the street side of the hall. Within a moment, Jennet came bursting in from the garden, William's servant following.

"I pray you forgive the interruption, mistress, Master Frost," Jennet bobbed her head. "But you will want to know. I thought it wise to follow young Jenkins as he departed. He was just stepping out onto Castlegate when a man slipped up behind him—I had no time to notice whence he had come. When he reached out to take Jenkins's arm, the young man cried out. I came forward as they were struggling. Then the attacker shouted and ran off, dodging carts and folk walking. I lost him. I thought you would want to know."

Kate noticed the servant holding something behind his back. "Are you hurt, Jenkins?"

"No. I wounded him." He brought his hand out to show the bloody knife.

Kate commended him. "Where should we look for the wound if we encounter him again?"

The young man looked to his master, back to Kate. "I believe it was his hand, perhaps his forearm. As he reached out for me. I should not have lashed out before I knew his intention. But he startled me. And with all the deaths . . ."

Kate crossed the hall to him, took his empty hand, looked him in the eyes. "You did well. Did you recognize the man?"

He shook his head. "He wore a hood."

"All I could tell was that he was of middling height and very fleet of foot," said Jennet.

"I think it best you wait for your master in the kitchen, eh?" said Kate. "Go now. A nip of brandywine might calm both of you."

Kate turned to William as Jennet nodded and shepherded the lad out the door. "Clearly he should not rush off to make your apologies after such an experience."

A tight shake of his head. "Of course not. Though I would ask you to leave it to me to order my servants about, Katherine. You do overstep." He waited. She did not see the need to respond. Finally he said, "Jenkins and I will continue to Thomas Graa's together, when I am finished here."

Ah. The merchant Graa had once been Simon's partner, almost as wealthy as Thomas Holme, and definitely a prominent citizen. "Good. Let us begin at the beginning."

William groaned.

"The man you set up in my guesthouse, was he the king's man?"

"Yes. Or so he said."

"And his name was Jon Underhill?"

A nod. "He carried a letter with the king's seal."

"Did you examine the seal closely?" she asked.

"The seal? I have a vague recollection. The white hart perhaps? I cannot recall details." He stared down into the goblet in his hands as if wishing he might see the letter once more. "I should have used more caution. He was secretive. Not what I had expected. Always before King Richard has sent men of a certain discretion and status. A merchant, a landowner." He looked up, pleading. "I fear for my family, Katherine. Faith, it was fear for my family that brought this trouble. I meant you no harm. I swear."

"Did he threaten you?"

"No. Quite the contrary. He offered his services to keep my family safe."

"From what?"

"For weeks I sensed I was being followed. Roger felt it, too. But whoever he was, he was adept at staying hidden."

"Why would someone be following you?"

"At first I thought, perhaps, Duke Henry. My wife—you know that her father and the duke's father were enemies. My wife had tried to remedy that with Duke Henry. I feared he had sent someone to follow me, see to whom I spoke. But to what end? I deal with merchants and landowners of all opinions. We are seeing to our lives, going about our business. We all wish we might forget the king's feud. But we all know the danger of that."

"Has a business transaction gone sour?"

"No. Nothing like that. Everything has been quiet."

"No king's men searching your ships?"

He shook his head. "I am known to be loyal."

"But your wife is not. Curious that the king accepts your household's divided loyalties."

"Perhaps the king has set someone on me. But then why Underhill? God's blood, I cannot see clearly." William pressed a hand to his face.

Kate waited for him to calm. In a few moments he dropped his hand, stared at it for a moment, then turned it a little as if examining his signet ring.

"I heard about your ship being searched," he said. "And that the king's men stole some spice?"

"Lionel told you?"

A nod.

"Is the man reaching out for Jenkins the first time he has done more than shadow your household?" she asked. "If it is the same man."

"No, not the first time. He frightened my wife and daughter."

Kate did not try to hide her eagerness as she leaned forward. "Tell me."

"Isabella and Hazel were shopping on Stonegate. A busy time of day. My daughter felt hands round her neck. She thought it her mother, but then noticed her several steps away. A man whispered, 'A little twist and your neck snaps. Tell your father he is watched.' She screamed. A man near her described someone in dark clothes, nothing distinguishable."

"So bold," Berend muttered. Both Kate and William glanced at him. "I am sorry for your daughter, Master Frost. That must have been terrifying for her."

William nodded, tears in his eyes that he tried to hide by leaning down to stroke the dogs' backs. Hazel was Isabella and William's only child, a delicate girl, unable to eat anything but the most plainly cooked meats and gruels. William adored her. Kate waited until he had composed himself. He sat up, tugging on his jacket. Back in control.

"A day later Underhill appeared," William continued, "carrying a letter of introduction from the king. Or what I took to be such. He wanted access to Lady Kirby. I told him I might not be the best person. Someone was following me. He offered his protection if I did all he said."

And Bale's letter carried Duke Henry's seal.

"Did he find the shadow?"

"No. But he had little time before Lady Kirkby arrived. And then—I have wondered whether he was strangled by the one who has been shadowing me. To prevent his interfering."

"So the dead man is Underhill?" Kate asked.

William bowed his head. "Yes," he whispered.

"Have you ever heard the name Hubert Bale?" Berend asked.

"No," William muttered, sounding miserable.

"What about Alice and Connor? How did they happen to be in the guesthouse that night?" Kate asked.

William rubbed his face, sat back, blinking. Kate could not remember when she had last seen him so disheveled. A long while ago, for certain. Isabella would hiss at his appearance when he joined her at the Graa residence. "Before this trouble began, Alice came to me requesting that I use my family's influence in Beverley to find Connor work there. At the minster, preferably. I agreed to try if she would allow me to visit our son Tom, to let him know that I was someone to whom he might turn if ever he needed help. I did not ask her to identify me as his father. She meant to wed Connor, so that should have been his role. The boy would call me 'uncle.' It would be something. And I promised to help with his education.

That night we were to meet at the guesthouse so that I could advise Connor about how to comport himself with the dean and chapter of Beverley. But Underhill came to me that day with the plan."

"Was it he who arranged Matt's accident?" Kate asked.

"He mentioned that he would ensure that Matt was elsewhere that night. I never imagined he would injure him."

"And you did not think to insist that no one be harmed?"

"I trusted him. The king's man." William threw up his hands. Lille opened an eye, and Ghent raised his head. "I am glad to see Matt has recovered."

"Perhaps you did not notice his limp? That he must walk with a crutch?"

Kate let him stew in that for a moment. In the silence she heard the thaw continuing up above, ice sliding down the roof. The ice jam was breached. The sound of dripping water surrounded her. For the next few days she would feel as if she were moving underwater. "When did you tell Alice of the change of plan?"

"Roger told her when he escorted her to the guesthouse."

"William! You did not ask her? You simply sent her there?"

He glanced away.

"Of course you did not ask her. You knew she would refuse, and for good cause. Once again you cast her in the role of whore. How could you?"

"I know. I see now how—it all went so wrong. So wrong."

Kate slapped him before she was even aware she had put thought into action. It was Geoff's voice in her head—*Steady, Kate*—and Berend's hand on hers that brought her back.

William's eyes were as round as a child's when waking from a nightmare.

"You treated her like a piece of property, William. Like a slave. Alice. The mother of your son. How could you do such a thing?"

He felt round for blood on his face. There was none, of course. She had not hit him that hard, or with the hand on which she wore a ring.

"How could you?" she whispered.

"I was frightened for my family."

"She is the mother of your only son. Is he not at least family?"

"I will pay for her burial," William said softly, "and masses for her soul."

"And your son? I know that you cannot have custody of him, but will you support him?"

"In any way her sister Tessa will permit."

"What of Isabella? Can you hide such expenses from her?"

He colored, cleared his throat.

"Ah, I see. You already hide much."

"For Hazel's sake. To keep peace in the household."

Of course. Just for that. Not to make life easier for him. "Have you learned anything of what happened at my guesthouse that night?" she asked.

"Nothing."

"Did you see Alice afterward?" He bowed his head. "William, did you see her after the murder in the guesthouse? Was that a nod?"

He straightened up with such effort it was as if he were pushing against a weight, his face drawn, his eyes red. He admitted that he had seen Alice. She had been lurking in an alley just down Stonegate from where he had parted from Kate outside the goldsmith's shop. "Alice accosted me, hissing that I had ruined her again. I—I pushed her back into the alleyway and warned her that she would go to the stocks, that I would name her as a scold if she tried to contact me again."

"William! How can you accuse her of defaming you? *You* were the one to cause injury, not Alice."

"I am ashamed to admit it. But I have told you."

"Did she say anything else?"

"She said something about being followed. She was disheveled. I asked where she had slept. That is when she threw up her hands and walked back into the dark alley."

In the silence, Kate could hear his jagged breathing, as if he were crying within. Enough. She had bullied him enough to force him to recall what she guessed he had tried to forget.

"What of your shadow?" she asked softly. "Is he gone?"

A shrug. "I have sensed eyes on me, but I might be conjuring them out of my own fear. Roger believes the danger is past."

"You doubt him."

William raked a hand through his hair, knocking off his hat. "I know not what to believe at present."

Berend silently retrieved the hat and put it on William's lap.

"What do you know of Roger's loyalties?" Kate asked. "Does he serve only you?"

She watched as he realized what she was asking.

"He has served me faithfully."

And so William never questioned his loyalty. He gave Roger a comfortable life; what more could he want? Like Alice, Roger was property.

William shook his head, trying to clear it, his eyes moving as if he were weighing the evidence.

Are you toying with him? You do not believe Roger is part of this, do you?

Are you suddenly William's advocate, Geoff?

You know better. I never cared for the man. But he is in pain.

She reconsidered. "Roger might believe the danger past. Or wish to calm you. Is it not his duty to guard your family, keep the three of you safe? This might embarrass him."

"I think it might." William held up his goblet. "A little more?"

His hand shook as he lifted the cup after she poured. He no longer tried to mask it. Giving him a moment to collect himself, she flipped over a corner of the cloak Sam's shadow had been wearing, looked at the matted fur lining. Well made, but old, worn.

"That is an old piece," said William. "Are you giving that to Dame Jocasta?"

"I bought it from her."

He let out a sharp laugh. "Why?"

She told him about the man who had followed Sam.

That sobered him. "Your servants are followed as well? What is happening, Katherine? Who can we trust? It certainly was not Roger. Sam would have recognized him."

"I did not mean to accuse Roger."

William seemed beyond any consolation. "Call Sam in here, would you? I would like to ask him myself."

"He left for Beverley after the incident, to see whether Alice Hatten had simply gone home. He has not returned."

"He traveled that road in the snow?"

"I know. Even after I had told him to delay it. I am worried, of course. The snow, the deaths." *Or he might have made his escape,* she thought. Could she trust Sam?

"What are we to do, Katherine?"

"Did you bury Underhill, or did you weigh him down in the river?"

"Buried. With prayers. And any time now the king will send someone to find out what happened to him. But I did it for you. You wanted him out of the guesthouse."

"His presence would have been difficult to explain to Lady Kirkby."

William shrugged. "I am just reminding you why I was in such haste. I had no time to think of a way to have him discovered along the road. I have thought about that over and again. How I might have simply left him with some other cord round his neck. Or nothing. Let the sheriff try to guess what had been used to strangle him." He paused. "Why do you now want to know what I did with his corpse?"

"We have no time to lose," she said. "It is too late now, but tomorrow you will take me to the grave. Berend will help you dig it up."

"Dig him up? Why?"

"To see whether we recognize Underhill."

"How would you?" He noticed her looking at Berend and turned to regard him. "Do you think you know him?"

"I heard rumors that someone I once knew had been seen in York." Berend bowed to William.

William looked to Kate, back to Berend. "You know more than you are telling me."

"We know nothing," said Kate. Though they suspected much. "Immediately after the morning service, come to the guesthouse. We will leave from there."

"On the Sabbath?"

"Would you prefer to miss the requiem masses on Monday?"

He nodded. "Tomorrow. I will be there. Now might I continue on to Thomas Graa's?"

"Of course. I will see you in the morning."

After dinner, when Jennet had gone up to tidy the chamber and get some sleep, and Matt took Lille and Ghent to the hall to settle for the night, Kate sat with Berend in front of the kitchen fire, reviewing the interview with William and what she had learned from her uncle. She stared into the flames, frustrated, unable to see the way forward.

"The more we learn, the less we know," she said.

"Do you trust that he will come tomorrow?" Berend asked.

"If he does not, we collect him."

Berend grunted.

Kate sat up and turned to study her companion's scarred face. He did not flinch, nor did he smile.

"What is it?" she asked.

"I felt a ghost in the hall when you described the suffering of that poor woman. You have seen this before. It awakened old anger, old fear."

"And if it did?"

He shrugged. "I am your servant."

"Forget for now that you are my servant, Berend. You are my comrade in arms. What do you need to say?"

"A warrior needs a clear head. Perhaps if you told me about this ghost, what her death meant to you, it might exorcise her, and help prevent—"

"The slap?"

"And the unnecessarily vivid description of how it might have been carried out."

"You think I should have taken a gentler approach with William." She waited, hearing in Berend's silence his earlier question. "And if he does not come to the guesthouse tomorrow, I am to blame."

"No. Not entirely. He is hoping that somehow this storm will rush past, that perhaps the king is too busy to notice his man has not returned. He might hope he can wait it out, that something will happen that negates the need to disinter a man he buried in haste, in fear."

Kate held out a cup for more ale. Berend poured.

Are you going to tell him the story?

I will tell him about Maud. Perhaps he does sense her here.

But not the rest?

No. I need his trust.

Faintly, Kate heard barking. A moment later Matt burst through the door. "Lille and Ghent have caught the scent of someone in the alleyway. It was all I could do to squeeze through the door without letting them out."

"I will give you some training in handling them later," Kate said as she clamped on her pattens. She was out the door just behind Berend, who carried a lantern. She had not reckoned on the chill of the evening glazing the puddles and stumbled against Berend.

Steadying her, he suggested she wait by the kitchen door while he checked the garden and the alleyway, watching for movement. She itched to cross the garden and let loose the hounds, but it was more important to be Berend's extra set of eyes.

In the end, he found nothing, and when she brought Lille and Ghent out on leashes they lost the scent in St. Mary's churchyard across the road. She led them back to the hall and gave Matt a quick lesson in signals for stay and lie down, for which he thanked her.

Berend had watched the exchange, and quietly suggested she go up to bed. Their conversation could wait.

Kate did not argue. It seemed days ago that her uncle's servant had come for her. She left the pattens by the door and made her way up to the solar, sensing the absence of her wards, their often troubling but no less dear presences. Jennet snored in the great bed, an arm and a leg dangling out. Kate climbed in beside her and lay on her back, gazing up at the canopy, praying that Phillip and Marie were securely tucked in at the deanery, and would remain safe.

12

RAISING THE DEAD

—❦—

Sunday morning, standing in the watery sunshine on the porch of St. Mary's, Castlegate, Kate wished she were anywhere else as every member of the congregation took her arm or her hand and asked after young Phillip. How horrible for a young boy to witness such an end. How shocking. Was he at home abed? Was he injured? Each looked her in the eyes, hoping they might be the one in whom she would confide precious details they might repeat as points of pride. She had been aware of people craning their necks to count her companions throughout the mass, whispering that neither of her wards was with her. As soon as she could, she broke away to collect Lille and Ghent, then joined Berend and Jennet for the walk to High Petergate; but first she waded through more acquaintances feigning concern in the hope of gaining more information. With all the snow, the two deaths and Lady Kirkby's presence were the only news anyone had heard in weeks, and Kate was the wellspring. God help her if any learned of the first death, the one in her guesthouse.

Despite her delay, she arrived at the house on High Petergate ahead of William. She wondered whether he would come.

As soon as she had stepped across the threshold she was swept aside by Lady Margery, who whispered that she had something to discuss. She led Kate to a small table by the rear window where Griselde and one of Margery's guards waited, both looking ill at ease. Kate prepared herself for more bad tidings.

"Odo Marsden, your tenant across the alley, came pounding on the door quite late last evening complaining of sounds in the undercroft," Lady Margery began. The undercroft next door was the one in which Kate warehoused her most expensive spices. "He says it is not the first time he has heard someone down there." Margery leaned close, her perfume quite dizzying. "You have grounds to evict him for neglecting to inform you, Katherine. Considering what I am about to tell you I recommend you do just that—evict him. Your spice stock is too valuable to risk." She leaned back, nodding. "I sent two of my men over to look around." She motioned to the one who sat beside Griselde, a warm-eyed man who filled his clothes as if he were as thickly muscled as Berend. "Tell Dame Katherine what you found, Alan."

He bobbed his head in respect to Kate before speaking. "We found the padlock on the door open. It had been cleverly put back so that you cannot see that it is unlocked unless you reach for it. Inside, in the far corner, we found a pallet and some blankets, an empty jug, and other items that suggest someone has been biding there. Unless you have a guard who does so?"

She shook her head, her mind searching for how long it had been since she had been in the undercroft. Lionel should have been there this past week. But it had been awhile since Kate had checked it.

"But you found no intruder last night?" The guard shook his head. "And have you watched it since?"

"We have, Mistress Clifford. Whoever it is has not returned."

"I want to talk to Odo." Kate rose, inviting the guard to accompany her. She called to Berend to join them.

Odo grumbled at the guard when he came to the door, then apologized when Kate stepped forward and moved past him into the hall, her nose tickled by the air emanating from the large room.

"What is this smoke?" She could barely make out the opposite wall for the thickness of the air. "When was the last time you cleared the chimney?" When was the last time she had inspected up here? She could not recall. "We will talk about this later. At the moment . . ." Her eyes were tearing and her lungs felt tight. She asked Berend and Alan to open the shutters and the doors.

"But the cold!" Odo reached out a gnarled hand as if to stop Berend, who simply brushed past him.

"As my tenant you are responsible for maintaining the house in a safe condition. Such smoke is a prelude to fire. You are also responsible for alerting me at once to any trouble on the premises, and a faulty chimney is one. Intruders in the undercroft is another. How often have you heard someone down there?"

He shook his head. "I never said because I thought he was your man. But so late on the night before the Sabbath . . . Or was it something else?"

"Such as?"

He frowned, tilting his head as if trying to recall what he had been saying. Giving up, he demanded, "Are you evicting me?"

"We will speak of this in a few days. You say he has been here before, but you said nothing until last night. What happened last night?"

"Noise." He shook his head. "I wanted it to stop."

"But why last night?"

Odo just kept repeating that he wanted the noise to stop.

"What noise?"

He looked confused.

Kate dragged a high-backed bench toward the doorway, where the outside air tempered the smoke, and ordered him to sit beside her. He shuffled over and settled down, muttering that it was the Sabbath, and a man should be left in peace on the Sabbath.

When Berend and Alan had opened the shutters and doors, she sent them down to the undercroft—Berend knew how they had last left it. How long had it been? A fortnight? More?

When they withdrew, she turned back to her elderly tenant, who was shivering and whining about the cold despite the cloak he had draped round himself. Dirt had settled into his wrinkles, accentuating them, and his eyes were rheumy and bloodshot. Perhaps he was ill. Who would not be ill living in this smoke? "Tell me about the intruder. From the beginning."

As the man spoke of noises down below, his account wandering, Kate began to see him in a different light. He was not simply a churlish man set in his ways, but an aged man frightened by failing health, failing sight, and a mind that danced away from him, down paths in which he became lost. One moment he knew it was the Sabbath, the next he complained about slipping on the autumn leaves when he went out to the midden. Odo needed care. Perhaps St. Leonard's Hospital would take him.

"Have you any kin in York, Odo?" she asked, interrupting his wandering. She had heard enough to guess that the intruder might have been down there for several weeks. Which made her wonder where Lionel had warehoused the most recent shipment of spice.

Odo shook his head. "All my kin are long gone."

"I thought they were long-lived."

He frowned, started to talk about his brother's accident on the road south—a broken axle, his being thrown from the cart, his head hitting a rock. "No pain," he whispered. "They said he felt nothing."

Kate patted his hand. "We will see what we can do for you. Tell me about the noise. What is the noise the intruder makes?"

He hummed a tune that was no tune. "Like that," he said, then shrugged and told her of a whistle his father had given him one Christmas, his voice trailing off as his head nodded.

"I will send Seth, the Fletchers' boy, over to help you. And I will see to having the chimney cleared. Have you any food in the house?"

Chin to chest, Odo began to snore.

Kate blinked her eyes to ease the sting of the smoke as she rose and toured the hall, groaning in frustration at the damage—the gouges in the walls, the wall paintings blackened by the smoke, the stench in a corner that was either Odo's indoor cesspit or that of an animal companion she had not yet discovered. Tears of frustration joined those caused by the smoky air. She cursed herself for avoiding the old man. She had loved this house. Now her poor stewardship had ruined it. Another crisis. How was it that they were all arising at once?

No. That was the wrong question. More to the point, what did this have to do with the deaths? She did not believe in coincidence. How was the intruder connected with her other problems?

"What has happened here?" Jennet asked from the doorway. "Has there been a fire?"

Kate skirted a pile of debris to join Jennet by the snoring tenant. "I will explain."

Jennet gazed down on Odo. "How he has aged since the accident."

"What accident? When?"

"A few months past, he and his brother had a cart accident. The axle snapped, tossing both of them and Odo's elderly servant onto the road. His brother and the servant died. Odo survived, but it looks as if he was far more seriously injured than anyone realized."

"How did I not hear of this?"

Jennet shook her head. "It is the sort of thing I would have reported to you, him being your tenant. I am surprised that Griselde did not notice the condition of the hall. I thought they were friends."

"I do recall her saying that she and Odo had argued. Much complaining on her part about his stubbornness. After a while I stopped listening." Kate pressed her fingertips to her eyes. "I pray you came to tell me my cousin has arrived."

"I did. He and his man Roger. We are ready."

So William had kept his word. Kate bent down to Odo, lifted his hands, felt the gnarled joints and the too-thin flesh without warmth. He required more help than Seth would know how to give. Jocasta Sharp would surely know of someone willing to take on the task for a little while. Kate would send Seth with the request. While he was gone one of Lady Margery's servants could stay with Odo.

It seemed so little, and Kate felt wretched leaving Odo. It took but a moment to cross the alleyway, but she had been so busy with her own troubles that she had neglected her tenant, conveniently assuming he was a man never pleased, never satisfied. She had become so focused on her goals that she had become willfully blind to the suffering round her. One visit had lifted the veil from her eyes.

Or perhaps Alice's death had lifted the veil. She had lain awake in the night imagining Alice's last night, last day. How her heart must have ached when she discovered that William was trading her to a stranger. No doubt she believed he had never meant to help Connor, that he had intended from the start to betray her. Then the horror of the attack. Her escape. How frightened she must have been. And William's callousness.

She had tried to focus on the problems, not the suffering, reminding herself to ask Phillip whether something Connor said in his cups, something he did not realize as significant, might provide a hint about what had happened in the guest chamber that night. What had Alice witnessed? How had the attacker ensured she would not interfere? The wine. Had Alice, Griselde, and Clement all had something in their wine to make them sleep through the attack? William had entrusted Kate's servants and the mother of his son to a stranger without questioning how he might treat them. And the next day, William himself threatened Alice with the stocks if she approached him again. When had the murderer caught Alice? Had it been at the other end of the alley? Kate had been sick in the night, imagining Alice's terror.

Now she struggled to regain her composure so that she might smile at William, who had kept his word. What she yearned to do was kick him in the groin.

"Ready?" Jennet asked.

"Go on ahead. Tell Lady Margery that I need one of her servants to watch over Odo. And send Seth to me. I will wait with Odo until they come and all is settled. Tell William that he should be ready to leave very soon."

It worked. Giving instructions, seeing to Odo, Kate fell into her coping pattern and was soon able to cross the alleyway, enter the guesthouse hall, and hold her tongue as William rose from his place beside Lady Margery. He took Kate's hand, leaning close to whisper that he had not slept, having prayed all night for Alice, for forgiveness, for the courage to be a better man. Indeed he looked haggard, but she was miles from forgiveness.

She simply nodded. "We have work to do."

As they were leaving, Griselde told Kate she would send some hot food next door and began to apologize for holding a grudge against Odo that had stopped her from checking on him. "I always used to. Odo's servant was aging along with him, and I often did some tidying, some cooking. But he made me so angry. . . ." She covered her face with her apron.

Kate pressed her arm, assured Griselde that she was not the only one who had avoided the man. "He was my tenant. I neglected my responsibility. All we can do is move forward with better grace, eh?"

They were a solemn party, William, Roger, Kate, Jennet, Berend—though Lille and Ghent thought it a rare treat to lead her out Bootham Bar into the wide world beyond. The Forest of Galtres was surely their idea of the heavenly abode. They strained against their leashes, eager to run, but with the Sunday afternoon strollers Kate did not think it wise to let them loose. Besides, they were a marked group, she and William each connected in some way to the scandalous deaths the past week. Well might folk stare at them, wonder where they were wayfaring on a Sabbath afternoon.

But as the group moved out beyond the walls of St. Mary's Abbey, the dogs' ears began to twitch as if they sensed someone coming up behind. Kate, too, sensed that someone behind them watched too closely. Now Berend lifted his head, glanced round. Jennet, too. Roger exchanged a look with Jennet.

Quietly, Kate suggested that she and Jennet could be spared, for they would not be digging up the body. And the dogs were best at tracking a tracker. Berend and the others would continue, while she and Jennet would hang back and do what they could to catch their shadow, then either escort him back into York or bring him along. The latter only if she believed it was the murderer. Anyone else should not see the grave in the forest.

The plan agreed, the men went on ahead as Kate and Jennet lagged behind with Lille and Ghent. As they entered the cover of the first dense grove of trees, they pretended to be stopping for a rest beneath a venerable oak a little way off the road. Even in the weak winter sun the oak cast a shadow with its thick limbs. Snowdrifts like frozen waves made walking a challenge, and Kate felt the dampness seeping into her boots and her skirts growing heavy as they brushed along the melting surface. Crouching down, she unfastened the dogs' leashes. They shook themselves off, then gracefully picked their way through the drifts, noses to the ground, curious about who had been there before them. Kate and Jennet leaned against the wide trunk, softly talking about nothing in particular, their ears pricked for the sound of someone stealing up on them. Both held their knives hidden beneath the folds of their cloaks, at the ready.

Perhaps this was the beginning of the end of the search. The murderer might have underestimated Kate. He might reveal himself.

"Do you think we imagined being followed?" Jennet asked.

As if her question had been taken as a signal, someone approached, trying hard to move silently. But the crusty snow made stealth impossible. Crouching down, Kate whispered to Lille and Ghent, "Find."

They took off into the brush, and in no time at all she heard Lille's proud bark, and the sound of someone attempting to run. Kate and Jennet took up the pursuit, eventually seeing a man moving surprisingly quickly through the trees. But Lille and Ghent were gaining on him, spurring him to become reckless, and at last he pitched forward with a thud and a curse.

"Skirt round, see if he had a companion," Kate whispered to Jennet, then hastened toward the downed spy.

He lay on his back trying to blow aside the fur collar that had twisted round and covered his mouth as he fell. Ghent's forepaws on his chest prevented the use of the one hand not stuck beneath the cloak. "Clever Ghent," she said, "pinning down that arm." Lille stood near the man's head, growling.

"Call them off, I beg you, Mistress Clifford."

Kate cursed as she recognized the man. Lionel Neville's manservant, Fitch.

"Has your master sent you to spy on me, Fitch?" Kate asked.

He tried to talk, but he'd managed to twist the collar even tighter, preventing speech.

Kate motioned for Ghent to ease away, but stay alert.

Fitch sat up, straightening his collar, pulling off his hat to shake off the snow, spitting the fur from his mouth.

"Well?"

"No, Mistress Clifford. No. Course not. I thought maybe you were out seeking Sam. I am worried for him."

She did not for a moment believe him, but it was a curious choice, to mention Sam. "Has Sam been spying on me for your master?"

"No! We are just friends. Old friends. Like I said, I am worried for him, with all the deaths, and him taking off to Beverley in the snow."

That interested her. And, looking more closely at his fur-collared cloak, she remembered another one. An older one that had been tossed into

Jocasta Sharp's cart. Of course she'd seen that old one before. And this one. They were Lionel Neville's castoffs. "And when did Sam tell you he was off to Beverley?"

She saw the dawning on the man's face, how odd it would be for her servant to stop at Lionel's home, to tell this servant, friend or no, that he was leaving on a mission for her. Though heading out Walmgate was one route out of York toward Beverley, still, she did not believe Sam would take the time. Unless he had been asked to do so.

"I have no idea of Sam's whereabouts," she said.

He glanced on down the track as if hoping to catch sight of Berend and the others, then started as Jennet came up behind him.

"Well, this is a surprise," she said. "You are a good runner, Fitch. We might have lost you had it not been for the snow."

He straightened and began to give her a long-toothed smile, then caught himself. "I am looking for Sam."

Jennet laughed. "You are a poor liar." In a sudden move she grabbed his right arm and pushed up his sleeve. Bandaged. Seeping. So it was a fairly fresh wound. "See, Mistress Clifford? This is where Jenkins cut him last night. What were you doing lurking in the alleyway, Fitch? Waiting for Sam?"

Jerking his arm from her grasp he shrugged and mumbled something Kate could not hear. No matter.

"Jennet was about to turn back, were you not?" Jennet would not need Kate or the dogs to keep Fitch in line.

Jennet grinned. "Happy to have your company on the walk back to the city, Fitch."

He rose gingerly, brushing off his cloak with an injured air. "I am not headed back just yet."

"Yes, you are," said Kate.

"I have a right to walk out into the forest of a Sunday."

"Of course you do. And my friends have a right to be spared my brother-in-law's inept servant spying on their flirtations with the young ladies of Easingwold." She pretended dismay at divulging the reason for the outing, and, stepping close to him, said, "If I discover you have told anyone what I just said, I will gut you." Jennet caught his wrists and jerked them back as Kate put the knife to his stomach. "Now. Why have you been haunting my alleyway, and why were you following us today?"

Sweating despite the cold air, his eyes wild, Fitch still swore he was worried about Sam.

"Well, that sort of worry . . ." She lowered the knife to his groin. "Hm. That sounds as if he is your lover. Are you a sodomite, Fitch? Not that I would condemn you for it. We cannot help who we love, can we?"

He gulped. "No. No," he whispered. "He is not my lover."

"Then I do not believe your story. Tell me another one."

"Master Lionel, he asked me to watch your house, tell him all I noticed."

"Why?"

Fitch shook his head. "He did not explain."

She slid the knife up to his throat. "He told you nothing?"

"A man came to him. A man like Berend, strong, dangerous. He wanted to know about Lady Kirkby's mission. The master sent him away. I did not hear how he managed it. A few days later, once Lady Kirkby was in York, he ordered me to watch your house, especially in the evenings and early mornings."

"Why then?"

"I have other duties throughout the day. It has been difficult. I have had little sleep."

"But Lady Kirkby is lodged at my guesthouse on Petergate, not at my home."

"I do not question Master Lionel's orders." Fitch was shivering. "I am cold, Mistress Clifford. The snow soaked my leggings and the icy water is going down into my shoes. Have mercy." His teeth began to chatter.

"What about today? How did you know to follow us today?"

"The master gives me leave to walk out into the countryside after mass on the Sabbath. I saw the lot of you and thought he would be pleased to know what you were about. I am sorry, Mistress Clifford. I pray you. I need to move. Get warm."

Kate lowered the knife. "You will pretend for your master that you are still going about your task, yes?"

A nod. "I s-swear."

"Go on with Jennet."

Lionel was a terrible judge of men. Fortunate for her. Even more fortunate that they had caught Fitch and turned him back before he saw the body buried in the forest. But perhaps most useful was his account of the man who came to Lionel for information about Lady Kirkby. Hubert Bale? She must think how to draw out her brother-in-law.

She waited beneath the oak until Jennet and Fitch were out of sight, then told Lille and Ghent to lead her to Berend. They trotted off, choosing the smaller track that branched off toward Wigginton, eventually leading her off through the brush to a line of ancient hollies. The sound of shovels came from just beyond the prickly hedge, and when she had found a way through, she saw the men's cloaks and jackets hanging on the thick limbs of a willow at the edge of a clearing. Berend and Roger were bent over, digging.

A flash of memory. Her brother Walter watching as her father and a servant dug a grave, a bundled body lying to one side. Dread rose up, chilling her hands and her feet, blurring her vision.

Steady, Kate, Geoff whispered.

She took a deep breath and the memory dissolved. Ghent leaned into her, sensing Geoff.

That was Father digging? Geoff whispered.

Who else was left?

There is so much I have not seen. How have you hidden these memories from me?

I've hidden them from myself. I am not sure why they are breaking loose. It worried her. They weakened her.

I am here to strengthen you.

I would prefer to have you here in the flesh. Now be quiet. I need a clear head.

Lille whined. She'd already caught the stench of death from the grave. Gently, Kate commanded the dogs to stay back beneath the tree, stroking both of them, reassuring them. Herself as well. They steadied her.

As she stepped into the clearing she assured Berend's bent back that all was calm. He and Roger leaned into the work, the shovels short-handled, the best that could be done since they needed to fit in a sack Berend could conceal beneath his cloak. He had deemed it best not to call attention to himself with such tools on the Sabbath, particularly if they were being watched. The two were shoveling out the dirt, as William raked the piles away from the edge with a spade he must have brought with him. Or, rather, Roger. She could not imagine William being aware he owned such a tool.

"Our shadow was Lionel Neville's manservant Fitch. Jennet is escorting him back to the city," she said as she joined them. "He will not give her trouble."

"Fitch?" Berend glanced up, chuckling. "Poor man if he tries. So Neville set a servant to spy on us?" He nodded. "Of course he would want to know what we were about."

William leaned on the spade. "Lionel Neville? Why?"

"No doubt to find a way to deprive me of my share in the business. He is ever hopeful of finding something scandalous so that he might demand the business in return for his silence."

"Would he do that?"

"Of course he would. He's a Neville. He believes himself far worthier than I am. He has lost hope that I will forget the terms of Simon's will and tumble into marriage, thereby forfeiting my share. So he is looking for another way in. Which is why I am so cautious." She gave her cousin a look that she hoped reminded him of the trouble he had brought her. In truth, Lionel was not so different from William, who hoped to get her married off so he would feel less responsibility, though in truth he had done more to ruin her than any other.

But William simply muttered, "That Neville bastard," and resumed his work raking the dirt. Until he began to gasp, then dropped the spade and turned away from the grave with a gloved hand to his mouth. "God in heaven," he groaned.

Kate smelled it as well and lifted a corner of her cloak to cover her face.

"Yes, we are there." Berend tossed aside the shovel and knelt by the grave.

"Pity the thaw has begun." Roger adjusted the scarf over the lower half of his face.

Berend wore one as well. Even so, Kate wondered at how they went about their business, leaning into the grave, brushing the dirt from the shrouded body with their gloved hands.

Roger tugged open the top of the shroud. "Good we did not sew him in," he said. "Well, there he is. Not a pretty sight."

Berend sat back on his heels, slowly shaking his head as if not believing what he saw. "Hubert Bale. I never would have credited it had I not seen it with my own eyes. The man was invincible."

"I do not care to think what that means about our adversary," said Roger. "Was he an assassin?" Berend gave a curt nod. "Then whoever murdered him was also well skilled in the art of death."

Holding his gloved hands over his nose and mouth, William crept close to the grave, peering down.

"So this man was not Jon Underhill, but Hubert Bale?" he asked Berend, who nodded. "An assassin? Not King Richard's man?"

"He would serve whoever could afford him—kings, dukes, wealthy merchants."

"Do you still have the letter he showed you, William?" Kate asked. "The one from the king?"

He backed away from the grave looking pale. "He kept it. I checked his clothing." He licked his lips. "Found nothing." He coughed into his hand. "He had a pack when Roger escorted him to the guesthouse. Not there when we collected his body. I do not feel—" He covered his mouth and rushed past her, making it just past the dogs. Poor man. His retching went on for a good long while.

So the pack had been Bale's, and he had carried a letter of introduction from both the duke and the king. She wondered for whom he was actually working? Either of them? Another? And who had moved the pack to the shed, then removed it?

13

VOWS AND SECRETS

———⌁⌁⌁———

It was dark by the time they returned to Castlegate. In the comforting warmth of her own kitchen, Kate relaxed as she watched Berend moving about, freshening Lille and Ghent's water bowl. He laughingly rewarded their shameless begging with a bit of meat despite all they had eaten at the guesthouse, sharing the generosity with Lady Margery's dogs. When they were settled, Berend sank his large, scarred hands into the bread dough that would rise during the night. She wondered at his ability to move after his exertion in the forest. No, she did understand. His heart was heavy tonight. She had felt it as they walked home across the city, his distraction, his weighted silence. If a gentle rain had not begun as they walked home, she would be out in the garden quieting herself with her bow.

"You grieve for Hubert Bale?" she asked.

She thought he had not heard her question, lost in his own mind. Belatedly, she was glad he had not heard. It would only remind him if he had succeeded in pushing his thoughts away.

But after kneading the dough for several moments he paused, nodding. "I do. I doubt that he had a chance to make his peace with God at the moment of death. I am sorry for that. We all deserve that. I will find a way to give him a proper Christian burial."

"Ask Jocasta Sharp to help."

"Thank you, but I have my own resources, Dame Katherine." He pressed the dough, lifted it, slapped it down, kneaded it. "I was blessed with a second chance. To reform, to find peace and wholeness in nurturing and protecting this household. I have discovered the comfort of daily tasks—day after day, cooking, baking, repairing things round the property, shopping." He paused again, with the ghost of a grin. "Assassin to housekeeper. I suppose Bale must have thought me mad. One head wound too many. But my heart is at ease. I never would have believed it possible." He kneaded awhile longer.

She wondered at his ability to smile at himself, he, who had come face-to-face with his own mortality in seeing someone he knew lying in an unblessed grave. But he was not entirely free of his own past, or at least he blamed his occasional disappearances on a need to go off and clear his mind. He would return a few days later exhausted, but calm.

She found herself unable to find the humor in her own situation, and she knew that for a bad sign. Even amid the violence her family had always found things to laugh about. But all she could think tonight was how her dream of achieving the financial ease that would afford the liberty of choosing when and with whom she would wed was ever farther beyond her reach. If Hubert Bale had come to York on a mission for King Richard, he would be missed, and others would come asking questions, turning over every report of his movements until they arrived on her doorstep, her secret scheme exposed, her reputation ruined. And that was just one of her worries. Alice's and Connor's deaths were linked to Bale's murder. What of Phillip? Would the murderer fear what Connor had told him? Or whether Phillip had seen him with Connor the morning of his murder in the chapter house? Might he decide to eliminate any possibility of Phillip identifying him? This she feared even more since seeing Phillip at the deanery in the late afternoon.

Lille and Ghent came over to settle, one on either side of her, warming her flanks. She stroked their wiry fur, grateful for being pulled out of her worries.

"They sensed you fretting," said Berend, covering the dough with a large wooden bowl.

He cut thick slices of bread, slathered them with butter, and handed one down to her as he came to settle beside her, careful not to disturb Lille.

"Three slices, Berend?"

"The dig, the walk, Griselde's less than inspiring stew . . ."

He made her smile. "She does not have your magic in the kitchen." But it had been a comfort to be in Lady Margery's bright company. William, too, seemed glad of it. Lady Margery had met him at the door on their return and said, "I do not suppose this is the time to discuss my husband's peace effort?" William, dusty, drooping with exhaustion, had surprised them all by saying, "No better time. I welcome the distraction. In truth, I used you as my excuse for coming to the guesthouse."

Margery had laughed. "We must come up with a clever explanation for the dirt on your shoes, leggings, and cloak. Perhaps I attacked you in the garden?"

Kate had been pleased to see the two of them laughing together. Something good might come of all the sorrow.

"Seeing Hubert Bale in that grave . . ." Berend shook his head. "He and I, all the assassins, we were ever aware that we balanced on the edge of death, but we imagined glorious ends, cut down in the midst of combat with a worthy adversary. As the Norsemen believed that they would enter Valhalla if they died with sword in hand. But Bale's was a pathetic death. Strangled with the silken rope from bed hangings." Berend sighed.

Kate put a hand on his strong forearm. "Courage seemed its own protection. I thought my brothers invincible. I doubt it will be of any comfort to you, but my fear is that he *did* die at the hands of a worthy adversary. And that bodes all the worse for us." She leaned over to pour more ale. "This is maddening. The murderer has us dancing to his tune. He acts, we react. What if that is his intention? To keep us too busy to see what is right in front of us?"

Berend popped the last bit of bread into his mouth and reached for the bowl of ale at his feet, laughing as Lille, the shameless flirt, sniffed at his hands then rolled over for a stomach rub. It was awhile before he settled back, bowl in hand.

"So what have I not seen?" Kate asked. "Is it possible the murderer has been in my undercroft on High Petergate all along, observing how we dealt with Bale's body, watching the rhythms of the household? And if so, is this all about the guesthouse? Or Lady Kirkby?"

Berend sipped his ale, staring into the fire. His brows knit together as they did when he was puzzling something out.

"What are you thinking?" she asked when the silence stretched on.

"What if we are looking at the wrong pattern?"

"Is there a pattern other than connections to William, Lady Kirkby, someone watching them?"

"That is the question. We have assumed William Frost to be at the center of it all. Or possibly Lady Kirkby and her mission."

"Someone had been following William," said Kate. "The first murder was in the guesthouse, and Bale wanted access to Griselde and Clement."

"How did he intend to win their cooperation? According to Phillip, it sounds as if he did add something to the wine so that they heard nothing. But how was that to win them over? Would you tell me again all that Phillip told you?"

⁂

While they had been at the guesthouse, Kate's uncle had sent a servant with the request that she come to the deanery—Phillip said it was urgent that he talk to her. Her ward was not one to call anything urgent. Lady Margery assured her that all was in hand. Two of her servants were caring for Odo; Griselde had seen that he had a hot meal and would continue to do so.

The hall of the deanery was large and airy. In one corner several armoires and a large table with benches marked the area where clerks were usually hard at work, though not today, on the Sabbath. In the middle of the room, near the central hearth, an elegant settle and several high-backed chairs were clustered for conversation and piled with colorful embroidered cushions. Tapestries in rich jewel colors adorned the walls. It was a comfortable hall, inviting.

Dean Richard rose from one of the cushioned chairs to welcome her, garbed in a simple houppelande. His indoor shoes were an elegant brocade, with long, pointed toes. He enjoyed his pleasures. He plied her with questions about her meeting with William as soon as she took her seat. She had told him much of it when she escorted Marie to the deanery the previous evening, and he said he had been trying to make sense of it ever since.

"So am I, uncle. But this afternoon I came at Phillip's request, did I not?"

"Of course." He sent a servant to inform the boy that she had arrived. "After mass this morning he asked for advice about vows, promises, especially those made to the dead. He has been pacing ever since—in the hall, then in the kitchen where his sister complained that if she must tolerate his pacing she deserved to know what it was about. He escaped to his bedchamber."

"Have you any idea what it is about?"

"None. I see you went out to the grave?" He gestured toward her mud-caked hem. "Did you recognize the first victim?"

"Berend did. It is Hubert Bale, although he had introduced himself to William as Jon Underhill."

"So his attacker is still an unknown. I am sorry." He reached down to pet Lille and Ghent, who were already happily asleep at Kate's feet. "What was Bale's mission?" Richard asked when he straightened.

She told him what William had told her.

"Access to Lady Margery? And William agreed to it? Why would he do that? Why did he not simply go to the sheriffs with the report of someone following him? No, of course, I know, the tension between the king's supporters and the Lancastrians. No one knows whom to trust. And his wife, being a Gisburne, well, they might fear the sheriffs would be more sympathetic to their enemies than to them."

"To be fair, William's guest was the victim, not the attacker."

"Who knows what led to the strangling?"

Kate leaned back against the chair, her head beginning to pound.

"Forgive me," said her uncle. "You have had a trying day. Week. You will be glad to hear that I have the archbishop's permission to say a mass for Connor in the early morning, in the Magdalene chapel, for his fellows. Grantham will be present, and his wife. We will quietly bury him in one of the churchyards in the city, preferably one in the minster liberty. I am not yet certain."

She took a deep breath, willing herself calm. "This is good of you, uncle. How did you convince the archbishop to permit the mass?" Suicide was a mortal sin, depriving the dead of the benefit of burial in blessed ground. "You told him it was murder?"

"I had no choice. But I emphasized the importance of secrecy, and reminded him that we do not wish the sheriffs involved in searching for the murderer. In order to avoid that, we allow the city to believe that Connor murdered Alice in a fit of jealousy, then took his own life. Unfortunately, the secrecy prevents what I thought most fitting, that he should be buried with Alice Hatten. Dame Jocasta warned me that Alice's sister is quite the gossip."

"I am touched that you thought of that."

"I have a heart. So, apparently, has Scrope."

"I never doubted your heart, uncle. And it is not only William and the archbishop who wish to avoid involving the sheriffs."

"No."

"So Scrope knows. How much does he know?"

The servant returned with the message that Phillip would prefer to talk to Kate in the privacy of his bedchamber.

Kate said she would go to him in a moment.

The servant withdrew.

"I regret that I found it necessary to tell His Grace about everything, including the murder in the guesthouse. But not your delicate business there. Although I suspect that his lack of further questions suggests he knows of it."

"How?"

"I have no idea."

So the archbishop did have spies in the city. Of course he did. Kate leaned across to her uncle, kissing his cheek. "I am grateful that there will be a mass for Connor in the morning. I will attend."

She found her way down the passage to the outer steps that took her up to Phillip's room. He opened his door to her knock, thanking her as he stepped aside and welcomed her into the room. The guest room was warm and furnished almost as comfortably as her uncle's room, where she had spoken to Phillip yesterday—had it been only the day before? Helen had clearly fussed with it, using tapestries, cushions, several lamps, and a colorful bedcovering to brighten the room.

Phillip looked no better. His beautiful eyes were sunken in shadows. How sad he looked, how tired. He led her to a bench beneath the window. Reaching behind it, he drew up a pack.

Kate gasped. "Phillip, this is Hubert Bale's traveling pack."

"You have seen this before?"

"Yes. In one of the garden sheds at the guesthouse. And then it disappeared. Where did you get it?"

"Connor gave it to me. For safekeeping. He said he did not trust that he would not sell the contents for drink."

"Where has it been?"

"In my own pack. I promised him I would give it to no one. I promised. But now that he's gone . . . Dean Richard helped me see that my responsibility is to the living."

Bless Uncle Richard. "I am grateful to you, Phillip. How did it come into his possession?"

"One night Connor told me a tale—he had been drinking, so I wondered how much of this was true, but—he said he had gone to your guesthouse to meet Master Frost and Alice Hatten, his wife-to-be. She had coaxed him to go, telling him that Master Frost promised to help him find a place in the stoneyard at Beverley Minster. So the meeting that evening was so Master Frost might advise him how to please the dean and chapter as well as the master mason there. Connor was late—he had stopped for a tankard of ale, for courage, he said—and when he arrived, well, it was all wrong. He found two strangers, large men, both of them, struggling. And suddenly one had a rope round the neck of the other, strangling him."

"Did Connor recognize either of them?"

Phillip shook his head.

"Was Alice there?"

"Yes. She was slumped over near the door, drunk or poisoned, he could not tell. All Connor cared about was getting her away safely."

"The two men did not notice him?"

Phillip shrugged.

"How did he get her out of there?"

Shifting so that he was sitting cross-legged on the bench, Phillip began to use gestures as he spoke, something he had not done since finding Connor's body.

"He said he hoisted her over his shoulder, picked up a pack by the door—he never said why he picked up the pack—and he carried her down to one of the garden sheds, where he tried to wake her. He was frightened—she was so limp he feared she would stop breathing. He managed to wake her a little, but not enough for her to walk, even with his help. He kept expecting someone to come looking for them, so he could not linger. He searched the pack and found some money and a letter in a little purse. He put that in his own scrip, then picked her up and carried her to his lodging."

"So he did not take the pack?"

"He went back for it sometime. The next day?" He frowned at her. "I forget. I only half-believed him. But you do. Is this important? Did the man die? Or was he the one who killed Connor?"

"The man who owned this pack is dead. Whether his murderer then went on to silence Alice and Connor? I think it very likely. You must swear to tell no one. Not Marie, not anyone."

"I swear." He drew out a purse. "This is the purse he took. The money is gone, but the letter is here. When I finally looked at the letter I thought I had best tell you. The letter is signed by King Richard himself. It says that Jon Underhill is his man. But you said it was someone else's pack."

"Jon Underhill is the name he used with my cousin William. But Berend knew him as Hubert Bale. The man who was strangled. There was another letter in the pack with that name on it."

"So that is why Alice and Connor had to die? Because of those men?"

"I cannot think of another reason. My cousin has explained why Hubert Bale was there, and perhaps why Alice was in such a state. But who the attacker was, and what he wants, that we still do not know. Did Connor describe him?"

Phillip shook his head.

"Think. Perhaps he said something."

"Just that they were both big men, that they looked too strong for him to take down without a weapon." A sigh. "I hope something in the pack will help you find the murderer. He must pay for what he's done." Phillip turned round to push open the shutter, his breath coming in little gasps, as if he were fighting tears. The window looked out onto the stoneyard. "I would give anything to bring Connor back."

A visceral memory, kneeling on a bench to look out the high window in her bedchamber, seeing herself running out the gate hand in hand with Geoff, asking God to bring him back, bargaining—*Anything, Lord, I will do anything to bring him back.* She felt Geoff's warmth in her mind.

Perhaps that is why I am here.

I meant as you had been.

God has his own ways.

"Or at least clear Connor's name," Phillip said. "It is not fair that he is blamed for Alice's death." His arm still outstretched, the boy ducked his head, wiping his eyes on his sleeve.

"No, Phillip, it is not fair."

She dropped her head, her heart full.

Berend softly thanked her for recounting the conversation. "He is a good lad. His heart is broken."

As is mine. Kate forced herself to keep her attention with Berend. "If only Connor had described the man. Still so many questions, so few answers."

Berend rose with a grunt, raised his arms to the ceiling beam, stretching. "But we know more than we did. We know how Alice escaped."

Yes, that mystery was solved. "The greater mystery is how William could be so cold, abandoning Alice, the mother of his son, to her fate."

"Fear for his daughter, Hazel?"

"And his honor. His precious honor."

Kate started to rise just as Berend settled back down with more ale, reminding her that she had promised to tell him "about the one who died like Alice," the memory, or rather the ghost who led to her ill-timed attack on William.

"That is the last thing I wish to dredge up before sleep."

"I confided in you."

Seeing the challenge in Berend's eyes, Kate relented. If she meant him to be her comrade in arms, they must know each other so well they could predict the other's reaction. She fetched more ale, settled back beside him, forced herself to speak of what she had hidden for so long.

"Maud Allen. She was my good friend, and my brother Roland's true love. Her family's land bordered on ours, and we were together in the fields and the woods when the weather was fair and our fathers considered it safe. Raids happened mostly at night, but sometimes . . ." She shook her head. Stay with the story.

"Our particular enemies were the family of Andrew Caverton just across the border. Our families had been feuding for generations. They poached our cattle, our sheep, put fire to our barns when we had them filled with hay. And we did likewise. It took but an instant to light a fuse that would burn for months. That spring, when the roads were muddy, a cart had upended on the way to market and the goods toppled out onto what they said was their property. It was the road, how it went along the border there, that was often the excuse for the troubles. Roland and the eldest Caverton brother, who was called young Andrew, came to blows. Roland sliced open Andrew's face from his right temple to the right side of his mouth and cut off his ear. From that moment, young Andrew wanted revenge. He was vain, always strutting in front of the women. After Roland disfigured his face, he burned with a hate so fierce."

"That is a lot for a young man to suffer."

Tell him about Walter's hand.

"I do not claim we were better than the Cavertons. But my eldest brother had lost a hand to the brutes a year earlier."

"I did not mean to judge. Forgive me for interrupting. Maud Allen?"

"Maud was a beauty, a year older than me, and the previous winter she had flowered. That spring she was clearly a woman. Roland and she—both families guessed they had better not delay their marriage. The wedding was planned for after the harvest. The countryside was abuzz with it, so the Caverton boys knew that she was the pearl of great price, the theft that would tear out my brother's heart.

"They raped her and threatened her with a bloody death if she told, knowing she would. Knowing Roland would see her black eyes and swollen lips, her torn nails, and keep at her until he knew. Or guessed. She told me, she whispered it between sobs. One held her down while the other . . . They took turns, three brothers. And they had friends come watch. And jeer. And . . ." Kate shook her head to scuttle the memories.

How sick you were, Geoff whispered. *I held you as you heaved in the barn. Then you cried and cried, beating the wall of the stall until your hands were bloodied.*

Berend crossed himself. "I am sorry it pains you so to speak of it. But I need to hear it all."

Will it help to speak of it? To admit my guilt aloud?

It was not your fault, Geoff whispered. *Maud told Roland as well.*

But not in such detail, Geoff.

"Your twin is here," Berend said.

"How do you know?"

"I sense it. I feel you as two, not one. I do not mean to be cruel."

"You are never cruel to me, Berend. It is hard to speak of it. I was a child, and so frightened. I feared that the same would happen to me. My brothers feared it as well." Kate reminded herself that these were memories, in the past. "Maud did not realize that Geoff would learn all of it from me. There was no hiding anything from him. I doubt she would have shared so much detail with me had she known."

"But you were her friend. Perhaps the only one to whom she could talk so freely."

"I know my own part in it, Berend."

He apologized for interrupting.

"My brothers went mad with grief for Maud, and their hatred of the Cavertons deepened. They planned a raid. They would go as soon as Father returned. He had been called away on some business with the warden of the march.

"One afternoon Geoff and I were out with Lille and Ghent. They were just puppies. We were walking our land with them, familiarizing them with it. As we climbed down a rocky hillside the pups became agitated, hanging back and whining. Fearful. They picked up the scent of blood. Geoff told me to stay there with the pups while he climbed down. He . . . I could tell when he heard the flies, and smelled blood himself. Just the way he straightened, like a rod had been shoved down his back. Fighting stance. I knew. I just knew it was Maud. I called out to him to come back, we should go for her father. But he moved on.

"I could not stay behind. He needed me there with him. They were all a little in love with Maud. She was gentle, so kind to everyone. There was space in her heart for all." Kate closed her eyes. Took a few deep, deep breaths. The scene was there, spread out before her. The warmth of the sun, the breeze coming down off the high hills chilling her legs as she gathered up her skirts and scrambled down the rocks, the tug of the puppies on their leashes. They were so reluctant, hanging back, whimpering. But how could she know they would be safe up above? The bloody Cavertons might be anywhere. They were known for their stealth—one moment you were alone, the next you were surrounded.

"Dame Katherine?"

The hillside dissolved, the kitchen returned.

"The blood had soaked through Maud's clothing and into the ground. She was already cold. But maybe that was the loss of so much blood. Her jaw was wide open, the blood . . ." She needed to pause a moment, breathe. "But it was her eyes that frightened me most, the terror in them. They followed me everywhere for days and days."

"Roland and your twin died avenging her murder?"

Not Geoff, but that was not for tonight. "Her honor, her beauty, her innocence. The brutality. They feared for me."

"That is why your mother brought you to York?"

"So she said."

"What of the Cavertons?"

"Two of the brothers are dead, Bryce and James, and their father, Andrew. But young Andrew—I always thought him the worst of the lot, the eldest brother, the heir to his father's evil—one-eared, scarred Andrew disappeared."

"Your brothers killed the others?"

She ignored the question. "The Cliffords, the Allens, and many neighbors spent weeks searching for him. But they just drove him farther north, too far across the border for a quick retreat."

"How has your oldest brother survived up there?"

"Survived? Walter is a walking corpse, Berend. A man possessed. All fear him. He leaves a deathly chill in his wake as he moves across the land. That is what a friend told me a few years ago. His tenants fear him, but stay on in memory of Father, Roland, Geoffrey." Kate bent to Lille and Ghent, rubbing their ears for comfort. "Alice's suffering must have been terrible. And her fear that last day. But Maud's suffering—she lived with the horror for a week before she spoke to me, and then, every snap of a twig, every creak in the house must have terrified her. And to carry her to our property . . . I had never seen her in that place. She was no climber. So she knew she was being taken to her death." Kate bowed her head.

Yes, that is enough, Geoff assured her.

Berend quietly thanked her.

"I know that I said far more than I needed to William. But now you see why."

"I do." Berend rose, offered his hand to help her up. "It grows late. We have a mass to attend in the morning. And then you dine with Master Lionel."

Lionel had left a message with Matt inviting Kate to dine with him at an inn on Micklegate the following day. He'd told Matt nothing of his purpose.

"No doubt Fitch's misadventure inspired it," said Kate. "I shall enjoy watching Lionel make his excuses."

Berend snorted. "I should like to hear it. I do not suppose I might serve the two of you?"

"I need you at the house on Petergate, the house Odo has neglected. I have neglected. You must arrange for the workmen, show them what to do." She shook out her skirts. "And you and Clement need to do an inventory of the stores in the undercroft. Find out how long it has been since Lionel was there." She thought of the filth in which the tenant had been living. "Poor Odo."

"He was not your responsibility, Dame Katherine. He was a tenant, nothing more."

"Then I should have paid more attention to the state of my property."

Berend did not disagree.

Wrapping her cloak round her, Kate called the dogs to her and wished Berend a good night. Out in the quiet garden, she paused to gaze up at the stars. Maud, Roland, her father, Geoff—

No. I am right here.

"Yes, you are," she said aloud. "Though I know not how. But so many are not. And now Hubert Bale, Alice, Connor have joined them." She crossed herself and continued on to the hall door, where Lille and Ghent waited.

Matt snored by the hearth fire, but reared up as she entered. He clutched a knife. "Who goes there?"

"It is Dame Katherine and the dogs, Matt. Be at ease." She waved him quiet as he began to apologize. "I am glad to see you so ready to defend the household."

The dogs settled down near Matt. Kate lit an oil lamp and wished them all a good night, then climbed up to the solar, Matt's snores fading, Jennet's growing louder. She prayed they might all make it safely through the night.

14

A REQUIEM

———⁘———

A thick mist enveloped Kate and her companions as they stepped out onto Castlegate before dawn. Her pattens clicked on the wet cobbles, and she held her skirts away from the piles of slushy snow that had been pushed about by passing carts. It was a mild morning, such a contrast to a few days earlier when she had hurried beside her uncle's secretary. The cobbles had been icy and treacherous then, and the cold had numbed her face. Now it was the stench that assailed her, weeks of dung, piss, and refuse uncovered by the thaw. Jennet and Berend carried lanterns, but their lights did little to distinguish between puddles and rain-slicked cobbles.

As they passed a garden she heard an owl cry, then the shriek of a small animal. Past Ousegate, two cats bolted across their path. Jennet crossed herself. Berend teased her. A drunk argued with a watchman in St. Helen's Square, two apprentices knocked on a goldsmith's shop, the opening door throwing light and warmth out onto Stonegate for a moment.

The dean's cook and housekeeper welcomed them at the deanery door with small bowls of ale, inviting them to get warm by the roaring fire in the hearth. A servant would come to escort them across to the minster when the dean and his servers were ready for them.

Slowly they were joined by Connor's fellows from the stoneyard. They wore their work clothes, for it was the start of their week, but all had made an effort to brush the stone dust from their clothes and drag wet combs through their hair for the solemn occasion. One young man carried sprigs of holly heavy with bright red berries.

He shrugged shyly as Helen admired them. "No flowers yet, so I thought these might brighten the chapel."

"You are a dear." Helen patted his cheek. "Oh, there are the young ones." She lowered her voice and leaned toward Kate. "They have fallen out with each other and are quite snappish this morning. Just a warning."

Kate's wards stood in the passage that led from the kitchen, searching the crowd with their eyes. Marie was the first to see Kate, hurrying over without a word to her brother.

"I do not want to stay here," she announced. Chin high, she glared at Phillip as he joined them.

Phillip gave Kate a little bow and interrupted her response to Marie to thank her for rising so early.

Kate nodded to him and was telling Marie they would discuss her wishes later when a small company burst into the hall—Lady Margery and Dame Jocasta, with several servants following. The stonemasons parted to allow the women passage.

"Our parties converged in the yard," Lady Margery exclaimed. She wore a deep red cloak lined in pale fur. "I sent word to Dame Jocasta last night that this morning's mass is for both Alice and Connor."

"I am moved by Dean Richard's gesture," said Dame Jocasta. "It felt right to attend this mass before taking Alice on her final journey. You must pardon my traveling robes. My serving men have taken Alice's coffin to the friary. We will leave for her sister's house as soon as the service is over."

Kate said a silent prayer of thanks for the diversion. She needed Marie safely tucked away here in the deanery, out of trouble. "You are making the journey with the coffin?"

"I cannot do otherwise," said Jocasta. "My heart needs to see my dear Alice well buried. I hoped to bury her here in York, but her sister chose otherwise." A little shrug. "It is her right. I do not know how long I will be away. But if I hear anything of help regarding your missing servant, I will try to send word to you."

Sam. God help her, Kate had forgotten all about him. She thanked Jocasta for thinking of him.

Lady Margery asked Phillip and Marie if they were enjoying the deanery. "Such a warm, inviting house, I suppose I do not need to ask. Of course you are."

Marie shrugged.

Phillip excused himself to go greet the Granthams. "They paid for a fine coffin for Connor. And the candles," he said. As Phillip passed a small group of stonecutters, Kate heard him ask one of them, "Were you in the stoneyard early this morning?" The man shook his head and asked why. "I thought I saw you. No matter." He nodded and moved on.

Kate glanced down at Marie, who was frowning in her brother's direction. "He saw someone in the stoneyard earlier?"

"He tells me nothing." She kept her eyes on her brother who was now smiling at the Granthams. "There was a time he did. But no more. I hate him."

"I hated it when my brothers kept secrets from me."

"How many brothers do you have?"

"I had three."

"Where are they?"

Kate was saved from answering by Lady Margery, who asked if they might talk, then smiled down at Marie. "Might I borrow Dame Katherine for a moment?"

The girl ignored her. "Is the mass in the chapel of St. Mary Magdalene because Connor's precious love was a whore like my mother?" she demanded of Kate.

Saturday's sweetness had quickly gone sour. "No. We wanted to keep it quiet. Private. So we chose a chapel in the crypt," Kate told her.

Lady Margery crouched down to Marie. "The Magdalene's story is one of forgiveness and redemption, child. Connor would be honored that he and Alice are sharing a service in a chapel dedicated to her."

The child cocked an eyebrow. "Do you think the dead care about such things?"

"Go to your brother," said Kate. "I will come join you when it is time."

The girl sighed and turned away. Lady Margery led Kate into the corner by the armoires, where Berend and Jennet awaited them.

"Is she always so perverse?" Lady Margery asked.

"When she is disappointed, yes," said Kate. "What is it? Has something happened?"

"Yes. And I thought you should all hear this," Margery began. "It happened last night. Your man Seth, who is caring for your elderly tenant across the alleyway, heard someone at the rear door of the hall. We were already uneasy—Troilus and Criseyde had been running in circles by the door, barking. So when Seth came for one of my guards, we were awake and ready to assist. Together they went out to search the gardens. The door to one of the sheds in the guesthouse garden was open, and blocking the doorway was a wheelbarrow with a pile of rags crusty with dried blood. A great deal of blood."

Kate crossed herself. "Alice's blood?"

"I wondered the same. And according to Odo, while Seth was out in the garden, the intruder who hums out of tune was down in the undercroft, setting a fire."

"God help us. Did you catch him? Was there damage?" Kate asked.

"No and very little. Fortunately we had aired the hall so well in the afternoon that they smelled the smoke at once. Someone had lit the pallet. They were able to drag it out and beat out the few spots that had caught."

"A gesture not intended to actually burn down the house," Berend suggested.

"What can this person want?" asked Margery.

"He is showing us how easily he moves among us. Like we did as children," said Kate.

"Perhaps you did," said Lady Margery. "We were never so clever."

"No further disturbance?" Kate asked.

"No, God be thanked. It was quite enough for one evening. I woke at every creak of the house throughout the night. Such a pity. I had felt good after my conversation with William Frost. He promised to speak up in my favor to his colleagues."

"I suppose he sees it as an attempt at atonement," said Kate. It would have been far better had he helped Alice. She asked Margery whether she was still comfortable in the guesthouse. "I would not blame you for seeking other lodgings."

"My mission is far too important to us all to waver in the face of such cowardly attempts to frighten me off."

In truth, it felt to Kate as if *she* were the object of attack, not Margery. But that was an argument for another time. "I meant no insult. You are my guest, and I feel responsible for your welfare."

Margery pressed Kate's hand. "Bless you."

One of the dean's clerks rang a bell for attention, announcing that he would now lead the procession to the chapel, begging them to proceed in an orderly fashion.

Kate excused herself and slipped through the gathered mourners to join Phillip and Marie, and together they walked out into the minster yard behind the Granthams as the first hints of dawn silvered the sky. At the southeast door, Dean Richard's secretary waited with a tray of tapers, handing one to each mourner. Each taper was then lit by a servant standing beside him.

"I do not like this place," Marie muttered as they moved forward into the aisle. "There are too many shadows."

Usually Kate would agree, but this morning she caught her breath at the beauty of the line of light moving through the darkness as the mourners' footsteps echoed in the soaring space. At the door to the crypt, a clerk advised them to move down the steps one at a time. "With care," he whispered. "They are narrow and uneven."

The stairwell had been brightened with white paint and crossed with red lines to give the look of ashlar, but no natural light illuminated the descent, and the stones seemed alive as the candles flickered in a strong draft. The line of mourners moved down, down, until they bent beneath a stone lintel and entered the chapel of St. Mary Magdalene. The low-roofed space, far more welcoming than that above, was fragrant with the warm scent of beeswax. A clerk showed them where to place their tapers, so that the chapel became a constellation of light.

Hugh and Martha Grantham, Phillip, Marie, Kate, and Dame Jocasta were directed to stand behind Connor's coffin before the altar. The Granthams were subdued, showing signs of sleeplessness and tears. The masons gathered behind them, standing with heads bowed, their rough hands pressed together in prayer.

A murmur went through the crowd, and all turned their heads to observe Archbishop Scrope step into the chapel. Dressed in modest clerical robes, he bowed toward the altar, then took a place at the back beside Margery Kirkby. She smiled, pressing His Grace's forearm in greeting, right hand to her heart.

So they were friends. That surprised Kate, considering Scrope's mentor, Thomas Arundel, and his rumored alliance with Duke Henry on the continent. Would Scrope support King Richard if he reconciled with Duke Henry?

Kate was pondering that when Phillip tapped her arm, asking her quietly if that was truly the archbishop come to pray for Connor's soul. Her nod lit the boy's face. "Such prayers will surely speed Connor's welcome in heaven," he said.

She was struck by her ward's earnest devotion, and wondered whether what irked Marie was a touch of jealousy—if she saw Connor as a rival, even in death. Kate must think how to convince the child to stay at the deanery.

As her uncle began the mass, Kate bowed her head and prayed that God, the Blessed Virgin Mary, and all the saints and angels welcomed Alice and Connor. *I pray you, gather them to your hearts and hold them close, comforting them. And gently, gently ease the heart of my ward, Phillip. Help him to forget the horror of what he saw.*

And help me understand young Marie so that I might protect her.

As an afterthought she added, *Help me see my way to loving both my wards as they deserve.*

Toward the end of the requiem the sounds of the Lady Mass being sung in the choir drifted down to them, and as she turned to leave Kate noticed smiles on many of the tearstained faces. She glanced back to see whether she could observe her uncle's reaction. He looked pleased. Yes, he had planned this uplifting final movement. Bless him.

—❦—

At the deanery after the service, Kate introduced Phillip to the archbishop as Connor's apprentice. The boy beamed as Richard Scrope described how he had happened on Connor in the masons' lodge.

He had watched Connor forming the curl of a leaf. "Bent over his work, unaware of his audience, he hummed a little under his breath. I admired his focused attention and the easy joy with which he worked such magic in stone."

The archbishop shifted his gaze to Kate as he assured Phillip that Connor's murderer would be found. He would pay for his terrible crime, and for desecrating the cathedral with bloodshed. In that steady gaze, Kate read a challenge, not a reassurance. Her uncle had sensed that Scrope knew of Kate's secret enterprise. Did he judge her? Unfortunately, he slipped away before she had a chance to speak with him further, to explore whether she had simply imagined the message.

15

THE LION

‒‒‒‒‒‒◦୧⊙୨◦‒‒‒‒‒‒

The sun had been low in the sky as the mourners departed the minster, but now, as Kate stepped from the deanery, it warmed her uplifted face and brightened her heart. She was grateful to have been called out so early, for the breeze carried a chill and the scent of rain; she might easily have missed this glorious moment. Breathing in, she filled her lungs with the freshness of the morning, and, for a little while, let her mind go blank, forgetting her cares.

Cares. Such an innocent word, suggesting domestic trifles or misunderstandings among friends. Not three unsolved murders, a missing servant, and a killer so confident as to stay in the city and taunt her by trying to burn down one of her properties. Lady Margery might see it as her battle to fight, but Kate was not so certain as to risk the safety of her wards.

Which is why she had turned a deaf eye and ear to Marie when she appeared in the hall of the deanery with her pack, demanding to return to the house on Castlegate. Kate had relieved Marie of her burden, taken her firmly by the hand, and led her back to the kitchen, placing her in Helen's competent care.

"I will watch her like a hawk, Dame Katherine," the cook promised.

Kate had slipped away before Phillip could take up Marie's cause. No doubt he would feel the wrath of his sister—she would blame him for inviting her there in the first place. And, knowing Marie, she would extend that to his affection for Connor. Had he not befriended the dead man, they would both be back on Castlegate. Not that the girl seemed happy there. It was a matter of control. Kate understood, but she would not bend to the child's latest whim.

A scent of roses announced Lady Margery just before she slipped her arm through Kate's. "I thought my daughters had vile tempers at certain ages, but your ward Marie—there is a special place in heaven for you, taking in that child and giving her such good care. At least you cannot blame your blood. She is all Neville. Her poor mother. No wonder she died young. Now, where are you headed?"

"To see whether the workmen have arrived to repair the once-lovely residence I own next to the guesthouse."

"Then let us be off." Margery signaled to her servants to follow.

Jennet broke away from her examination of the deanery yard, quietly reporting to Kate that she had found no broken locks or loosened shutters that might invite a trespasser. Berend had gone on ahead to organize the workmen and see whether Clement felt capable of some work in the undercroft.

"Forgive me for bringing up my trivial concerns when you have so much on your shoulders." Lady Margery pressed Kate's arm. "But far from being frightened away by recent events, I would like to extend my stay for a few days beyond the fortnight we had arranged. Once your cousin William recommends me to his colleagues I hope to have quite a few visitors. I will pay, of course."

But not long-term, as did Kate's regular clients. In faith, if the troubles were aimed at frightening Lady Margery away, Kate looked forward to her departure. "Invite a half-dozen couples to each gathering," Kate said. "Better to entertain the merchants in the company of their peers—it will shame the reluctant into committing some funds for your husband's mission. The guesthouse hall is quite large, and you can borrow additional seating and tables from the deanery."

"Then your answer is no?" A pretty pout. "You have clients waiting?"

"Are you not expected elsewhere?"

Margery shrugged. "Lincoln is next. But the wealth is here, in York." No pout this time, instead a winsome sigh. "Ah me. Perhaps your dear uncle would accommodate me at the deanery. . . ."

Better him than me, Kate thought. "The guesthouse is not an extension of my home, but a trade concern, Lady Margery. Had I the room in my home to welcome your entourage, I would." Not quite true, but courteous, and apparently well received.

Smiling, Margery assured Kate that she understood, and, arm in arm, they turned onto High Petergate, greeting passersby as they progressed toward the guesthouse. One or two paused to ask them about the shouts and smoke the previous evening. Lady Margery was at her best, telling a tale of elderly, befuddled Odo and an attempt to light a lamp in the undercroft. No one questioned his being down there. All clearly found Lady Margery charming.

A neighbor glanced up as young Seth and Odo approached. "Poor old man. He is so fortunate to have such care in the two of you gentlewomen."

In fact, Odo looked scrubbed, tidy, and alert, doffing his hat to them before Kate had spoken a word.

"We are out for a brief walk to escape from the hammering," Seth explained. "The workmen arrived eager to begin, and Berend has them repairing the shutters and doors first."

"I would like a word with both of you," said Kate. "Come to the guest-house when you have had your walk. Goodwife Griselde will not begrudge us her kitchen for a little while."

Odo began to turn to follow the women, but young Seth stopped him. "The walk will do you good. Once down to the crossing and we will return," he said, encouraging Odo forward.

"You have remarkable servants," said Margery. "No doubt because they are yours to choose, unlike your late husband's." She gave a little laugh.

"Simon's servants? Oh, you mean Sam? He seemed better than the others at the time." Or perhaps she had simply worried that he was too old to find different employment.

"Was he Simon's man? That explains much. But I meant . . ." Margery sighed.

"His bastards? True. But there are times I am glad to have them with me."

"The boy, yes, he is a dear. But Marie?"

As they turned into the alleyway they found Berend stepping out from the undercroft, shaking his head at Clement, who breathed hard as he leaned against the wall next to the entrance.

The invalid gave Kate a wry smile. "I saw Odo shuffling down the alleyway and imagined myself nimble in comparison. The truth is not so sanguine."

"We have kept the door opened and guarded all night," said Lady Margery. "How is the air in there, Berend? Is it still too foul for Clement's weak chest?"

"It is far better than I had expected." But Berend asked Clement whether he was sure he felt strong enough to spend the day in there. Clement assured him that he was quite capable of breathing some smoky air.

"Speaking of that . . ." Berend asked if he might have a word with Kate.

While Lady Margery continued on into the guesthouse, her lapdogs barking wildly to see her, Kate stepped aside with Berend.

"The workmen discovered rags stuffed in all the smoke holes," he said. "No wonder Odo's fires created such smoke. Fortunately there are gaps all over the house and roof, and a serious leak over the solar. He would be dead if the house were in proper repair."

"So whoever lit the fire last night had prepared the house?"

"And Odo was to be the next to die."

Kate told Berend she would come speak with him more after she talked to Odo.

—◦⊚◦—

In between spoonfuls of Griselde's meaty stew, Odo excused himself for not telling Kate of the intruder from the start.

"I just thought it was Master Neville. He always makes a fuss when he comes to the undercroft, and he whistles a few notes over and over." Simon had complained endlessly about his brother's whistling. On Channel crossings he swore he was some day going to silence the man with his fist. "But the other one hums just off the note so it makes me grind my teeth," said Odo.

"The only difference is the humming off-key rather than the whistling?" Kate asked.

Odo frowned down at the food. "I could not swear to that. But if there is something else, I cannot recall it." And he was helpless regarding when anything had occurred or whether he remembered hearing someone up on the roof. He was quiet for a while, happily eating, then suddenly looked up. "Is Master Neville now in charge of this guesthouse?"

"No. Why do you ask?"

"I saw his servant Sam over here. As he is Master Neville's manservant . . ." He waggled his head, reaching for the small bowl of ale beside the trencher.

Kate put her hand on his, staying him for a moment. "Sam works for me, Odo."

"Good. That should make Sam's brother happy."

"Why should it matter to Sam's brother?"

"He and Sam had a falling out over Master Neville. I heard them in the alleyway, arguing. His brother said Sam had shifted his loyalties, working for 'the Lion,' the bastard they all hate on the staithes, the one who had almost lost him his work, accusing him of stealing a pouch his own servant had set aside. He never apologized."

Nor would he. No wonder Lionel had so few allies. "This argument, was that after you had seen Sam over at the guesthouse just the other day?"

"Maybe before that?" He shook his head. "My mind is a muddle."

Kate remembered how Lionel had asked after Sam the night of the murder in the guesthouse. She thanked Odo and handed him the bowl of ale.

Seth sat shaking his head, his bowl long empty. Kate had already asked him about the fire the previous night, but learned nothing new.

"What of you, Griselde?" Kate asked as she rose from the table. "Have you ever seen Sam and Lionel together, or Sam lurking about before?"

"I am certain I have seen him come and go, Mistress Clifford, like the day of—you know." She glanced over at Odo and young Seth, lowered her voice. "He came with Master Frost's boy Tib to deliver the barrel of wine. The gift for putting us out. Though I cannot say I ever noticed Master Lionel. I never thought to question Sam being about as you own both these houses." She leaned close to add, "The old man is fairly muddled in his mind. If you want the truth of it, you might wish to talk to Sam's brother Cam. He works on the King's Staithe. He looks much like Sam before his hair went white."

"Sam accompanied Tib with the wine?"

"It was Sam who carried the barrel to the kitchen. I thought it peculiar—it is Tib who has the muscle—but you had offered Sam's help earlier. As I recall Sam took his time about it. He helped himself to a bowl, you see. Left it sitting there with a drop in it, bold as could be. I never did understand why you kept him on after Master Simon passed."

"You never spoke up to warn me against him."

"Clement had betrayed you in so many ways, all that he kept from you. I could not warn you against doing for Sam what you were so kind to do for us. But he has always been a man looking to make some money on the side."

Kate thanked her, thanked Odo and young Seth, and returned to the hall. She found Jennet talking to one of Lady Margery's men. She must be back from examining Connor's lodgings. She rose to join Kate.

"Are we off to see Master Neville?"

"With a stop at the King's Staithe. But first I want a word with Clement. Did you learn anything?"

"Connor's landlord already has a new lodger in the room. I spoke to the landlord's wife, who had cleaned it, and she said Connor had left only some clothes, some tools." She held up a pack. "They are all here. She was going to sell them in a few days. I have not given it a good look."

"We will do that later. Has Lady Kirkby's man told you anything of use?"

"He noticed a lad poking about the outbuildings the other day, and thinks he has seen him before. Slight, about Marie's age. Wears an over-large hat and runs like a girl, he said."

They exchanged a look.

"Not you?" Kate smiled.

"No, but we know why she might be dressed so. A boy is a wee bit safer out on his own than a young girl."

"Tell him to tell the others to watch out for the child. Perhaps our intruder has a helper. Or the child might have noticed something. We need all the help we can get. And ask Odo if he recalls a youth hanging around. Then join me in the undercroft."

Lady Margery was hastening down the outer steps from the solar when Kate stepped out of the hall. "When you see Lionel Neville, tell him to call on me this evening."

Kate frowned up at her guest. "You have changed your mind?"

"I should like to know what his cousins are thinking about the king and the duke."

"You should not expect him to be honest with you."

Margery chuckled. "I am quite aware of that. But how he lies might reveal quite a lot."

"Why now?"

"Have you not wondered whether your late husband's family is behind all that has happened? Nothing deters a Neville from his ambition—or hers, I daresay. My husband warned me that their loyalty will shift from moment to moment. If I have the misfortune to be perceived as in their way, well, I may learn something from him."

Had Sam seen his service as to the Neville family, not simply to her late husband? Kate nodded. "I shall tell him."

"I know that your uncle Sir Thomas Clifford has served as Warden of the West March with Sir Ralph Neville, now Earl of Westmoreland, and I might think I insult you by questioning the honor of that family. But you seem to have no love for them."

"I feel much the same as you. And so does my uncle Sir Thomas."

"There was a time when Sir Ralph, the head of the family, mind you, supported King Richard. But as his second wife is a Lancaster . . ."

Kate shrugged. "At present I suspect the Nevilles cannot fathom that someone could be loyal to the king without being an enemy of the duke."

"Precisely," said Margery. "This man who was murdered here, with letters of introduction from both the king and the duke, reeks of Neville."

Dean Richard was certainly keeping Margery informed. All for the best, it seemed to Kate. Lady Margery's suggestion, that Simon's family was behind all the recent trouble, warranted consideration.

"Come first thing tomorrow," said Lady Margery. "I will tell you all I observed. And Katherine, have a care when you meet Lionel today. If he has been sent by his powerful cousins . . ."

"Jennet is accompanying me. We will both be armed."

Lady Margery raised her eyebrows. "I did not mean that, but—you are a woman of many talents." She kissed Kate's cheek. "I wish my sons were not so young. I should welcome such a daughter-in-law into my family."

"I pray you, do not sour our friendship by matchmaking." Kate pressed her hand and excused herself.

In the undercroft, Clement and Berend sat at a table piled high with ledgers, stacks of counters, and weights. A clerk stood at the ready to hand them the caskets, barrels, packs of spices.

Kate told the clerk to step out into the alleyway for a moment while she had a word with Clement. As the man hustled out, Berend rose, giving her his seat, and began to leave. "No, stay. You should hear this." She told Clement what Griselde had said about Sam—the barrel of wine, her impression of him.

"Tell me all that you know about Sam."

Jennet appeared in the doorway. Kate nodded to her, returned her attention to Clement.

His eyes were bright with interest. "Do you think he meddled with the wine? Is that why we slept so soundly?"

Clement's body might be broken, but his mind was still sharp. "He had the opportunity," said Kate. "And the bowl Griselde found, could it not be where he mixed something, poured it back in?"

Closing his eyes, Clement slowly shook his head, his jowls swinging. "You never know about folk, do you? Not really."

"Tell me about Sam."

He scratched his head, looked down at his shoes. "He was loyal to Master Simon. No question. Never spoke a word against him. He liked traveling with the master, always ready to jump to his orders. But he was a tattler when it came to his fellow servants and those of us above him in the household. We all knew to go quiet when he was slithering about. More than one of us paid him for silence."

"Paid him?"

"I am shamed to say so, but we did."

"What sort of secrets?" Jennet asked.

"I am not a tattler, Jennet. Never have been. I will tell Mistress Clifford what she needs to know, but that is as far as I go."

"Why did you not warn me about Sam when Simon died?" Kate asked.

"I expected you knew, that you would have heard the servants talking. Women have the ear for whispered conversations, it seems to me."

Apparently Kate did not. "Anything else I should know about him?"

"Of course he knew of Mistress Anne and the children in Calais. But I am not surprised he would not speak of that with you."

She left him with the request to tell Berend whatever else he might recall.

"Bring home anything you find in here today that does not seem to belong," she told Berend. "Anything."

Connor's pack they left with him as well. No need to scurry about with it.

—◦⊙◦—

By the time Kate and Jennet reached the King's Staithe, clouds hid the sun and a sharp breeze snapped the sails of a ship at anchor. Many of the dockworkers greeted her, some expressing their outrage that her ship had been boarded by the king's men in Hull—"That would never happen here," one bragged, "I wouldn't let them past me, Mistress Clifford"—and some asking after young Phillip, poor lad, finding Connor hanging in the minster. One asked whether it was true Connor had killed Alice Hatten. She spoke the truth by saying she did not know who had killed Alice, but a terrible thing it was. They were quick to point out Sam's brother Cam when she asked after him. She realized that she had met him once before, unloading one of her ships.

He seemed oddly happy to see her, quickly explained by his asking, "Has my brother returned, Mistress Clifford?"

177

Of course he would wonder. "I fear I have no news to give you, Cam. But I have just heard something that concerns me. Is it true that Sam works for Lionel Neville as well as for me?"

"Lionel Neville." Cam turned the name in his mouth as if it were spoiled fruit, then suggested they step aside so they might not be overheard. "I hope that my brother took my advice and stayed well away. He feels caught between the Nevilles and you. Master Lionel says my brother owes it to Master Simon's memory to help him, tell him things."

"What sort of things?"

"He would not say, but what else would it be but to round upon someone, give Neville something he can use against them? For the life of me I cannot think why he would choose Sam for that. What could Sam hear?"

There was plenty Sam might tell Lionel. Had he? "Sam felt he could not refuse?"

"He has no backbone, my brother. Do you think he got in trouble for something Master Lionel put him up to? Is that how he went missing?"

"As far as I know he went off to Beverley for me. He left before Alice Hatten was found. He was to see whether she had simply gone home without telling anyone."

Cam looked doubtful. "I would not trust that Master Lionel had naught to do with my brother's disappearance. He's always nosing round in folks' affairs. We all know to shut our mouths when word goes along the staithe that 'the Lion' is about. If he did that with someone powerful, and Sam was caught at it—" He cursed, then apologized.

So Sam and Lionel were two of a kind, though Kate could see Cam was blind to his brother's faults. She thanked him. "One thing more." She described Hubert Bale as best she could. "Did you ever see your brother with such a man?"

"I did." He looked pleased with himself.

"Can you remember when you saw him?"

"Not so long ago." He scratched his chin, then nodded. "Just before 'the Lion' came sailing in complaining of being boarded by the king's men downriver. I remember thinking you might do well to hire that bull to guard your ships. Will you?"

"Do you think it would discourage the king's men?"

Cam laughed. "No. Once they put on the livery you would think they were first knight, all of them."

She thanked him again and promised she would get word to him the moment they had any news of his brother.

Jennet had disappeared while Kate talked to Cam. Off hunting for information in her own manner, Kate guessed. She made her way back through the crowd of workers, pausing here and there to respond to their queries and concerns. She was proud of how they greeted her. When she had reached the bridge, she looked round, and not seeing her servant, she started across. Jennet joined her halfway, as Kate paused at a shop stall to admire a display of silk thread in jewel colors. The cushions in the deanery had inspired her to brighten her own home.

"Several men reported seeing Lionel and Sam together, and recently," Jennet quietly reported. "And perhaps Sam with Hubert Bale as well."

Together they continued on.

"Cam thought he had seen his brother with Bale, so I would guess that is true," said Kate. She told Jennet the rest. "To think that I laughed at Lionel's poor choice in servants when we caught Fitch. It seems I may have made an even poorer choice. Perhaps Fitch truly was hoping to see Sam, but not because they are friends."

"I could gut him," Jennet said.

"Sam or Lionel?"

"Both!"

"You warned me. You never trusted him."

"Nor Master Lionel, but you needed no warning about him."

They passed a crowd gathered round a juggling act and then glanced at some bows a man was hawking—good quality, most made from yew, but too ornate for Kate's taste. She liked her bows simple, supple, just the right length and heft.

The question that nagged Kate was whether Lady Margery was right, that Bale was the creature of Sir Ralph Neville. If so, had Lionel sent him to William? Had Sam been the go-between? If Jennet did not gut Lionel, Kate might do it herself.

16

THE KNIGHT

———⁓◦⊙◦⁓———

The tavern Lionel had chosen was in the undercroft of a business fronting a substantial house on Micklegate. Private, no public rooms, an arrangement preferred by merchants doing business requiring discretion. Though Kate avoided the practice, preferring her fellow guild merchants to trust her, Simon had frequented the place, and the taverner greeted her warmly. He seemed excited as he informed her that her party had preceded her, quickly showing her into his best room. Cushioned chairs were drawn up to a table large enough to seat several merchants and their factors. Wall sconces and a brazier lit the windowless space, the latter made necessary by the stone floor and walls that glistened here and there with river damp and held in the winter chill.

Handsomely dressed in a brown velvet houppelande and deep green leggings, a brown velvet hat with a swooping feather covering his thinning hair, Lionel had clearly dressed up to the standard of his surprise companion, Sir Elric, a retainer of the powerful Ralph Neville, Earl of Westmoreland. Not a good sign.

"Sir Elric." Kate bobbed her head, irked by a fleeting sense of relief that she, too, was dressed in finery, in honor of Alice and Connor, and that Jennet was as well, wearing the dress Kate had altered for her. Yes, he was a handsome man, but she needed a cool head. "My brother-in-law did not mention I would be dining with a knight in the service of the Earl of Westmoreland. It has been several years since we have met. You seem in good health."

He replied in kind, asking after the health of her wards, expressing concern about Phillip's recent discovery in the chapter house. She assured him they were both well, the morning requiem a great comfort to Phillip.

Elric was a retainer answering directly to Sir Ralph Neville, in residence at the earl's castle of Sheriff Hutton in the Forest of Galtres. She had met him on numerous occasions when she and Simon attended feast day celebrations at the castle. Always Elric had dressed in fine velvets and silks, though he was clearly valued for his martial skill, demonstrating his swordplay as part of the entertainment out on the jousting field. A curious companion for this dinner. She suspected it was he who had called them together, and she wondered why.

Once they were seated and served with wine and the fish course, Lionel expressed concern about the fire in the undercroft on High Petergate the previous evening. "I passed by this morning, heard workmen hammering, and the undercroft door swung wide, a man in the Kirkby livery standing guard out front. A passing neighbor said the fire had been down below. Of course I am concerned about the spices."

"You have no need to worry on that count," said Kate. "The smoke was noticed at once, the fire doused before it did much damage."

"Was it your tenant who caused the fire?"

"No. Someone had lit the pallet that recently appeared in the undercroft. Yours, Lionel?" She tasted the salmon. Quite good.

"Mine?" He looked honestly surprised. "No. When I noticed it on my last visit, a week ago, I think, I reckoned you had someone guarding the undercroft while I was away. An excellent idea. I had found the lock undone on several occasions."

"And never informed me," Kate noted, quietly, which took great effort. "It is clear we need to bury our differences and learn to work together,

Lionel. We stand in danger of losing everything. For now, I may move the stores elsewhere once Clement and Berend complete the inventory."

"Inventory? When?"

"Now. They began this morning."

She noticed sweat beading on his forehead. Good. And Sir Elric, who had seemed content to savor the fish, regarded Lionel with the hint of a smile before turning to Kate. "I am here seeking news of a comrade who came to York on a mission for the earl and seems to have vanished. A great bear of a man, Jon Underhill." He described Hubert Bale.

"You are the second person this day to describe him to me. I have just learned that a servant gone missing for several days was seen in this man's company before he disappeared."

"Might it have been your cousin, William Frost, who mentioned this?" asked Sir Elric.

"No, it was not. It was my servant's brother and his fellows on the King's Staithe. William knows this man?"

She expected the knight to flinch at having said too much, but he merely shrugged. "When I last saw Underhill, he told me that your cousin William had some trouble with a man too curious about his family, a man who had frightened his daughter. Jon had offered to help your cousin resolve the matter."

Two could play this game of cool indifference. "Poor William. Well then surely you must ask my cousin about this man's whereabouts." She imagined poor William choking on his memory of Bale's decomposing body.

"I have. He tells me that he refused Underhill's offer and sent him on his way."

"Ah. I am afraid I cannot help you there. But perhaps Lionel might. It has been brought to my attention that he and his servant Fitch have been often in the company of my missing servant, Sam. In fact some have come to believe Sam serves Lionel, not me, they are so often together. And Sam has been seen with this Underhill." She shrugged. "In fact, Fitch was following Sam in the early hours of the day my servant disappeared. When I noticed Fitch behind Sam in the alley, he took off running. He shed his cloak, one of Lionel's castoffs, in a passing cart as he went. Is that not odd, Sir Elric?"

The knight sat back in his chair, regarding Lionel, who was grasping the edge of the table with his gloved hands. "Clearly it would be best that I see to this going forward, Lionel."

To Kate's surprise, Lionel rose, bowed to Kate, to Elric, and made to depart.

"One question before you depart, Lionel," said Kate. "How is it that Jon Underhill approached my cousin William? Your doing?"

It was Sir Elric who responded. "I will explain."

"Good. And Lionel, Lady Kirkby asks that you call on her at the guest-house this evening. She would hear you out."

Lionel expressed his surprise, and thanked her, bowing out.

"And now, Sir Elric, I trust you will do me the courtesy of explaining yourself," Kate said quietly, one hand on the dagger hidden in her skirts.

"Forgive me for not having invited you to dine myself, but I did not know whether you would come. However, Lionel . . . Well, you have much to discuss with him, so I brazenly used him to lure you. I pray your forgiveness."

"It would seem you have lived so long among the Nevilles that you have adopted their bad habits. I much prefer someone who is direct."

"Direct I shall be. But first, would you be so kind as to serve us?" he asked Jennet.

"Gladly, sir." Jennet jumped to the task, serving all three of them the meat course that had been set out on the sideboard and refreshing their barely tasted goblets.

Kate took a forkful of the meat. Venison. Delicately spiced. Elric and Jennet also tried a little.

"So," Elric began, "you are quite right about my lord's kinsman. Lionel has interfered with your servant. I learned that only this morning, and have sent out men to search the road to Beverley. And other destinations, in case he had other plans."

"Other plans?"

"If he was indeed working with Jon Underhill, or Hubert Bale as your servant Berend knew him—"

She looked up sharply. So he knew about the two identities. And that Jon was the king's man, Hubert the duke's? She wondered. But clearly he thought Bale still alive.

Elric was grinning at her surprise. "Yes, this man is known to the former assassin you call your cook. In any case, your man Sam, well, it is possible that Underhill offered him something more interesting than living out his years serving you."

"Because I am not a Neville?"

A shrug. "He did prove willing to betray you. But to a point. I am quite certain that Lionel is as yet unaware of the clients you regularly host in the house on High Petergate. Sam did not choose to betray you about that."

She began to protest, but it was foolish. He *knew*. "How did you learn about my guesthouse?"

"I no longer remember how I learned of it. But I applauded you when I did, Dame Katherine. Your late husband was not an honorable man. He and his brother seem two of a kind. Your secret is safe with me. You have nothing to fear from me on that count."

On *that* count. "You think Sam might have left the city in the company of Jon Underhill? Why? What was Underhill's mission?"

"Sir Thomas Kirkby has not always been a man of peace. My lord earl sent Underhill to gauge the mood of the citizens of York who dine with Lady Kirkby."

"So that is why he approached William Frost?"

"Yes. An influential, highly respected citizen of York."

"What do you fear this man has done instead?"

"I have no idea. But I will find out."

His steely gaze made Kate uneasy. This man would discover everything.

"And if you find my servant, what happens to him?"

"It depends on whether or not he is with Jon Underhill. If he is, he will be brought to me at Sheriff Hutton. If not, he shall be delivered to your doorstep." He glanced up at Jennet. "The other meat dish now, if you will."

"I cannot believe that Lady Kirkby's mission is anything other than what she claims it to be," said Kate. "Both the archbishop and the dean of York Minster have sanctioned her presence here."

"One is a Scrope, the other a Clifford. I doubt either of their families would remain neutral in a civil war."

"And the Nevilles would?"

A cough, a grin. "The earl merely wishes to know which way the citizens of York are bending."

"I see. So why our meeting?"

"My lord still needs an ear among the citizens of York. I hoped that might be you. Or, if you prefer, you might help me recruit your cousin Frost. No need to decide at once." He tasted the stew. "I must commend the taverner on his kitchen. The steward of Sheriff Hutton is in need of a new cook. Do you think I might lure the man away from the city?"

"I very much doubt it. He is his own man. His family is here, and the merchants pay him a handsome retainer for his services."

"Ah. Pity."

They moved to neutral topics for a while as they ate, such as the long winter, the sudden, welcome thaw, each sizing up the other.

Finally Elric pushed his plate away. He sat back, elbows on the arms of the chair, fingers steepled. He regarded her with cool blue eyes.

She allowed to herself that he was a handsome man, strong-jawed, well-spoken. She had watched him fight, remembered quite clearly his grace in motion, his skill. She was not immune to his charm. And for that reason, and more, she regarded him with great caution, so she fought a smile with his first words.

"I should very much like to have you as an ally, Dame Katherine. I believe we would work well together."

"No doubt you would like that. But what value should I find in it?"

"Trouble is coming, of that I have no doubt. You have chosen strong servants for your household, and you have powerful kin. But when civil war breaks out, you will need more than a former assassin and the resourceful Jennet to assist you in protecting your wards and your property. Sheriff Hutton might be a place of refuge for you in the storm to come, and the Earl of Westmoreland is certain to stand with the victors." He grinned at Kate's snort. "I am not blind to the self-serving nature of the family I serve. Your family by marriage, eh? I offer you protection, including protection from the petty meddling of my earl's kinsman, Lionel Neville." His smile was more dazzling than Matt's.

Time to escape. Kate rose.

Sir Elric rose.

"You have given me much to think about, Sir Elric."

"One thing more. I give you fair warning that I am investigating any rumors that come to my attention about several matters that touch on your interests. This fire in your undercroft, the deaths of Alice Hatten and her lover, your cousin's sudden fondness for the Forest of Galtres. I will, of course, share with you anything that I find. I merely mention this to spur your consideration of my offer. Were we to cooperate, we might resolve these mysteries in a more timely manner." He bowed to her.

Outside, a steady rain fell. Kate was pulling up her hood when Jennet caught her arm.

"Will you work for him?"

"The question is whether I actually have a choice."

"He knows too much?"

"If he does not now, he soon will."

"Sam, that crook-pated lout. He told Sir Elric all about us. My background, Berend's. If we find him at home, warming his feet in front of the fire, I've a mind to geld him."

"We will worry about what to do about Sam in due time. For the moment we have more important things to sort through." Kate pulled up her hood as she considered where to head. At this time of day, just after dinner, she might find William at home. Watching for puddles, she pushed through the crowds on Micklegate, heading for her cousin's house.

17

A COMB, A PAIR OF GLOVES

After the rain, the night was cold and clear, the stars bright. Kate shivered as she leaned out the window of her bedchamber, listening to an owl hunting in the gardens across Castlegate. She welcomed the chill wind stirring her hair, cooling her face. She would prefer to walk out into the darkness. She yearned to take the dogs and walk down to the river, but held herself back—the murders, the fire, Sir Elric's sudden interest—or, rather, the Earl of Westmoreland's. But it was Sir Elric's eyes that haunted her, and the sense of coiled life, ready to spring.

For tonight, Kate had sent Jennet back to her own bed in the little house at the street, not wanting to keep her awake with her inability to settle. But, most of all, she had done it to avoid Jennet's questions, to which Kate had not, as yet, any answers.

She had indeed found William at home. He had understood the import of Sir Elric's interest. For now he believed himself safe, convinced that the knight had believed his account of brushing off "Underhill's" offer, with his explanation that he feared he would be in worse trouble with such a man defending him.

"The key is to keep the lie simple. Liars elaborate," he told Kate. Moments later, his confidence had crumpled. "But if he finds the grave . . . Why would he think anything other than that I murdered the earl's man?"

Kate had assured him that he was free to tell Sir Elric about the night at the guesthouse, that he already knew about her clientele.

"But Isabella. If she should learn. Dear God. Whatever he wants of you, Katherine, I pray you, appease him."

"I stand in awe of the ease with which you ask the women in your life to give themselves freely to those who might help you, cousin. What a heady feeling it must be, your certainty that God chose you for great things, that we have been placed in your path as your handmaidens." She had goaded him, enjoying his discomfort.

Better than swimming in her own.

She hated that she kept remembering Sir Elric's eyes, and his form on the practice field. She had been too long without a man in her bed, that was her problem. What York needed was a brothel of men, for servicing women. Berend's hand on her arm this evening had burned her. Matt's smile tormented her. A good round in bed and she might have a clearer head. This is how women fell back into marriage—that yearning, that hunger.

Still leaning out the window in the hope that the chill night air might have some salutary effect, Kate distracted herself by recalling, in as much detail as possible, the conversation in the kitchen hours earlier.

Lille and Ghent had sat at her feet, sensing her need for comfort, butting her hands over and over so that she spent most of the evening rubbing them down as she listened and shared.

Clement's assessment of the inventory results, related through Berend, was that small quantities of spice were missing from almost every shipment. No ordinary thief would take the trouble to steal a small quantity from each container, yet each weighed less than expected. Or most did. Lionel had missed a few.

To Kate it seemed a petty issue compared with her other worries. But no wonder Lionel had become agitated when she mentioned that Clement and Berend were counting.

The two men had worked late, determined to complete the task, then left one of Lady Margery's men on guard. This time the arsonist might be Lionel, covering his guilt.

When it came her turn to recount what she had gleaned, Kate began with all she had learned about Sam, particularly his betrayals, and Lionel's part in encouraging them. "Sam went only so far. It seems he said nothing about the guesthouse. And he mentioned nothing about Bale's murder. I wonder what stayed him?"

"It matters not," said Jennet. "He has lost our trust."

Matt nodded.

Kate agreed. "I will need to think what to do about him if he returns unscathed."

Berend and Jennet exchanged looks. One thing was certain, Sam could no longer serve in her household. Not unless Kate was able to turn a blind eye to the "accidents" that would befall him.

"And what of his being seen with Hubert Bale?" Jennet asked. "What do you make of that?"

"Sam and Bale." Berend gazed into his empty cup. "So William Frost is somehow part of this?"

Kate did not believe that. "There is a far more powerful hand in the game now." She told them about Sir Elric's offer. And his threat. William's reaction.

Berend cursed softly.

"So." She had looked round at her three companions. "What do we know? Are we close to understanding what has been happening? Can we solve this before Sir Elric gets too close?"

"We know that Sam cannot be trusted," said Jennet. "At some point he was dancing to Hubert Bale's tune—when he added a sleeping potion to the wine."

"We know that Lionel Neville is untrustworthy," said Berend. "And that he has been stealing from you, his own partner. But he has little power in the family. Nor do I think Fitch, for all his sins, is connected to the murders. At worst, Lionel's failed attempt to spy on you has served as an unfortunate distraction."

Kate nodded. "Anything else?"

"Clement and Griselde knew of Sam's nature but said nothing to you," said Matt.

"Distrust all round," said Kate. "But about the murderer we still know nothing. Nothing." She felt the tension round the table, the defeat.

"What would it mean if we partnered with Sir Elric?" Matt had the courage to ask.

"We would become the creatures of the Earl of Westmoreland," said Berend.

"I need to think it through," said Kate. "I promise you this, that if I decide to accept his offer, the three of you are free to leave my service."

"Never," said Berend, pressing her arm in the emotion of the moment.

Kate had met his eyes as he touched her arm. That was the moment when she thought how wonderful it would be to curl up in his strength, his warmth, to make love to him. Surely her face had flushed.

"Never," said Jennet.

"If you have need of me, I am yours," Matt said.

Kate looked round at the three fierce faces. "Bless you."

"Sir Elric seemed certain that it will come to war," said Jennet.

A comment met with a silence so charged, Lille and Ghent rose up as if thinking Kate needed protection.

"We all need a good night's sleep," she said.

That had been hours ago. Kate drew back into the room, lit a second lamp off the first, and placed Connor's pack on the bed. Berend said he had added a few things found in the undercroft—a pair of gloves, a woman's comb, an empty flagon, a broken lock pick. She pulled out the items one by one, beginning with Connor's tools, carefully rolled up in leather. She untied it, let it roll out on the bed. Stoneworking tools, lovingly cleaned and oiled. Phillip would treasure them. She rolled them up and put them aside. The gloves were clearly not Connor's—though hardened from the weather, creased and well-worn, they were made of costly leather. The broken lock pick might belong to the intruder, but the pieces of metal held no clues as to who that might be. The flagon was a cheap one. Connor's shirt had been washed so many times it was remarkably soft, the elbows and wrists and stomach darned many times. His shoes had so much dust embedded in the inner soles they bore the shape of Connor's feet.

Alice and Connor had come so close to happiness. Kate breathed through the knot in her stomach as she drew out the rest of Connor's clothes and set them aside.

And then, caught on a loose thread—a woman's decorative comb, mother-of-pearl on a strip of silver, the comb the whitest ivory. Kate stopped breathing.

It is not possible, Geoff whispered in Kate's mind. *How is this possible?*

It had been her most precious possession, a gift from her father for her tenth birthday. To be strong like her brothers, to train with them, accompany them hunting, that was her obsession as a child. She kept secret her love of pretty things, her pride in her dark, thick, wildly curly hair that Roland called raven wings, her delight in whirling about the room in dance and the touch of silk and fine linen on her skin. Her father seemed to guess, always asking her to dance to Roland's livelier tunes, his face brightening when she appeared in her best gown. And when he tucked the comb in her hair, telling her that the moment he saw it he imagined it just so, a ray of light in her raven hair, her heart had swelled with love and pride. She had taken care to wear it only when she was in her best gown, sure to stay put, not rush out into the fields or climb the hills or muck about with the animals and chance losing it.

So she had never been certain how long it had been missing when she opened the small carved box in which she kept it, wrapped in a piece of velvet. The velvet and the box were there, but not the comb. She wanted to wear it for Roland's burial, a ray of light in her raven wings. She *must* wear it. She searched everywhere, accused everyone of stealing it. Her mother had finally confined her to her room for a week to pray for her soul. "All this for a comb, Katherine? You would seed distrust through our household because of a bauble? In this time of mourning?"

She reached for Geoff, to ask him what he remembered, but he was silent.

You know something about this.

Silence.

How did my comb come to be in the undercroft?

191

Geoff's silence was deafening. For the first time in all her recent troubles, Kate felt a cold fear gripping her heart. She had not felt this since the darkest days up on the border, when Geoff deserted her.

Forgive me. But I have no idea how it would come to be here in York, he whispered.

You hold something back.

Silence.

I will know in time.

Silence.

She pulled out Hubert Bale's pack. The letters of introduction, one for Jon Underhill, carrying King Richard's seal, one for Hubert Bale, carrying the duke's seal. According to Berend, Hubert Bale was the man's true name. And he had been here in the service of Westmoreland, who was married to a Lancaster. It fit. Apparently Sir Elric guessed William was the king's man, hence Bale had presented himself to him with the false name. Interesting, but not helpful. Returning them to the pouch, she slipped off the bed and hid it beneath the floorboards.

Settling back on the bed, she tried to forget the comb. It was no use. Again and again her eyes were drawn to it. She cupped it in her hands, held it to her heart.

A knock on the door. Jennet peered in. "I saw your light as I paced in the garden." She looked at the bed. "Have you learned anything?"

"I am not sure. Come in, do. I sent you away only so you might sleep." Now the questions Kate had wished to avoid would be most welcome. She laughed to see that Jennet was fully dressed. "Did you lie down at all?"

"I did. And slept awhile, not long. Then the lists began to march through my head and I thought a walk in the cold would freeze them." She looked down at the comb. "Pretty. Was that in one of the packs?"

"Berend found it in the undercroft. It is mine, Jennet. Lost when I was—twelve? Thirteen?"

Jennet looked up with a half smile, as if expecting Kate to admit she was teasing. The smile faded. "You are serious. How is it here? Now?"

Kate shook her head.

"Your cousin William?"

"He was not there at the time."

"This frightens you."

Alice's death was so like Maud's. And Maud's death killed Kate's dream of standing beside her brothers as their equal. It made real the danger that she had sensed but denied, believing she needed only be strong enough. From that day forward she had understood that the danger was real. Her fear turned to anger. To be born a woman was to be cheated of that easy confidence she so admired in her brothers. That anger grew as her brothers circled round her, determined to protect her.

"I am imagining things. It is very like a comb I had as a child."

"Hmpf." Jennet shrugged as she sat down on the bed, touching the scattered items. She picked up the gloves. "Worn. Fine, though. A man's gloves. A wide hand with stubby fingers." She wiggled one of the gloves at Kate.

Kate forced a laugh. Wide palm, short, fat fingers on muscled arms pushing her down. Stubby fingers gripping the axe, eyes burning. *You will pay for this.* Running, her lungs burning, her torn gown soaked in blood.

Jennet put the gloves aside, picked up the broken lock pick. "I have one very like it."

"You do. But this is not yours?"

Jennet patted her skirt. "I carry it always. I never know when I'll need to find a way in, or out." She frowned. "You are worried. Still the comb?"

Am I mad, Geoff? The gloves and the comb, are they part of a message? Did the Cavertons take my comb? The deaths all hurt me or someone close to me. Even the attempted fire fits. And if it is all traced back to my guesthouse, it could ruin me. Is this the pattern, Geoff? Is it possible?

Do not go out alone, Kate. Be safe. Take no risks.

But why? Why would the Cavertons come all this way? How could I matter so much? Your warning. You believe it's possible. That the Cavertons might be here.

You are the one with eyes and ears, Kate. I only feel your fear.

"Lovely tools. Will you give them to Phillip?"

Kate made herself pick up the chisel, feel the heft in her hand, slip it back into its loop in the leather case. "Yes. I think I will take them to him first thing this morning. On my way to see Lady Kirkby."

"You still mean to see her? Do you care what Lionel had to say now that you know Sir Handsome is the one in charge?" Jennet stuck her face close, peered up at Kate with a teasing grin. "I sensed the magic stirring between the two of you, do not think you can hide that from me."

"It would still be interesting to hear Lady Margery's impression. As for Sir Elric, his appeal will not sway me."

Jennet nodded. "I never doubted that." She rolled up the tools. "Young Phillip will be pleased. But Marie will expect something of equal worth. The comb?"

"No!" It was out before Kate could guard her tongue. "No. The teeth are too far apart for her fine hair. But you are right. I will promise her a new gown. We will choose the fabrics together."

A nod. A yawn. "Shall we try to sleep a little?"

Kate realized she was cold now. Hiding beneath the covers for a while held some appeal. They set the items carefully on the bench beneath the window and climbed into bed.

"Have you encountered any Scots in the city of late?" Kate asked as Jennet began to settle.

"The Cavertons? Do you think they stole the comb?"

On the night Kate caught Jennet thieving in the hall, she had recognized something in the young woman's eyes, the anger, the determination. Shortly after Jennet began to serve Kate, they shared bits of their stories. Jennet knew of the Cavertons, of Maud, of her brothers' deaths. Not everything, but enough.

"Young Andrew had wide palms, short, fat fingers, and spent his coin on fine gloves and boots."

"The one who got away? The scarred one?"

"Yes."

"Face pulled together on the right, and missing that ear." She was quiet a moment. "There is always talk of suspicious Northerners on the streets, and many badly scarred men about, but I have heard of no such newcomer."

Kate closed her eyes. "But you did not know to ask."

"No. You think Andrew Caverton has done all this as revenge?"

"It is madness, I know. All because of a comb that stirred memories."

"And the gloves. Both in the undercroft that was set on fire."

"So I might never have known they were there. A different culprit? Am I simply imagining the connections?"

It was not long past dawn when the men pounded on the door below, waking Lille and Ghent. And Kate, who was amazed to realize she had slept. She was alone in the bed, Jennet already up. Kate dressed with care, armed and ready to slip away to the deanery as soon as she could, grateful that she could be so clearheaded despite that pounding on the hall door.

Downstairs, a pair in the livery of Westmoreland stood in the doorway, the mud of the road on their clothes. One of them apologized for arriving so early. "But Sir Elric said you would want to know as soon as we found him," he said.

"My servant Sam? You have found my servant?"

"We believe it is him. From what we can tell, he fits the description. The cart is coming behind us. We were first through Walmgate Bar to wake you, Mistress Clifford."

From what they can tell? "Is he alive?"

"Only just, Mistress. He is breathing, not much more."

Matt quietly informed her that Jennet had just gone out to the kitchen, and he had been about to let the dogs out into the yard when the pounding began.

"Take Lille and Ghent out to the yard and poke your head in the kitchen. Tell Berend we will need hot water and rags." She turned back to the men. "Where did you find him?"

"Not far outside Walmgate Bar. We stayed there the night with him, in a farmhouse." The man who had so far done all the talking nodded, then stepped back, as if considering his duty finished.

His partner seemed ready to say more. Kate prodded him with a few questions. She had guessed right.

"We were on our way back to the city," he said. "Thirsty. We had been out there all afternoon, asking everyone we encountered about a white-haired man. So when we saw an alewife's sign, a bushel on a pole, we stopped. Fine ale, and as we drank, we told the alewife about the man we sought, headed to Beverley in the snow. She told us to take a look at the poor fellow in the lean-to, staying warm with her cow. He looked the part, white haired, slight of build. He had been there for a day. Her husband found him in the ditch by the road, brought him in."

Jennet and Berend entered the hall carrying water and rags. Matt followed and set about pulling his pallet over by the fire. Kate sent Jennet up to the solar for an old sheet, some blankets. Matt and Berend moved the chairs and table about to afford more room for nursing Sam.

"Are the dogs loose in the yard?" she asked Matt.

"No. I left them in the kitchen. I thought it best."

She asked the earl's men why they had not taken Sam to Sir Elric at Sheriff Hutton. The second began to answer, but the first rushed to talk over him. "We were to take him for questioning. But we doubt the man will wake, much less be able to tell us anything. His face . . . He is of no use to Sir Elric."

"And you found no sign of Underhill?"

"No. The others are still out searching for him."

At the sound of a cart creaking down the alleyway, Berend went out, Jennet following with a lantern. Kate heard Berend directing the men and suddenly thought of Lille and Ghent, imagining them at the window, ears pricked, investigating the unaccustomed noise.

She dug some old scissors out of a basket by the door. In case clothes needed to be cut away. Damn them for arriving just now. She had wanted to see that Phillip and Marie were safe at the deanery.

Berend escorted a man through the door carrying Sam in his arms. Kneeling by the pallet, Berend helped ease Sam down onto the old sheet. They were right that he would be of no use to Sir Elric. His breath was a death rattle. Jennet joined Kate at the pallet, whispering a prayer that Sam might be beyond pain. His face was caked with blood and filth, his mouth and jaw so battered he could not possibly speak, his eyes swollen shut, hair matted, clothes tattered and filthy. What cause had anyone to so beat old Sam about the head?

"Your servant, Mistress Clifford?" asked one of the men.

"What is left of him," she said. "Thank you for bringing him to us."

The man who had carried Sam in from the cart bobbed his head and departed, but the first two remained. "We are to report whether he lives, and whether he manages to say anything of use."

She looked up at them in disbelief. "How? How might he speak?"
The two men bowed their heads.

Kate told Matt to fetch his cousin, the healer Bella. Sam seemed beyond healing, but Bella might ease his pain.

Berend and Jennet were already cutting away Sam's clothes, the shears difficult to use on the fabric, which was stiff with blood and filth—mud, urine, feces, and, as Kate leaned closer, she detected pus, the scent of festering wounds. He had been suffering for days. She studied the horrific injuries to his face. And all the while something about him bothered her. He had been found too quickly, too easily.

Wetting a rag, she began to clean the muck from his forehead, eyes, temples, cheeks, nose. She sat back. Jennet glanced at her. Kate dabbed at the nose. Their eyes met. Sam had a prominent mole on his nose. This man did not.

Too easy, far too easy. A distraction? Though filthy, the clothes seemed to be Sam's. A deliberate ruse then. Such malevolence.

She crossed herself and said a prayer for the stranger's soul. Then she rose, telling Berend and Jennet she was going across the road for the priest. She waited until they had both looked up, indicating that they had heard. Taking her cloak, she was about to step out the door as Matt entered with Bella.

"God bless you for coming so quickly. I entrust him to you." Kate nodded to both of them and hurried out. Checking that no liveried men lingered in the yard, she paused, expecting some sound from Lille and Ghent—their claws scratching the door, or a bark demanding attention. They had been locked in the kitchen so long. But Kate heard nothing. She rushed across to the kitchen, flung open the door, careful to close it behind her. There was no need. Lille and Ghent would not dash out. They were gone.

Sam. Sam walked Lille and Ghent, they knew him and trusted him. And he knew how much they meant to her. But why? How? If it was Andrew Caverton behind all this, how had he enlisted Sam? Sam, of all people?

Because he knew her household so well. And he knew how to handle Lille and Ghent.

Wait for Berend and Jennet, Geoff warned.

No. He will not show himself if they are with me.

Andrew? Or Sam?

Either of them, the bastards. I'll gut them both.

She opened the kitchen door with care, slipped out, shutting it behind her, melting into the shadows beneath the eaves. The hall door opened. Jennet stepped out, hurried down the alley. It would take her a moment to cross over to St. Mary's and discover Kate was not there.

Opening the gate into Thomas Holme's yard, Kate crept along the fence, feeling her way, ducking past the lanterns her neighbor now kept lit through the night, past the Holme house and the small shops fronting the street. She paused there. Where would Sam advise Andrew Caverton to lie in wait? Where could he trust that the dogs would not call attention to them if they barked?

A little hand closed over hers. "Come with me."

18

UNFINISHED BUSINESS

———⚬⚬⚬———

She was not much taller than Marie, but not so slight. The hat, sized for the head of an adult, or to hide long hair, made her neck seem too thin. But the girl was young enough and filthy enough that she might simply be an undersized lad; one could tell little about what lay beneath the grime on her face in the pale light of dawn.

"Take me to Sam and the dogs. And Andrew Caverton."

"He said you would guess right quick. He knows you well." The Scots burr suggested the child had accompanied Andrew from the north. "Stay low as we cross the road." The child held on tight to Kate's hand as they crossed. Just then, Jennet stepped into the road, coming from the church. Kate stumbled, caught herself, moved on when certain Jennet had noticed her. She and the girl slipped behind a yew at the edge of Holme's gardens.

Jennet's voice, calling out to Berend. "Not at the church."

A tug on her hand. Kate missed Berend's reply as the child hurried her along. They zigzagged down the garden, staying beneath trees, behind hedges. The child knew this place well, quickly descending toward the

199

river, where the morning mist would help mask their passage. As Kate ran, she reviewed in her mind the weapons concealed in her skirts. It would depend how close he was, and whether Lille and Ghent were in the way, but the axe seemed her best chance at felling Andrew. A soft drizzle began, blending with the mist. Kate silently cursed. The mist would affect her vision, weakening her aim.

Then you must use your other senses.

She nodded to Geoff.

Stumbling again, Kate carefully fell to her knees, causing the girl to lose her grip. Kate whistled. A whimper. The dogs were near, muzzled. She released the axe from its sheath and drew out her knife, then turned. The girl grabbed Kate's left hand, yanked, and Kate used the momentum to come close with such suddenness the girl lost her balance. With her left arm, Kate hugged the child close, the knife, in her right hand, at her throat.

"Be silent, do as I say, and you will not be hurt," she whispered in the girl's ear. Keeping her ears pricked for sound, Kate walked them slowly down toward the water. She gambled that Sam would be busy restraining the dogs, so she need take only Andrew. She thought through how to let go of the girl and reach for her axe in a smooth movement, take him by surprise.

A rustle in the brush. She stopped, held her breath. A cat streaked past. Running away, not toward. Could be Sam with the dogs who spooked it, could be Andrew. Kate stood still, a firm grip on the wriggling girl, getting her bearings. A creeping in the underbrush. Close. Closer. She pushed the girl down and sideways, kicking her so she rolled down the hill. A form broke from the underbrush, hesitated. Kate aimed her axe just above the knee. A startled yelp. As the man lost his balance she caught his arms and yanked, bringing him down.

"Mother of God!" he howled.

The telltale *r*. It was Andrew. Good.

The dogs whimpered somewhere to her left. Kate remembered an old stone building near the water, masked by underbrush, where Lille and Ghent once cornered a young fox. She dragged the hobbled Andrew toward it, thanking God it was not far—she was strong, but he was heavy. The girl caught up as Kate felt a door behind her. Using her back to push it open, Kate dropped Andrew's arms and kicked him so he turned onto the axe with a shriek. She yanked the girl on top of him and used their confusion to drop and roll into the hut, knocking Sam down in the doorway and slicing his arm with her knife. He cried out. Away to the dogs who were plunging crazily. Their leashes were tied to an iron bar in a window opening and, as she'd guessed, their muzzles were on. Damnably clever Sam. She needed them off so the dogs could bite and tear. She was fumbling with Lille's muzzle when Andrew came for her. A cry of pain in the doorway—Sam?—and Jennet was there, launching herself at Andrew, knocking him to the floor, pressing his face into the ground, giving Kate enough time to succeed in removing Lille's muzzle and order her to catch the others. Ghent's muzzle was easier to open, and he was quick to follow, pinning Sam down. By then the girl was gone, Lille in pursuit.

Andrew reared, shaking Jennet off, but he could not stand. Kate yanked him into the light filtering in the barred window, stumbling a little. She hoped he, Sam, and the girl were sufficiently subdued that she did not need to test how much strength she had left.

"Murdering Clifford bitch, get the axe out of my leg." Andrew howled as he tried to do it himself. His right arm did not do what he wanted.

She must have pulled it out of joint. Good. She crouched beside him, took hold of the axe, nodding to Jennet who moved to hold down his legs, and pulled.

Andrew barked with the pain. Ghent answered.

Sam cursed and ordered Ghent off his chest. "You would bite me?" he cried. The dogs were trained not to bite down unless she signaled, or she was down, but Sam did not know that. She had not shared that part of their training with him. God be thanked she had not been a complete fool about him.

A scream outside, and Berend ducked into the shed, the girl tucked under one arm. "She is a fighter, but Lille subdued her."

He stepped aside to let Lille trot into the room. She immediately went to Sam and growled and snapped, then came to sit beside Kate, glaring at Andrew.

Kate rubbed Lille's ears, thanking her.

"You always were more comfortable in the stable than in the house," Andrew wheezed as he tried to shift all weight off the wounded leg. "Cruel to keep fine hunting dogs in the city."

"You are as ugly as I remember, Andrew Caverton," Kate said.

"Thanks to your brothers, Kitty Kitty Puss Puss."

The old taunt had Kate fingering the axe.

Steady, Kate, you have him. Learn something before you gut him.

So you are here. Proud of me, are you?

As ever.

As if he were a guest in her hall, Kate asked Andrew what brought him to York after all this time.

"What would you say if I told you it was your mother's pious preaching that woke the beast?"

His answer strayed so far from what she had expected that Kate was at a loss for a retort. The girl began to whimper. Berend eased her down. She lunged toward Kate. Lille went for her, but Jennet grabbed the girl and hoisted her onto her lap, pinning her arms to her side. With a grunt, Andrew leaned forward and swatted the girl's hat, knocking it off. Thick dark hair tumbled over her slender shoulders. Lille growled.

"She is proud of that hair. Remind you of someone, Kitty Kitty with the raven's wings? She's your niece, Petra. Walter's girl."

"My brother has a daughter?"

"Why do you think he lost the hand? He wooed my sister Mary, used her, flung her away. Twelve years old, she was, same as you. Sent away, to the north, to family, my poor sister, and there she died. Too young to give birth. Aye, Mary died, but Petra survived to remind us, ever remind us. And then the Clifford men closed round you, protecting their princess, Kitty Kitty Puss Puss, fearing what we might do to you, that we might be as cruel as your Walter. We almost succeeded."

I knew she'd been sent away, but I thought it was to torment Walter. Did you know about this, Geoff? That she was with child?

I guessed, but only later, after Maud. Walter denied it, said she was too young to conceive.

"That pretty comb we left for you among the spices that make you rich, I knew you would remember it. The precious comb your brother

Walter took from you to give to our Mary. Why are you not wearing it, Kitty Kitty Puss Puss? Or the one you wore that day Bryce and I caught you out alone. That bloody day." He reared forward, pushing Kate down before she could react, pressing himself to her, grinding his twisted lips against her mouth. Lille and Ghent charged at him.

Berend roared as he rushed between the dogs, lifting Andrew into the air and slamming him against the wall.

Kate rolled over, spitting out the taste of the bastard.

Berend held Andrew down with a foot to his chest, though the man's eyes were closed as he struggled to breathe. "Have you heard enough, Dame Katherine? Shall we end it?"

"Not yet." There were things she wanted to know, and things she did not want her servants to hear. "I want to talk to him alone. Take Sam out. Question him. Petra, too. Leave Lille and Ghent."

"Dame Katherine . . ."

She motioned Lille and Ghent to her side. They stood, alert.

"Go, Jennet, Berend!" she commanded.

Jennet lifted the girl, and Berend yanked Sam to his feet, kicking shut the door behind him. Kate took out her knife, set the axe beside her, took Andrew's foot and shook his wounded leg.

He sputtered awake. Lille and Ghent, who crouched on either side of him, growled a warning as he moved. "What is this? You give your dogs the honor of the kill? But you love to kill. You had such pleasure with—"

"Bryce was the devil's spawn. No child of God could have so boasted of his pleasure in cutting out Maud's tongue and pressing it up into her with his cock. He was no man born of woman. And how slowly he killed Geoff. A piece at a time until he bled to death." She suddenly saw it so clear in her mind she flinched, turned away to hide her emotion.

"Ah, she looks away. A woman's soft heart after all."

"The dogs will take you if you reach for me," she whispered, breathing deeply to steady herself.

I did not feel it after a while, said Geoff. *God protected me from the worst of it.*

"What did you mean about my mother?"

"I wondered when you would return to that." His words were slurring a little. Berend had done her no favor slamming the man's head into the stone wall. "Seems your mother, Saint Eleanor, wrote to Walter from across the Channel at Yuletide. Crazed Walter, all alone on your land on the border. Save your soul, Walter. Find Mary Caverton and help her and the child. You will feel so good, so righteous." He forced his voice high. Not so weakened then.

It was the sort of thing her mother might do, meddle in others' lives as if hers was so admirable, so above reproach. As if she hadn't abandoned her surviving children in following her new husband to Strasbourg. And she had lied to Kate, made her think Walter the victim, heartbroken over Mary. "So Walter tried to find Mary?"

"Aye. He went to the Bensons." A neutral family north of the border. "They told him Mary had died in childbirth seven years ago. But Benson promised to ask about the child. So he did. Now Walter is interested, I thought, and wondered why, for he'd never loved Mary. Even so, here he was asking, and I wondered how I might use it. So I took little Petra to meet her father."

"Then why are you here?"

"Well you might ask." He might be smug, but his labored cough betrayed his anguished breathing. "His betrothed—wealthy, young, ready to bear him more Clifford monsters—she forbade him to acknowledge such a creature as Petra, threatening to break the betrothal. Petra has lived wild, like me. She is strong, did you notice? Much, much stronger than your Norman ward, pretty, delicate Marie. Smarter than Phillip." He licked his lips, the thirst that came with loss of blood from his leg and a gash in his head. "Walter offered me money to take Petra away. He said there might be a place for her with your mother. She was returning to York to found a nunnery. So I took the money and came to present Saint Eleanor with her granddaughter. But she is not here."

"No. Your journey down from the borders was for naught."

Why would Walter send him here, Geoff?

Walter is lost, Kate. I pity his betrothed.

Andrew frowned at her. "Are you listening?"

"I am. So what will you do now that you know Walter lied to you?"

"No matter. I found you, young widow, living a comfortable life. With secrets. A bawdy house for the powerful citizens of York. Clever. Dangerous." She caught his foot as he tried to shift. He coughed. "I am dying here."

"Slowly bleeding to death like my twin, and Maud, and Alice. What I want to know is, why Hubert Bale, Alice, Connor? Why not kill me?"

"I wanted this, to watch you suffer. Grieve. Be tormented by a fear that you missed a chance to save them. I killed Walter too quickly. Snapped his neck and it was over. He suffered no more. Nothing to savor."

Kate had gone cold. Her last brother, dead. All the men in her family, dead. She and her mother all that remained. Her mother, her muddle-pated meddling mother, had provoked this bloody onslaught of vengeance.

"So I vowed not to rush your dying. I meant to give you the guilt, and ruin you as well. You challenged me more than I could have hoped. You are a clever one, burying the body right away." His chuckle was a gurgle. "William Frost struts about before his peers, but he crawls for you, eh?" He might be struggling to breathe, but Andrew's grimace was a smirk. He so enjoyed twisting the blade in Kate's heart. "He's no less your servant than Berend and Jennet—comrades in arms you like to think, but they call you 'dame' and 'mistress.' You order them about. You Cliffords."

Kate tightened her grip on her knife and fingered the axe. Enough? Had she heard enough now?

Andrew's chuckle had the tone of a death rattle. "You have me wondering. You pushed them out when you thought they would hear how you murdered my brother. How you slit his throat as he sat watching the cattle, peaceful as could be."

"My mother took me away before I could finish you."

"So why not let your comrades hear about your kill?"

It was not the killing. It was what came before, the day the two of them, Bryce and Andrew . . . I ran. If I had not run, if I had killed them then . . .

Two against one, Kate. You were right to run. My death was not your fault. They meant to kill all of us.

"What you did to Alice. She had done nothing to you. Nothing."

"Nor had Maud. But it changed you. Changed all of you." Andrew coughed. "One feeble girl's death destroyed you all."

She leaned over him, the knife to his neck. "Like Mary's death?" It was her mistake.

Something thudded against the door. Kate turned her head and, as the door swung open Andrew grabbed her hair with one hand, pulling her close.

Lille and Ghent sprang in. "Bite!" Kate commanded. They found a purchase on Andrew's arms. He screamed.

"No! Get the dogs away from him!" the girl shrieked from the doorway. She hurled herself out of Jennet's grasp, fell onto Kate.

Andrew lost his grip and Kate rolled away, pulling the girl with her and holding her tight though she flailed and kicked.

"Call off the dogs," Sir Elric commanded from the doorway.

Seeing his drawn bow, Kate whistled to Lille and Ghent, their command to drop their grip. To Elric she called, "Hold your shot, sir. He is mine."

But at that very moment the arrow pierced the bridge of Andrew's nose.

Petra shrieked again, then went limp beneath Kate, sobbing.

Kate lay there for a moment, holding the child, waiting for her heart to slow. Damn him. Damn his arrogance.

"Are you hurt?" Sir Elric crouched down beside her.

She did not look at him. "He was mine to kill." She lay still, holding the child until Berend plucked her from Kate's arms, took her out of the shed. Lille and Ghent nuzzled her face. She held them a moment, then shifted her weight and pulled herself up, glaring at the knight until he shrugged and went over to retrieve his arrow.

"His blood mingles with Alice's," said Jennet. She stood off to the side, examining the mud floor. "This is where she lay bleeding." She came to Kate then, offered a hand to help her stand up.

"Damn him to hell."

"He thought Andrew was attacking you."

"He assumed I needed rescue." She noticed how Jennet cradled her left arm. Blood soaked the lower end of her sleeve. "What happened?"

"Petra bites. Through good wool, no less."

"Get back to the house. Goodwife Bella might still be there. A bite needs attention at once. Tell Berend to follow, with the girl."

"And you?"

"I will come." Kate gathered the dogs' leashes. Her head was pounding from the stench of blood. Lille and Ghent whined to leave.

"He was not yours to kill," said Elric, startling her. She had not noticed he was still by the door. "He murdered my lord's man."

"You know this?"

"Your cousin William Frost told me all, where he buried him, how your cook identified him."

"So that is how you came to be here? You came for Berend?"

"No." He sounded offended. "My men told me they had found your man Sam. I came to see, but heard the disturbance down here."

"That Andrew murdered an assassin was nothing compared to what he and his brothers did to my family. My three brothers. My best friend. Alice Hatten and Connor." She saw the incomprehension. She called the dogs to follow and walked out, heading through the trees. Walter, dead. And the last of the Caverton brothers. She was hungry for revenge, but Elric had robbed her of that.

Let it go now, Kate. It is over. No one left to hate. Let it go. You are alive and that is precious to me, to know that you will go on.

Andrew and Bryce had come for her, two against one, and she had gone out that morning with only a knife to protect herself. She was searching for a ewe who had wandered off when she was about to yean—Kate's responsibility that spring. She had thought only of the ewe and the lamb, not her own safety. Had she been better armed she could have saved Geoff.

You were injured.

I still might have thrown my axe.

Peace, Kate.

At the edge of the trees Sam sat in the grass, watched by one of Elric's men.

"He bet you would choose the hounds over the lad," Sam said. "I did not believe him."

She started to curse him, then realized what he had said. "What do you mean, the hounds over the lad?"

"Your ward and the dogs go missing and you chose to save the dogs. I feared for them. If you did not come, he meant to kill them."

"Phillip's missing? From the deanery?"

"You did not know?"

Elric's man was nodding. She clutched his arm. "What do you know about this?"

"A man came to tell you. After you had gone."

God help me. "How?" The man shook his head. She grabbed Sam by the collar. "How? Where is he?"

"The lass. She slipped the boy a message. The Scot told me nothing about his plans for the lad, only that he was giving you a choice. I think it's one of Sir Elric's men who has Phillip. I'm not the only fool."

Her heart was pounding as she ran up the hill to the kitchen. The smell of seared flesh met Kate as she opened the door. Berend was holding Jennet as Goodwife Bella cauterized the bite.

Kate wondered at Bella's presence. "The man whom you've been tending?" Kate asked her.

"Dead. My cousin is sitting with him in the hall. Poor Matt, it is an unpleasant task for him."

Petra was curled up by the fire, bent over a chunk of bread. Kate yanked it out of her hands and tossed it in the fire, pulling the girl up onto her feet.

"Where is Phillip?"

A shake of the head, eyes steely, angry.

Kate took her by the shoulders and shook her. "Where is he?"

"Andrew gave me a note to give your boy before I came for you."

"You handed Phillip a note? In the deanery?"

"Easy to climb to his window."

"You did not read the note?"

"I don't read."

"Did Phillip say anything?"

"He just nodded."

"He did not question you, a stranger, appearing at his window?" What was wrong with Phillip?

"I've seen him in the stoneyard with that man."

"The man Andrew hanged?"

Petra looked to her feet.

"Did they talk to you there?"

"I watched them work and fetched things for them. The boy said I might work there someday."

"He thinks you're a lad."

"Most do."

Phillip, missing. Andrew's last piece of vengeance. If Sir Elric had not been so eager to draw his bow she might have made Andrew talk. Damn them to hell. Both Andrew and Elric.

Kate picked at the torn sleeve of her gown, thinking as she watched the midwife packing Jennet's wound with a poultice. "The comfrey will draw the heat from the burn and speed your healing," Bella said in a soothing voice. Jennet looked white as the midwife loosely wrapped the wound.

Berend poured water for Lille and Ghent, and reached for food.

"Just a little," said Kate. "They will be heading out again, so not too much."

"Eh?" Berend straightened from his task.

"One of Sir Elric's men has Phillip," she said, looking to Petra. "Is Sam right? Andrew turned one of the men who wear the earl's livery?" She nodded toward Elric as he bent to come through the kitchen door. "One of his men?"

"Not one of my men. I do not harbor traitors," he protested.

"'No Name,' that is what Andrew called him. Mean." Petra looked at Elric, a challenge in her eyes.

"You would trip on your pride, Sir Elric," said Kate. "Traitors are born out of dissatisfaction. Who among your men holds a grudge? Feels unappreciated? Unnoticed?" She saw the wince. "Too many to name. Well, Sam was not the only one Andrew recruited here. Someone in your guard joined his game, distracted us with a man who looked like Sam, and he has my ward Phillip."

"I will help."

"You blundered in before I learned what I needed to know, and now you want to help? Stay out of my way—you will frighten the boy. Berend, with me. Lille, Ghent." The dogs rose.

Berend nodded to Petra. "Serve yourself more bread and make yourself useful. See that the good knight does not follow us."

"Are you mad?" Kate exclaimed.

But the child stepped up to her. "I can help maybe. I know the hiding places."

"Why would you help?"

"Phillip is nice to me."

Kate glanced at Berend, who mouthed, *Trust her.* Perhaps he was right, time was of the essence. She reached out her hand to Petra.

The girl hid hers behind her back. "I will help for him, not you."

—•⊚•—

For the rest of the morning, Kate discovered abandoned cellars, boathouses, sheds, even an entire abandoned dwelling she had not known existed. Cobwebs, rats, decaying corpses of things the hounds shied away from—with each ghastly space Kate's heart darkened, dreading what she would find at the end of the search.

"How do you know these places?"

"We did not sleep in the same shelter twice."

At last the child suggested another "game" Andrew played, hiding something in plain sight. The deanery.

Marie squeaked at the sight of the filthy girl in the hall. "What is it?"

"She is helping us search for Phillip. Let her be," Kate warned, allowing the child to lead her to the cellar. "You know this building so well?"

"I practiced," said Petra. "I thought I might take the boy messages from down there, but the cat caught me every time."

As if on cue, Claws appeared at the foot of the ladder leading down to the undercroft, hissing.

"The boy is not here, then. That cat would have set up a howl if a stranger was down there." The child headed to the kitchens, demanding of Helen, "Are there any rooms no one goes in?"

Helen glanced at the child, her expression neutral. "Not with the children here."

"Outbuildings," Petra announced, and led the way out the door to the garden.

No Phillip.

Dean Richard joined them. "I am so sorry, Katherine. Phillip must have gone before the servants were up and about. We did not notice his absence until Marie complained that he was a slug-a-bed and Helen told her to go up to see if he was unwell. She found his chamber empty. We sent word."

"I know. Sir Elric's men took their time telling me. It was not your fault, uncle. The Earl of Westmoreland's men consider themselves too important to fret about a child lured away by a murderer."

"I should have come myself."

"I've no time to debate this."

The dean nodded toward Petra as she emerged from a garden shed. "Who is the urchin?"

"My niece. Walter's child. I will tell you her strange story when we have found Phillip. That comes first."

A church bell rang. Then another.

"Sext," said Berend. "Midday already. When Andrew does not send for them, what will happen, Petra?"

"The man will kill Phillip at sundown."

"By the rood, he would not do such a thing to an innocent," the dean exclaimed.

Petra fired a pitying glance at him.

As more bells joined in, Kate gazed up at the minster. "The chapter house." She left the dogs and Petra, who had begun to stumble with weariness, with Helen. When the girl protested, Kate promised that if they did not find Phillip in the minster, they would come back for her. "Eat something. Be ready to return to searching. Come, uncle, Berend."

They rushed across the yard and into the south aisle where workmen shook their heads. They had seen no one. But Phillip and his captor would have come through before they had arrived for work. They made their way through the assorted lawyers' booths in the north transept, stopping at a few to ask the clerks whether they had noticed anything unusual, heard anything. But no one had. Up the narrow steps, they came upon workers bustling about.

Kate gazed round in defeat. "Of course it is busy during the day. Nowhere to hide."

Dean Richard stopped one of the stonemasons. "The roof. Any workers up there?"

"No, Dom Richard, not today."

The dean looked to Kate, to Berend. "On the walk round the top there are blind spots where no one would see them from below."

Kate made sure her knife was easy to reach. Berend did likewise. They followed the dean to a ladderlike stairway. Dean Richard explained how the trap door was secured and they headed up in the darkness, Berend in the lead. Kate readied herself to be blinded by the light. They might need to move quickly despite poor vision. At the top, Berend found the hasp undone.

"You were right, I think," Kate whispered down to her uncle. "Go find some strong men—we may need to carry Phillip and his captor."

The dean nodded, blessed the two of them, and backed down.

Berend opened the hatch.

For a long while he stood quite still, so still that all Kate heard was the rush of the wind, the patter of rain, so still that, gazing up, she watched the fat drops of rain fall on his head and shoulders. Silently, like a cat moving a leg forward in slow motion, its eyes locked onto its prey, Berend moved his left leg up a rung, his right arm, paused, then right leg, slowly, cautiously, silently, left arm. He turned his head to listen with his good ear. Paused. And then, with great care, he crawled out onto the ledge. It was barely wide enough for his bow-legged stance when he rose to his feet. He looked round, nodded to Kate.

She tucked her skirts up in her girdle and climbed, her hands growing colder as she ascended, the rain, now whipped up by the wind, stinging her face like icy needles whenever she looked up to gauge her progress. As she crawled out onto the ledge, Berend, who had moved beyond her vision, reappeared. She sat back on her knees so she could see his face. She found no comfort in his grim expression.

"What did you find? Is Phillip up here?"

A nod. "Alive, both of them, but wounded."

"Both of them? Did Phillip wound his captor?"

"He must have. It wasn't *my* doing. The lad knows we have found him. He is pinned beneath the man, who is a dead weight, but still breathes. If I try to lift him and he makes a sudden move—"

Kate crossed herself.

Berend nodded. "We need the men who work up here. They will know how to secure them and safely move them down."

"But how—" Kate stopped. She would find out what had happened soon enough. Right now she must think only of climbing down and explaining what they needed, must not wonder how Phillip injured his captor, must not spin out her fear of what might happen when they tried to move two bodies on a high ledge. Phillip was alive, and she needed to help move him to safety.

At the bottom of the ladder, men waited with a lantern. Despite her chattering teeth, Kate managed to explain what Berend had found, so that by the time he joined her the men were talking among themselves, two moving off to fetch what they would need.

Dean Richard put an arm round Kate. "We are not needed here. Come. We will light some candles and pray at the deanery."

Berend agreed. "We will bring Phillip to you as soon as we have retrieved him."

❧

The girls were a study in contrasts. Marie sat poised at the edge of Phillip's bed, her gown carefully arranged round her, hair caught up in green ribbons. Her fingers were busy with paternoster beads, her lips silently shaping the prayers, her eyes set on her brother's still face. Petra, her face scrubbed, her hair caught back in a thick braid, sat on the floor near the door, her slender arms round her drawn up knees, rocking, eyes cast down. She still wore the tattered, pungent clothes of a boy—she had refused to borrow anything from Marie, who had made the offer while clearly bristling with resentment.

"My fault if he dies," had been Petra's response when Kate asked her why she had touched none of the food Helen had offered.

Phillip had awakened long enough to ask whether Elric's man was alive. When Kate told him he was, that he had been taken to the castle at Sheriff Hutton, where he would answer to the earl, his lord, Phillip had whispered a prayer of thanks. He feared he had killed the man.

And what matter if he had? But in truth Kate was grateful Phillip had not been blooded, prayed that he never would be. He was skilled with the knife, though, that was clear. The man had not counted on that, was wounded far more seriously than he had wounded Phillip—not fatally, but he had lost much blood.

"God be thanked he did not find your knife," said Kate, thinking it somewhat miraculous.

"Jennet set a sheath for it in my boot," said Phillip. "I didn't dare go for it until he was coming down on me. Then I pulled it. I thought I was dead anyway. I held it point up and closed my eyes. He couldn't avoid it without risking a fall off the ledge, I guess."

"God bless Jennet."

"God bless all of you," he said softly. "I have caused you much grief."

"Not you, Phillip. Never you." She kissed his forehead.

Kate had found the note in Phillip's pocket, signed as if from one of the stonemasons saying he had found something that might help prove Connor had not killed himself. Did the boy actually still believe Connor could have climbed up to the scaffold? She had thought he understood.

When we were his age, we never trusted that the adults told us the whole story, Geoff reminded her.

"What of the child?" her uncle had asked Kate. "She is all alone now. Caverton was a monster, but he fed and cared for her."

"I took in two bastard Nevilles, and I will do no less for a Clifford, my own brother's daughter. My foster daughter now."

"Another ward, and one with much healing to do?"

"We will do it together."

It had been a quiet moment before folk began to arrive wanting to hear the tale. Hugh and Martha Grantham, Lady Margery, Cousin William, Jennet bringing along Goodwife Bella to see to Phillip, Sir Elric, who watched from the doorway, uncertain of his welcome. She ignored him.

William held out his arms to her. "I am so sorry, Katherine. Sir Elric told me about Walter."

She let her cousin hold her. It felt good to soften for a moment.

"You have a valuable ally in Sir Elric," William whispered in her ear. "He vows to keep our part in hiding Bale's death out of the report to the earl. He regrets any harm his men brought to you and your household, including the body of the stranger."

Jennet had reported that the poor man had been prepared for burial, and he lay out in the shed behind the kitchen on Castlegate, along with Andrew Caverton. Sir Elric had ordered his men to tie Sam up in the shed with the bodies. "Let him contemplate the fruits of his betrayal." Jennet had nodded her approval.

All so busy tidying up, restoring order. As if all troubles were past.

Even her neighbor and partner Thomas Holme was of that mind, swearing to her as he arrived that he would tear down the old stone shed so that nothing like this could happen again.

City folk and their childlike belief that their walls and laws protected them from all danger. When Kate could listen to it no more, she had excused herself to sit with Phillip. Ignoring Helen's frown, she had brought Lille and Ghent with her. She sat now on a low stool beside Petra, stroking the dogs' wiry fur as they napped beside her. As ever, Kate found comfort in their companionship.

She touched Petra's cheek. For the two of them, life had never been tidy and ordered. Or for Marie and Phillip. They might be all the stronger for it, but how good it would be to rest. To find trust and a greater sense of safety.

Petra glanced up. "That woman in the kitchen said I look like you. She said you are my father's sister."

"She is right on both counts."

"She said I will live with you now. Like those two." She glanced at Marie, who saw her watching and bowed her head.

Softly, so that Marie could not hear, Kate said, "Not quite like them. Though I have come to love them as my own flesh and blood, they were kin to my dead husband. They are wards, but you are my niece, my blood kin."

"My father did not like me. He paid Andrew to take me away."

"My brother had little heart left, Petra."

All that had happened must be confusing to the child, and frightening, sad—though she had not yet seen Petra cry. "Have you always lived with Andrew?"

When the girl did not answer, Kate glanced over, saw that the child was shaking her head very slowly, over and over, as if lost in the motion, her eyes still downcast.

"Who did you live with before?"

"Old Mapes, with deep wrinkles and the whitest hair. She was the wise woman, the healer."

"Did you love her?"

"I guess. But she died. And then Andrew came."

"How long ago was that?"

A shrug. "She made my hat. Still have it."

So it was not so long ago, though the hat, a dark felt, was grimy and ragged at the seams and edges.

"Do you miss her?"

"I miss my cats and pony, and the goats. And Mapes." The child's throat closed over the healer's name.

Kate guessed the time of tears would soon begin. A long silence ensued in which Marie's prayers and Phillip's soft snore were the only human sounds in the room. She let herself drift off into her own prayers for her brother's soul, for Mary Caverton, Alice, Maud, Geoff, Connor—such a long list.

"Do I have a choice?" the child suddenly asked. "About living with you?" She had undone her braid and was twisting a wiry lock round and round a finger, studying it as if it were a crucial clue.

"No."

"I thought not."

"I think we might like each other."

A shrug, still studying the remarkable curl. "Why do those big dogs follow you about?"

"Because we grew up together. They are what I have left of my life up on the border."

"Will they bite me if I disobey?"

"No. They will bite only to defend themselves from attack, or to protect our household. Which includes you now."

"How do they know?"

"They know."

"Will I wear dresses?"

"Most of the time. But Jennet knows how to make them so you will move with ease."

"I think I will miss Andrew."

"I know. I will miss my brother Walter."

"Would you tell me about him?"

Where to begin?

With his goats, Geoff whispered.

Kate smiled. "So you are fond of goats?"

19

SOVEREIGN SEALS

—⁓⁓—

Jennet watched as Kate moved the chest and checked beneath the floor-boards for Hubert Bale's pouch and his letters of introduction from the king and the duke. Someone had searched Kate's bedchamber while she and Jennet were otherwise engaged with Andrew Caverton and the unfolding drama of the day. Jennet had discovered the intrusion while Kate was searching for Phillip—a male scent in the room, a few items subtly out of place. She had remarked to Kate that whoever had searched was experienced and had taken their time.

"The pouch and the letters are still here, God be thanked." Kate slumped back against the wall pressing the letters to her heart. The search had drained what little strength she could muster at the end of this most trying day.

"And nothing is missing?" Jennet asked, slipping off the bed. "Let me help you put it all back."

Kate touched Jennet's bandaged arm and shook her head. "Nothing is missing, and you must rest. I will put it back in a moment."

Jennet shrugged. "As you wish." She padded back to the bed. Settling back against the cushions, she sighed. "I'd wager it was Sir Elric. He was here at the house while we were in the gardens."

"I know." Of course he would be keen to find the letters and dispose of them. They were incriminating evidence of the Earl of Westmoreland's connection with an assassin claiming to represent both the king and the duke. Treason. "I foiled him."

"For now."

"I intend to continue to do so. I might need these if I am cornered."

"Sam must go away. He knows you have one of the letters. If he were to tell Sir Elric . . ."

"I thought of that." Hours ago Kate had paused for a quiet word with Goodwife Bella, instructing her to slip poppy juice in some wine and make certain that Sam drank it down. The healer had proposed a few additional ingredients to fog his memory. Checking on Sam awhile ago Kate had found him groggy and confused. She must remember to pay Bella well for her services. "I will talk to Dean Richard about a place for Sam on one of his properties well away from York." She forced herself up, tucking the pack back beneath the boards and arranging the furniture over the space.

"Sir Elric, here in your bedchamber, and he took nothing? Not even your silk shift as a memento." Jennet grinned. "He is an honorable knight."

Without comment Kate climbed into bed and slipped down beneath the covers, pulling them over her head. A romantic entanglement with Westmoreland's man in York was the last thing she needed. Tomorrow she would show the letters to her uncle the dean. As Keeper of the Privy Seal he should be able to tell her whether the seals were official.

◦◦◦

Lady Margery bent to the task, moving the letters so that they were in the best light from the casement window in the deanery hall. Dean Richard was not so familiar with Henry Bolingbroke's seals to know whether this was current, but Lord Kirkby had kept up a correspondence with the exiled duke; hence the consultation.

"I knew that he had copied King Richard in adding Edward the Confessor's arms, but I had not seen this motto: SOVEREYNE." Margery gave a little shiver as she glanced up at Kate and Dean Richard. "I wonder that my Thomas did not mention it. Perhaps he does not take it to mean what the three of us clearly do? It is my greatest fear that my husband is too trusting, that he is mistaken in trusting that the duke wants to make peace with his royal cousin, that he wishes to claim his inheritance and nothing more."

"At one time King Richard did name him as his heir," said Kate. "Might this refer to his expectations?"

"After all that has transpired, Bolingbroke cannot be so naïve as to presume that. And such a seal would serve only to fuel King Richard's suspicions." Margery's hands trembled as she folded the letters and handed them to Kate.

"This has troubled you. I am sorry." Kate pressed Margery's hand.

"Better to know."

"So I am right in thinking this is an authentic letter, and the one introducing Underhill as King Richard's man is a counterfeit?" Kate asked.

Both her uncle and Lady Margery nodded.

"Hide these well," Margery whispered.

—◦◦◦—

On Lady Kirkby's last day in York, Dean Richard hosted a small, select dinner in her honor, attended by Archbishop Richard Scrope, Sir Elric, William Frost, and Kate. The conversation slid time and again to King Richard's expedition to Ireland and the growing unease of the barons. Kate watched the archbishop and Sir Elric, trying to gauge whether they were friend or foe. Elric knew all her secrets, except for the letters, and she believed her uncle was correct in guessing that the archbishop knew far more than she found comfortable. How would they use her? But the dinner was a triumph for Lady Margery, who received the archbishop's thanks for working for peace. He proved a complex man.

"Alas, we never had the opportunity to read Geoffrey Chaucer's wonderful love poem," Margery sighed as she and Kate parted at High Petergate.

"I look forward to doing so on your next visit," said Kate. She meant it. Though eager to have the guesthouse available to her regular clients once more, and still of the opinion that the quest for peace was naïve and destined to fail, Kate was fonder of Margery than ever, particularly since that awful day when Phillip went missing. Margery had offered help in a hundred different ways, exhibiting a particular skill in guiding Marie and Petra to communicate beyond insults. She had even found suitable clothing for Petra to wear. Recalling that Drusilla Seaton had a grand-daughter slightly older than Petra, she had paid the widow a visit and returned with a wardrobe. "May God watch over you and your husband on your noble mission," Kate said.

Margery kissed Kate's cheek and whispered, "Have a care, my friend. Danger surrounds us."

Sir Elric bowed to Lady Margery and wished her a safe journey.

"I will miss little Petra most of all. She is so like my youngest when he was her age." Margery pressed something into Kate's hand. "One for each of them, so they do not fuss." Kissing Kate's cheek again, Margery hurried off.

Gold filigree pins shaped as nests, with tiny jet beads tucked within. Kate placed them in her scrip.

"She is a generous woman," Sir Elric noted as they continued down Stonegate. He had insisted on escorting Kate home, despite Jennet's presence. Jennet now walked behind them with the squire Harry, a youth with a honking laugh. "Forgive my curiosity, Dame Katherine, but I wondered what you decided about your wayward servant, Sam?"

"My uncle the dean has offered him a penance of hard work, menial labor befitting a man of his years, in the kennels on an estate. He is good with dogs." She enjoyed the surprise on the knight's chiseled face. "Cliffords prefer to use problems, not destroy them."

"I see."

And Sam's gratitude would silence him about the letters. Or so she prayed. "And you, Sir Elric, what will be the fate of your wayward henchman?"

"Alas, the wound in his groin festered, and with little will to live knowing he would be a cripple, he went to sleep and never woke." A shrug.

Kate felt a chill down her spine. She must remember to warn her uncle never to reveal the whereabouts of Sam to this man.

"What do you think of Lady Kirkby's mission now that you have dined with her? And witnessed the archbishop's response?" she asked as they crossed into Davygate.

"I believe Lord Kirkby sincere in suing for peace, but he will fail. He understands neither Duke Henry nor the Lancastrians. The duke is a man besotted with his own image as first knight, a man who needs to be the hero of every tourney in which he participates. It is this that makes him dangerous. He dislikes that his cousin the king does not appreciate his military prowess. The king publicly embarrasses him by pointing out that a tourney is to the battlefield what a puppet show is to life, and that he has had little to no experience in actual battle. The duke has no wish to make peace with his royal cousin. The barons encourage the duke in his resentment, especially the Lancastrians. They see no benefit to peace."

It seemed Kate and Elric were of one mind in this.

For a while they relaxed into casual comments on the state of the streets, the weather, the folk who greeted her, so many with questions in their expressions—she certainly had been a source of much excitement of late. It worried her. And now to be seen on the arm of a handsome knight . . . She shrugged to herself. Perhaps Sir Elric's interest might be to her advantage, serving to ward off would-be suitors.

"Have you considered my proposal?" he asked as they crossed into Nessgate, almost home. "My silence and protection for your information?"

"And if I refuse?"

A small smile. "You are a formidable warrior, Dame Katherine. I prefer to be your ally, not your foe."

"Then perhaps we understand each other." She thanked him for the escort and excused herself for not inviting him in. "Petra is with her tutor today in the hall. I prefer that we not disturb them."

"Ah. How is she fitting in your household?"

Kate shook her head. "Phillip has chosen to stay with the Granthams for a while, until Marie becomes accustomed to Petra's presence." She smiled. "It is an uneasy peace. Like ours."

She nodded to him, signaled to Jennet, and was turning down the alley when Elric barred her way.

"One more thing, Dame Katherine." Curious how chilly blue eyes could be. "Your cousin William mentioned that Jon Underhill had shown him a letter carrying King Richard's seal. We found no such letter on the corpse."

"So you have exhumed him? To give him a proper burial, I hope?"

An ambiguous shrug. "Frost said Underhill had a pack with him when he was escorted to your guesthouse that fateful night. Is that in your possession?"

"You know that it is, Sir Elric. You searched for it yourself up in my bedchamber."

He cleared his throat and looked down at his boots for a moment. So he had a conscience. "Forgive me, Dame Katherine, but I had orders. And for all that I found no letter."

"Of course not."

"But you know of the letters."

"I know of the one William glimpsed. Was there another?"

A slight twitch beneath his left eye. "You miss nothing, do you?"

Kate merely arched a brow. "It grows cold out here."

"Of course. Forgive me for keeping you, Dame Katherine. I pray I have not jeopardized our partnership with my trespass."

"And I pray it is not repeated." She wished him a safe journey back to Sheriff Hutton Castle, then strode on down the alley, her heart pounding. She must find a safer place for the letters than the floor of her solar, somewhere they would be secure even should someone set fire to her home.

20

MOTHER AND DAUGHTER, OIL AND WATER

———⚬≈⚬≈⚬≈———

Early April 1399

Dame Eleanor felt a shiver of anticipation as her traveling party approached Micklegate Bar, its battlements guarding the south gate of the great city of York. More than six years had passed since she had paused before mounting her horse, taking one last look at the city wall, fixing it in her mind's eye so that she might revisit it in memory from time to time. She had been on her way to a new adventure, having married a wealthy spice merchant from Strasbourg, and was quite certain she would never return. Even her daughter's marriage had not drawn her back. Yet now, here she stood, having dismounted in order to lead her horse through that well-guarded gate and into the city.

She shivered and pulled up the fur-lined hood of her traveling cloak against the chill rain that had begun falling just as the city came into view. Still cold in early April. But of course. It would be even colder in Northumberland, where she had spent most of her first marriage. At least her son Walter's wedding was a month away. By May the weather might prove felicitous for journeying north to celebrate it.

Already she missed Strasbourg. Though it sat at the foot of the Alps, it enjoyed a more temperate climate than York. Or had Ulrich's love simply made it feel warmer?

"Dame Eleanor?" Her man Griffin peered at her face, shadowed by the hood. "Are we to proceed?"

"Yes. Of course." She glanced over at her companions and saw how their shoulders crept toward their ears. Brigida was visibly shivering. "Come along, my dears. We shall soon be warming our hands at my nephew's hearth. His manse is just within this gate." She prayed that was so, that they were expected. The decision to leave Strasbourg and set up her Martha House in York had been sudden, of necessity. She had written a letter, but whether it had preceded her to York she could not know until she was face-to-face with her nephew William. He had procured his late father-in-law's great house on Micklegate, a manse large enough to house Eleanor and her three companions, as well as the two servants and Griffin. It was only a temporary sanctuary, until Eleanor persuaded her daughter Katherine to part with one of the sweet houses on High Petergate that had been part of her dower. There might be tenants to evict, but surely for her mother, and to the benefit of her immortal soul . . . Eleanor, though, had never mastered the art of predicting how her daughter might respond.

Griffin knocked on the substantial oaken door to William's fine house. The confusion evident on the face of the servant who answered was disappointing.

"I pray your master informed you that he was expecting us," said Eleanor.

A large woman stepped in front of the servant with such determination that the keys on her gold and silver girdle tinkled delicately. All in velvet in late morning, and it was not even a feast day. Isabella Gisburne Frost.

She was certainly her father's daughter, keen to remind all how much she was worth. Eleanor prayed her nephew had not caught the malaise. He had been an honest, worthy man when she had parted with him. But he had made a name for himself, and such things did go to a man's head. "I know nothing of my husband expecting guests. You are—?"

"I have come to see my nephew, William Frost. I am his aunt, Eleanor Clifford. You do not recognize me?"

"Dame Eleanor who lives in Strasbourg?" The chilly gaze warmed slightly, but the narrow, colorless lips remained pursed as if she detected a bad smell. "It has been a long while."

My, what an unattractive woman William had wed. Eleanor did not remember her as quite so long in the face, the eyes so close together and small, the nose so sharp, the torso so . . . abundant. They ate well in this household. Too well for some.

"*Lived*, my dear Isabella. I have returned to York as a widow, a wealthy widow, and William has welcomed me to bide with you until I have set up my own household." Or he would, were he the man she believed him to be. Hoped him to be.

"William said nothing to me—"

"It is raining again," Eleanor remarked, stepping aside and motioning Dina, Clara, and Brigida to enter. "I had thought delaying the journey to arrive in April I might avoid such dreadful cold. Alas, it seems I have forgotten how long winter lingers here." She slipped past her reluctant hostess and shepherded the young women toward the hearth. A hearth, not a fire circle. How forward-looking. "Did your father install this, or was this my nephew's addition to the hall?"

"My father, of course. Though my husband installed another for our dear Hazel's bedchamber. It is better for her lungs."

So their one child was cursed with her father's weak lungs. "Yes, of course, poor William. He was the youngest, you know. The runt of the litter. His lungs were weak from birth. That is why he spent summers with us up north, breathing and strengthening. My sons put him through his paces. Put muscle on him."

"Your sons. Yes." For a moment the woman's face softened with sadness. But only a moment. "Who are these women, Dame Eleanor?" Isabella's beady eyes looked down the considerable length of her nose at the young women timidly holding their hands out to the fire.

"They are Beguines, Isabella. Lay sisters, poor sisters. I am not certain what you call them here. They will set up the Martha House I am founding in York, to tend to the souls and welfare of the poor. Dina, Clara, Brigida." The three young woman bowed and offered a blessing in French.

Isabella frowned. Difficulty with the accents, perhaps, or perhaps she was the sort who felt uneasy around pious virgins. "And this man?" Isabella gestured toward Griffin, who had remained near the door, arms folded, as the two servants hustled past him with Eleanor's baggage.

"Griffin. My late husband's factor." And armed retainer. But naming him a factor, a man of business, was clearly what would reassure this woman that the man was not a barbarian come to ravage her. He had served as Eleanor's escort—three young virgins, precious cargo, God knows. Griffin had been armed and ready to defend them.

"A factor? Do you intend to trade here in York?"

"Perhaps." Eleanor looked around. "Where *is* my nephew?"

"At the council chambers or . . . He is a busy man. But I expect him for dinner." The woman's eyes were suddenly far away, probably thinking how to extend the food for the unexpected guests. Or praying that her husband had not forgotten to inform her that he was dining elsewhere, forcing her to entertain Eleanor and her three women without him. "Would you not be more comfortable in your daughter's home? Do you remember it, situated next to Thomas Holme's lovely manse, and across Castlegate from the gardens that lead down to the Foss?"

Eleanor remembered Simon Neville's house as much too small for her traveling party. It was her daughter's additional houses in the city that interested her. But she must approach Katherine with care. Her daughter could be quite stubborn when she felt pushed. "This will suit us very well, Isabella my dear. If you would just show us where we might shed our traveling clothes and wash?"

CANDACE ROBB

Kate and Griselde stood in the repaired and refurbished hall next to the guesthouse, discussing whether or not to lease the house with furnishings or without. Odo was now comfortably lodged in the home of a midwife in Fishergate, and Berend had just supervised the transfer of the spices to the small house in front of her own on Castlegate. Much to Lionel's dismay, she had hired a clerk whose sole job was keeper of the spice. Young Seth was delighted with the work.

"Furnished is best," Griselde concluded. "Then it is always at the ready."

They were about to climb to the solar when Jennet rushed in. "Dame Katherine!"

"God help us, what has happened now?" Kate asked, seeing Jennet's flushed face, the mud on her hem.

"It's your mother. Dame Eleanor. She has just arrived in the city."

Kate felt her heart turn over.

God help you, Kate, Geoff muttered.

"Mother is here?" Kate groaned. "Did Ulrich decide to return to York?"

Jennet shook her head. "Apparently she is a widow again, and she has brought three poor sisters with her, to open a house here. To serve the poor of the city."

"That part of Walter's story was true?"

"You will hear soon enough. She is biding at Master Frost's house on Micklegate and Mistress Frost has sent Tib with an invitation for you to dine there today."

She could not. No. It was too soon. "Does she know about Walter?"

"Tib says she has proposed that the Frosts make the journey north with her, for the wedding. Dame Isabella wants you there now. She says it is your duty to break the news."

Kate muttered a curse. Nothing was so bad that her mother's presence would not make it worse. Far worse. And to be the one to deliver such news, such blame.

⸺◦◦◦◦⸺

The dinner had been almost a comedy of discomfort, everyone talking around the death that negated Eleanor's elaborate plans for the journey north. The last course had barely been served when Kate could sit no longer.

"Would you join me in the garden, Mother? We must talk."

"I am eating, Katherine. And it is raining."

"Wear your cloak."

"You are welcome to use my office," said William. "Tib will unlock it for you and bring you some wine."

Kate strode out, calling to her mother to follow. Huffing and tsking, Eleanor arrived in the lamp-lit building just across from the front entrance and immediately assumed the role of hostess, adding cushions to the chairs Tib arranged by a brazier. Another servant followed with wine and goblets, then stoked the fire.

As soon as the servants withdrew, Kate launched into an account of the past few weeks, sparing her mother nothing. She needed to know. When her mother would interrupt, Kate raised her voice and carried on. Eventually, Eleanor simply bowed her head and listened through to the end. When Kate finished, her hand shook as she lifted the goblet of wine to her lips. It was not the story, but her mother's presence.

Have I not suffered enough? Kate asked God.

Apparently not, said Geoff.

Eleanor's silence was brief. "No. No, I cannot be blamed for all this. You and your brothers—I brought you to York to stop your talk of going north to track Andrew. Let him go, I said. Let the blood feud die."

"Me and my brothers? It was Father who instilled in us a distrust of all Scots and a particular enmity with the Cavertons. If you must blame one of your children, place the blame where it belongs—Walter."

A sob. "My poor son."

Kate closed her eyes and silently said a few Hail Marys. She would never forgive her mother, never. But it was no use venting her anger at the woman. Eleanor was not one to accept fault. She was adept at twisting criticism so that it reflected back on the critic. Kate judged it best to talk of something else before she began fingering the dagger hidden in her skirt. "Tell me about your three poor sisters. Beguines, you called them? How did you come to be their escort here?"

"Their families were all known to my dear Ulrich."

"Why have they chosen York for a new house?"

"I chose it. I am establishing a house here, as I was just telling William and Isabella. You were at the table."

"Why?" Seeing the spots of color on her mother's cheeks, Kate softened the question. "You had so short a time with Ulrich. Your grief—is this foundation in his memory? Will they be praying for his soul? And perhaps those of my brothers? Our father?"

"All of that. Of course." Eleanor fussed with the flagon of wine on the table, shifting it slightly to the left.

"You do know that my partner and neighbor, Thomas Holme, founded a maison dieu attached to our parish church in Castlegate? With poor sisters. Perhaps he might advise you, Mother."

"I do not need his help."

"It would be a courtesy to consult with him."

"It is he who should consult with me. What does he know of poor sisters? I have observed them closely, their good works."

Kate felt her anger building again. "I pray you, Mother, do not antagonize him. I need his friendship. I have worked hard to build—"

"York needs this."

"What do you know of this city and its needs?" Eleanor and her cursed meddling. "Who are you to judge? You, who pushed Walter toward the Cavertons? How could you not see the danger in that? Do you realize the enormity of what happened here? The deaths? The threat to my wards? To me?"

"My sisters will pray for you as well."

"I do not want prayers. It is too late for prayers. What I need now is some peace. Peace in which to calm my business partners and reassure them that all is well. But of course all is not well. We are all holding our breaths as we wait to see how Henry of Lancaster responds to the king's threats to deny his inheritance. The king's men boarded my ship. Did you know of that?"

Too late Kate saw the trembling mouth, the tears. She was out of practice with the woman.

"No," Eleanor said quietly. "No, I did not know of that." She drew a deep breath and shook her arms as if fluffing her feathers. "Tell me about your dinner with Archbishop Scrope and Dean Richard. And what about this knight, Sir Elric? I understand he is not married."

Kate stared at her mother, bereft of words for several heartbeats.

Long enough that her mother continued. "You are the heiress now, you know. The land in Northumberland is yours now that Walter is dead. You need a husband to help you with the estate."

"I need no husband to do that," said Kate. "Nor do I want the manor up north. I will entrust William to arrange with some family member to exchange the land for property near York. I have built a life here."

"William? But, Katherine."

"How can you do this? You have just learned of the death of your last surviving son and you talk of this?"

"I will pray for him anon. You are my remaining responsibility. What about Walter's daughter—Petra, did you call her?" Eleanor rose to exchange one of the cushions on her chair for one across the room, then settled back, shaking her head. "What an odd name, Petra."

Kate felt the outline of the hidden dagger. "What about Petra?"

"Katherine, dear, bringing her up with Simon's French bastards. Is it seemly?"

"Will you shun bastards in your Martha House? Will your holy women refuse them prayers? Or charity? You do realize that Petra is a bastard?"

They regarded each other for a good long while. Kate noticed the new lines radiating from the corners of her mother's eyes and her upper lip, as if she had developed a habit of squinting and pursing her lips in disapproval. Charity? Piety? Not her mother. Kate guessed the poor sisters were no more than a convenient cause to fill the void left by Ulrich's death. She pitied the next man her mother snared, and the unfortunate sisters who would be left stranded in a foreign country.

At last Eleanor sighed. "You must admit that your household is peculiar, Katherine."

"No more than yours, Mother. Three young Alsatian women and an armed retainer you call a factor, with an accent suggesting he originated in Wales but has lived for quite a while in the Holy Roman Empire. A mercenary? And I'm curious about the one sister—Brigida? She speaks

Parisian French, and though her gown is simple, the fabric is expensive. New cloth. Just a merchant's daughter?"

"My, you have learned much in your time here. But not enough. Wealthy merchants often hire Parisian tutors for their children."

"For girls?"

"Her parents had expected her to marry well." Eleanor wrinkled her nose and leaned forward, taking Kate's hands. "What of Geoffrey? Do you still believe he is with you?"

"My brothers are dead," Kate said, with finality.

Kate?

My brothers, Geoff, not my twin.

Eleanor smiled—she still had a lovely, warm smile that lit up her green eyes—and let go Kate's hands with an encouraging little shake. "Good. I am glad you are over that. Now, my dear, I have a request. I should like the use of one of your sweet houses on High Petergate for my Beguines."

"Straight on to your latest scheme. You must be mad to ask that of me."

"Katherine, this is holy work. My women will pray for Walter's soul. For the souls of all our departed kin."

For just an instant Kate entertained the notion of installing her mother's holy sisters in the house that Odo Marsden had vacated, then waiting for her to puzzle out the comings and goings in the guesthouse next door. But of course that was too dangerous. Her mother did not know the meaning of discretion.

"No, Mother. You have outlived three husbands, the last quite wealthy. You do not need my charity. And I want nothing to do with your Beguines."

"Katherine, you are unkind."

"I am practical, seeing to my own affairs." She would not have her properties at risk when the true reason her mother had returned to York came to light. Ulrich had employed a former mercenary as an armed retainer for a reason, and Eleanor had departed Strasbourg in such haste upon his death that she'd arrived before the letter she had sent to William. It was only a matter of time before her mother's troubles caught up with her. Kate rose. "Please make my excuses to Isabella and William, and tell Jennet to meet me back at the house."

"You blame me for Walter's death."

"Andrew Caverton murdered my brother. But your interference served the same purpose as Walter's deflowering of Mary—it rekindled the feud. Pray God it died with Andrew, that another branch of the family doesn't mean to carry it forward."

Kate was at the door when she heard her mother's whisper. "I shall never forgive myself."

Oh, but she would. "Peace, Mother. My marriage to Simon taught me to look to my own interests, and let others look to theirs."

The End

ACKNOWLEDGMENTS

As always, I am indebted to scores of friends and colleagues who inspired, informed, assisted, and supported me throughout the research and writing of this book, albeit sometimes unknowingly. Thank you, all of you.

But some must be mentioned by name. I am grateful to my friend Richard Shephard for inviting me into the places and spaces in York Minster and the close that I'd not yet seen, setting up a yearning that drew me back to a York setting; to Chris Given-Wilson, Louise Hampson, Jennifer Kolpakoff Dean, and Doug Biggs for research that's all spun together to form this story, and for their generosity in answering my questions; to my nephew Nathaniel Weberding, DO, for inspiring medical discussions; to my agent/advocate Jennifer Weltz for her enthusiasm and support for the project from the beginning, her inspired feedback all along the way, and for finding a wonderful home for the series; to my dear friends Joyce Gibb and Mary Morse for their thoughtful readings and suggestions; to my editor Maia Larson for her perceptive and engaged editing; and all the team at Pegasus Books for their creative and talented support.

And last, but never least, I am so grateful to my beloved Charlie—mapmaker, research companion, sounding board, advocate, and all-round best friend and soul mate.